Imagi

"The most unique series of anthologies being published today."
— Allen Steele, author of *Coyote*

"Some of the best new writers in science fiction join a handful of veterans in getting their groove on. If you want to be in at the beginning of some stellar careers, this anthology is the place to start."
— Lucius Shepard, author of *Valentine*

"When you read *Imagination Fully Dilated*, you feel as if you're creeping up to the attic and stumbling across a long-lost treasure chest you've never opened before. Inside are pictures (cleverly drawn by the talented Alan M. Clark) of alien worlds, Seattle's Pike Place Market—even an interstellar brothel! And all of these snapshots come with the best stories penned by today's up-and-coming writers. Sit back, read, and enjoy. You've found a true collection of literary riches!"
— Eric Nylund, author of *Signal to Noise*

"Startling and original. Step through the artwork into the minds of this highly talented crew. Strap in tight!"
— Kay Kenyon, author of *The Braided World*

"Look at the pictures that inspired these stories; distorted images of recognizable themes with secrets hidden beneath their familiarity. That's a good description of these stories as well: familiar themes, beloved environments (a whorehouse with aliens, the surface of Mars) with something new contained within their text for your enjoyment.

"Therese Pieczynski and A. Alice Doty's story 'Cleave' was perhaps the high point of the book for me (if you don't count Elisabeth DeVos' 'Out of the Fire,' a happy — mordant — snort of a story from start to finish). David Levine's 'Legacy' will give you a chill up and down your spine — much like the one you got when you heard about a particular Northwest incident that I can't mention for fear of spoiling the story. Melissa Scott's 'The Sweet Not-Yet' is richly imagined and wonderfully alive, Syne Mitchell's 'Stately's Pleasure Dome' is a hoot and a half, but James Van Pelt's 'Lashawnda at the End' took me back to the sense of wonder I remember from my childhood reading science fiction for the very first time like nothing outside Ray Bradbury ever has. But everything's good. You'll want to read it all. Do yourself a favor and don't miss it!"
— Susan Matthews, author of *The Devil and Deep Space*

IMAGINATION FULLY DILATED: SCIENCE FICTION

THE LITERATED ARTWORK OF ALAN M. CLARK

edited by Robert Kruger & Patrick Swenson

Fairwood Press

Auburn·Seattle

Imagination Fully Dilated: SF

A Fairwood Press Book
August 2003

Fairwood Press
5203 Quincy Ave SE
Auburn, WA   98092
info@fairwoodpress.com
www.fairwoodpress.com

Cover art © Alan M. Clark
Cover and Book Design by Patrick Swenson

ISBN: 0-9668184-9-0
First Fairwood Press Edition: August 2003
Printed in the United States of America

also available from ElectricStory.com
in several e-book formats. See their website for details.
www.electricstory.com

IMAGINATION FULLY DILATED:
SCIENCE FICTION

ACKNOWLEDGEMENTS

"Introduction" © 2003 by Alan M. Clark
"A Word of Appreciation" © 2003 by Robert Kruger
"A Fully Dilated Introduction" © 2003 by Patrick Swenson
"The Sweet Not-Yet" © 2003 by Melissa Scott
"Threesome" © 2003 by Leslie What
"Area Seven" © 2003 by Robert Onopa
"The Dream of Vibo" © 2003 by Patrick O'Leary
"The Artist Makes a Splash" © 2003 by Jerry Oltion
"Fired" © 2003 by Ray Vukcevich
"Nohow Permanent" © 2003 by Nancy Jane Moore
"By Any Other Name" © 2003 by Steve Beai
"Stately's Pleasure Dome" © 2003 by Syne Mitchell
"Between the Lines" © 2003 by Arinn Dembo
"Dilated" © 2003 by Robert E. Furey
"Let My Right Hand Forget Her Cunning" © 2003 by Tom Piccirilli
"Cleave" © 2003 by Therese Pieczynski & A. Alicia Doty
"Out of the Fire" © 2003 by Elisabeth DeVos
"Legacy" © 2003 by David Levine
"Lashawnda at the End" © 2003 by James Van Pelt
All illustrations © 2003 by Alan M. Clark, except for
"Chattacon Collaboration" © 2003 by
Alan M. Clark and Kevin Ward

CONTENTS

INTRODUCTION
ALAN M. CLARK

*Illustrate v. — to provide with pictures or designs
for elucidation or adornment.*

Usually illustrators create visual interpretations of stories. This is an extremely satisfying pursuit, and as a freelance illustrator I have done this countless times. But I have also been unusually and terrifically honored to have had my work interpreted by great writers in three volumes of fiction: *Imagination Fully Dilated, Imagination Fully Dilated Volume II*—both edited by Elizabeth Engstrom—and now, the book you are reading, *Imagination Fully Dilated: Science Fiction.*

*Literate v. — to elucidate or enlighten
with words or phrases.*

The definition above doesn't appear in any dictionary, but it is useful here.

Audience participation has always been important to me, but I'm not talking about just a reaction to the colors, the composition, the technique, the subject matter of a piece of art. No, I want the audience involved in the "telling" of the image. My artwork tells stories, and just as with a piece of fiction in which the writer doesn't "tell" everything, the audience has work to do. I want my audience to bring their own emotional experience to the viewing of my images. This seems to make it a memorable experience.

That this was important to me was not something I appreciated consciously until I began to meet writers in the mid-'90s who had written stories or scenes in novels based on pieces of my artwork. They had seen a piece in an art show or bought a piece that inspired them. After this had happened four or five times the idea was hatched to do an anthology of these stories and include the artwork.

The process was fairly simple. For each volume a Web page was created containing about forty pieces of my artwork. Writers were invited to go look at the images and if they were inspired by one of them and wanted to participate in the anthology, they were given a high resolution print of the image to consider while they worked. The only rules for this particular volume were a limit of 7,000 words and that the stories should be Science Fiction.

Always fascinated to hear reactions to my work, I've had a tendency to eavesdrop on people looking at my paintings in art shows. They often take the suggestion of a story contained in a piece and elaborate on it, coming up with wonderful ideas. These are most often completely different and sometimes immeasurably more delightful than what I'd had in mind.

The writers in this and the preceding two volumes have done this with incredible results. Being a part of the editorial team for each of the *Imagination Fully Dilated* volumes has been the ultimate exploration into this process of audience participation. The writers have brought to it a wealth of imagination and storytelling ability. I am very proud to be a part of it.

Before reading these stories, you might flip through the book and look at the pieces of art. If they begin to suggest stories, allow yourself to add to them. Then when you are reading, see how this experience compares to what has been written.

I hope you will be as fascinated as I have been.

—*Alan M. Clark, May 1, 2003*
Publisher, Artist
IFD Publishing

A WORD OF APPRECIATION
ROBERT KRUGER

A lot has happened in the two years since Patrick and I first discussed this project with (the patient and forbearing) Alan Clark. Patrick and Honna became parents, ElectricStory published over a dozen more books, Fairwood Press put out several magazines and a couple of story collections, Patrick got his Master of Education degree, my daughter turned two and then three, I picked up a couple of computer-programming certifications (if you're going to run an Internet business, I've belatedly found, you'd better know something about the Internet), and we worked with terrific new authors, many showcased here.

I've had some prior experience with solicited-story anthologies (given the demands of this project—making sure that each author wrote to a different piece of art—choosing writers ahead of time was the only feasible arrangement); but the contributors to *Imagination Fully Dilated: Science Fiction* taught me new lessons in professionalism. Every author we invited had already achieved some literary success (and many, a Ph.D.!) and was a pleasure to work with, even when we had to respectfully turn down work. Some authors wrote us completely new stories when we decided to pass on the first ones, and as it turns out, you'll find all of those proudly here.

Based on my recent experience, I've made a revised note to myself on being a professional writer: taking it as a given that they have ability, pros may or may not get it brilliantly right the first time, but if they're interested and have time, they doggedly approach rejection as a problem to be solved; and if they don't have the time or inclination, they cut their losses and cordially drop out. Patrick and I had the incredible good fortune to work only with professionals, and all of you have my very deep and humble respect. Thank you!

—Bob Kruger, June 1, 2003
Publisher
ElectricStory.com

A FULLY DILATED INTRODUCTION
PATRICK SWENSON

Bob and Alan had already talked about doing an e-book for the third *Imagination Fully Dilated*, and were wondering about the print version when I just *happened* to insinuate myself into their conversation at a convention party. I said yes before I knew what I was getting myself into. Bob had the solicited-story anthology experience, but I did not. Sure, I choose stories for *Talebones* magazine, but none of them are solicited, and only a handful of them are chosen each issue from hundreds of possibilities. The *IFD* process was truly an eye-opening experience for me. Thanks to Bob and Alan for their invaluable help, and also our authors for being so understanding along the way.

If you haven't seen the first two Alan Clark *IFD* books, you're missing out. These beautiful limited-edition books are works of art themselves, with full-color plates lovingly placed by hand for each story. The stories, like the artwork, deal with darker, horrific themes. Alan is a versatile artist, however, and his SF artwork needed "literating" too. This third edition of *IFD* came to be in response to that.

The challenge on my end (the print version) was to duplicate the spirit of the earlier anthologies while keeping the price of *this* anthology affordable. My limitations meant that the interior graphics would not be in color. From the start I worked on a plan to get every color graphic into the covers of both print editions. I hope you like this solution.

As it turns out (and of course there was never any doubt), Alan's artwork translates beautifully to grayscale, and it's like having thirty-two images in the anthology instead of sixteen. The stories within do an amazing job capturing the subtleties of Alan Clark's SF artwork, color or not. Thanks, writers, for doing such wonderful, creative work. Readers, you have hours of captivating reading ahead of you. Enjoy!

—*Patrick Swenson, June 6, 2003*
Publisher
Fairwood Press, Inc.

THE SWEET NOT-YET
MELISSA SCOTT

Breakfast, the prosthesis said. I looked where it pointed me, and took a meal bar out of the box. Achronics often didn't feel hunger, it explained, as I undid the wrapper and took a bite out of the oily bar. We lost the sensitivity to any but the grossest physical symptoms; it was better to eat small meals before we knew we wanted them than to wait until we noticed something was wrong.

Hurry, it said. *You're late.*

I ate as I walked, letting the machine prompt me through the tangle of unmarked and white-painted corridors that it identified as our Glasstown complex. I could smell things the prosthesis named hot metal and fiber-form and acid; heard noises that were labeled as coming from the shop and the support line and the office; saw faces that smiled and nodded as the prosthesis attached names. I came at last to a short flight of stairs, and a red light flared in the center of the door jamb: the house mainframe, the pros-thesis whispered, and its voice belonged to my dead grandfather, whose personality lived on in memory.

"You're late," that voice said, an old man's, no more familiar than that, and another voice said, "Leave him be, Pappy."

Your father, the prosthesis said, and I braced myself, realizing I wouldn't know him, either. The face that looked down at me was all angles like the one I'd seen in my mirror, just lined and older, the hair white and cropped to a stiff and bushy halo, the nose tilted out of true like someone had hit him. Someone probably had, from the things the prosthesis was whisper-ing about him, and the stranger looked down at me for a second longer before he stepped back out of the door.

"Morning, Cass."

"Morning, Daddy," I answered, and in the moment I met his eyes I saw both our hopes defeated.

He looked away, busied himself with a big urn that took up half the service console behind the workstation. "Pappy bring you up to speed?"

"Not really," I said, and took the cup he handed me.

Daddy glanced at the node that glowed red in the upper corner of the room, and Pappy said, "The boy didn't get up till just now. And you know how long it takes him to get going now."

A personality construct shouldn't be able to sound accusing, but this one did. Daddy ignored it, and nodded me toward one of the chairs.

"We got a problem."

We had lots of problems, according to the prosthesis—the family shipping business was barely breaking even, and we couldn't supplement it with racing since I'd wrecked myself and the family ship and there wasn't anybody left who could take my place, plus there was new competition from Echt-Hanson, who were planning to build a transfer station in the Merredin system that would take even more of our business—and I made a soft and hopefully encouraging noise, wondering what it would be this time.

"We got a runner," Daddy said.

"It ain't ours," Pappy corrected, and I blinked once before the prosthesis caught me up to them.

"Who is it?" Runners happened when the workhorse, the artificial life that was supposed to mediate between the driver and the ship's systems, seized control of the ship and bolted, heading for some destination known only to its circuits. Most of the time, the drivers just bailed, but sometimes they hung on, trying to retake control, and the horse made its jump with them still on board. That was a runner. There wasn't a very high survival rate among runners.

But that never stopped us from looking. If a workhorse bolted and took the driver with it, every spaceworthy ship in the system went out after it, on the off-chance that one of our own horses might spot it—quantum-processor-based, they could see a little way into the adjacent possible—or if the driver regained control and forced it back out a jump point, at least there would be someone there to pick him up. It all depended on where the ship had gone missing.

"Where'd it happen?" I said, just a few seconds too late, and saw my father wince.

"About two minutes off the N-2 jump, coming from J-8."

The prosthesis presented me with a map, Merredin's system and the jump points that honey-combed local space/time, and there was a part of me, down in the muscle memory, that understood how the ship had been heading, how it would have felt under the driver's hands.

"And," Daddy said, "it was Alrei Jedrey."

The name sparked anger, contextless and disconcerting. I blinked again, waiting for the prosthesis to supply something, anything, that would explain the feeling, but all I got was a passionless biography. Alrei Jedrey was a pilot, too, a racer and the son of a racer, just like I was. We were of an age, we'd raced against each other dozens of times; I'd won a few more than him, but we'd both lost more to the current—make that last year's—champion. There was no reason to be angry—but the feeling was there, unmistakable, a core of heat down in my gut, and I savored it, nursed it, disconnected as it was. It was the closest thing I'd had in a long time to a real memory of my own, and I shivered with the excitement. Whatever was between us, it had to be something big to have imprinted itself that deep, beyond normal memory....

"Old Man Jedrey's asking for all hands," Daddy said. "And that includes us."

That was a problem, too, I could read it in his face, and I dragged myself away from my own exciting anger, focused instead on the way his hands flexed on his coffee cup and then relaxed, as though he was afraid of breaking it. Once again the prosthesis gave no reasons, and I rummaged in its front-brain storage—the artificial memory that was supposed to give me immediate contexts in conversation—for possibilities.

"Don't we have something that can fly?" I asked, drawing the words out a little to give the prosthesis a chance to correct me if it needed to. No, it assured me, we had ships capable of running the local jumps—even my wrecked racer was pretty much ready for launch, just a few cosmetic repairs still to be done.

"What we don't have is a pilot," Daddy said bluntly. "I'm too old, and you're not up for it."

"I can fly."

The panic at the back of my words scared me. If I couldn't fly, what the hell else was there for me to do? I'd never done anything else in my life. More than that, it was the one thing I knew bone-deep, worked so far down into the muscle memory that I could actually almost remember it, could function as though I did consciously remember it, the sense of the controls against my hands and feet, the way the horse and the ship responded to my lightest touch. I'd proved it in sims, the prosthesis reminded me, hours and hours of them, the only time I felt like myself, and Daddy knew it.

"I can do it," I said again, and Daddy shook his head.

"You haven't been out the house for 241 days," Pappy said.

"That ain't right," I said. "Can't be."

"It's right," Daddy said, grim-faced. "And that's why I say you can't do it, never mind the sims. And Colton Jedrey can—" He broke off, shaking his head, mouth clamped tight over bitter words.

And what in hell's name do we have against the Jedreys? The prosthesis was silent, and Daddy went on as though the words were forced out of him.

"We've lost enough." He wouldn't meet my eyes, and I knew he was talking about me.

"The law says we have to go," Pappy said. "The company charter mandates it."

"We don't have a rated pilot," Daddy said. "Ty's out-system, Dee's not due in until day after tomorrow, and Cass—Cass can't do it."

"Then you're just asking for somebody to sue to get your charter," Pappy said. "And they'll win, too."

The prosthesis whispered in my head, confirming local law. Merredin was a poor planet, and not particularly law-abiding, either. We didn't have much of a local search-and-rescue group, relied instead on deputizing all available shipping in the event of an emergency, and those terms were written into the charter that let the family operate. Pappy was right; if we didn't send a ship, someone could take the charter away from us, and the anger in my belly made me wonder if it would be the Jedreys who'd try.

"Pappy's right," I said. "You know we have to do it."

"We're obliged to send somebody," Daddy said. "Not necessarily you."

"You just said you didn't have anybody else," I said.

"Peeky's in Cah'ville," Daddy said. "That's only a couple hours away; we could hire him to take the flight."

"Peeky Toms?" I laughed even before the prosthesis finished feeding me the details. "Peeky hasn't flown anything but sub-light for—oh, it must be six, seven years. I bet he doesn't even have a jump license anymore."

"The boy's right," Pappy said. "Peeky's not an option."

I looked at my father. "You got to send me. We can't risk losing the charter."

Daddy scowled, the frustration plain on his face. "Goddammit, I shouldn't have to keep telling you this—and the very fact that I do is the reason I don't want you doing it. You already lost most of your perceptors. You only got six minutes of natural memory. You lose that, even that goddamn prosthesis won't do you any good."

"I ain't actually stupid," I began, and Daddy slammed his cup down on the table, not caring that the coffee splashed across the scarred fiber.

"You sure are acting it. You remember the last time you went outside?"

No. I bit back the word, knowing the question was rhetorical, knowing that attitude wouldn't do me any good. The prosthesis answered his question anyway, spilling pictures into my mind as it accessed images I could no longer create. A chaos of light and color, explanation lagging behind the perceived shapes; my feet stumbling on a flat walkway, splashing through liquid color that became advertising that became a puddle…. There had been friends there, people that I knew before the accident, but I'd been too busy trying to learn to see again that I hadn't remembered to tell the prosthesis to remember who they were. The Glasstown skyline loomed in memory, jagged color against the sunset, and I felt remembered nausea— anger, too, that so many people had been there to see. I guessed Daddy had been one of them, but I didn't, couldn't, remember.

"Yeah," I said, reluctantly, and Daddy glared at me.

"You still think you can fly."

"It's different," I said, and knew it sounded feeble. But it was different, a different kind of memory…. "Besides, somebody's got to do it."

"He's right," Pappy said again. "You know the law."

Daddy muttered something under his breath.

Pappy said, "What about this? Send the racer up—send the tender with the racer grappled on. The tender crew can do the real looking, and the boy will be on-board as the jump pilot."

"What if they find Alrei?" Daddy asked.

"Odds are 283.2 to one against it," Pappy said. "That's based on the number of ships the charter-holders are throwing up there."

"I don't like it," Daddy muttered.

I said it before Pappy could. "I don't think we got a choice."

Once the decision was made, it didn't take long to get things moving. We had procedures in place for this kind of emergency, just like any charter holder, and they pretty much worked the way they were supposed to, so that by nightfall we were on our way to the port for a midnight launch. We went in a closed runabout, passenger windows blanked as though it was full daylight, screening out Glasstown's lighted towers. I kept my head down for the walk into the hangers, and the queasiness I had been expecting did not recur. It was a struggle, though, the prosthesis always a heartbeat behind what I needed, and I knew there were people I should have known who I passed without a greeting. *That* I'd expected, been braced for, but somehow I'd thought I'd still know our tender. I'd thought that knowledge would be burned into me at the same level as piloting itself, but the heavy ship that hung in the launch cradle was just another round-bellied modified lifter. I recognized it only by the family logo splashed across its nose.

We slipped aboard without fuss, and I found myself at the door of the pilot's cabin without knowing how I got there. A little dark woman was waiting there with a stack of data—the prosthesis identified her as Tetia

Curry, the ship boss, and I looked away, seeing her hair uncovered. Tetia was Alari, the prosthesis reminded me, not Merredina; she didn't mind being seen without a scarf. But she'd seen my mistake, and her eyes were sad as I took the multi-colored wafers and retreated into the cabin. Not knowing the tender had depressed me, even if I had been able to find my own cabin without trouble; messing up with Tetia depressed me even more. I knew I ought to review the data, it was bound to be stuff I needed to know, like the exact approach Alrei Jedrey had been taking, and the local space/time weather, but I couldn't bring myself to do it. Anyway, it was late enough that I had an excuse, and I stripped and rolled myself into the familiar bunk. The lights faded automatically, but I stopped them with a wave of my hand. There was a scratch pad where I expected to find it, the top film curled from long disuse. I tore it away, and wrote on the next one, leaving myself a message for the next day.

Why do I hate Alrei Jedrey?

I woke to familiar vibration and a voice repeating a name. I moved, listening, and the light strengthened, bringing color back out of the gray. I lay there, sorting perceptions of an unremembered place. The vibration was right, though, comforting; the bed was large, pleasantly warm beneath a weight of covers. The air outside the blankets was cold, my hand pale and tingling as though I'd slept on it, and the light was strong and cool now, a light to match the delicate trembling in the air.

Your name is Cass Lairmore. You are achronic. Connect your prosthesis before engaging in further activity.

I didn't remember a prosthesis—but, of course, if I were achronic, I wouldn't remember it. I sat up, the movement triggering the room lights and a whirring that carried warmth, and saw an odd, skin-colored ovoid lying on the ledge that had been above my head. A jack lay loose on top of it—no, extended from it, a short, flat head, clear plastic that showed a hint of gold in its depths. I reached for it, picked up the seashell round, smaller and flatter and softer than I had expected, and found myself reaching behind my left ear. There was a jack there, not consciously expected or even fully recognized, but my fingers had gone to it immediately, and the connection seemed clear. I slid the head into the socket, the ovoid nestling cozily against my skin, and—expanded. The world brightened, gained depth and context, and I took a deep breath, letting the prosthesis's information cascade through me.

I was Cass Lairmore, all right, and that meant I was a pilot, a jump-and-JSTL pilot. I had been a moonlighter not all that many years back, and now I was a hauler, a legit shipper, and a sometime racer and the hope of the family. I had six minutes of natural memory left, plus whatever implicit and muscle memory could give me—it was implicit memory that led my fingers to the prosthesis's jack—and everything else, any past six minutes earlier than my permanent *now*, was backed up in memory, stored somewhere in the family mainframe to be accessed by the machine. The prosthesis kept me updated, kept a few important things always in that six-minute window and prompted me for the rest, so that in practice I could keep up with about a day's worth of events. It had to download every night, and I started over every morning. Except that we were on the tender, going out on a rescue run, so the prosthesis was working from the ship's copy: no real difference, except that I would have to be sure to check that everything I stored here was downloaded when we got back. The process was supposed to be automatic, but the prosthesis reminded me it never hurt to double-check.

I'd heard most of this before, and often enough that it was kind of like an echo, not exactly remembering, but enough like it that I pushed myself out of bed and began my morning listening with half an ear while I washed and shaved. I'd been a moonlighter because my father was a moonlighter before me, back when it was serious business—the prosthesis reminded me of the tax reforms that made it less profitable, and the two years Daddy'd spent in federal suspension, both of which probably had a lot to do with the decision to stick to legal work. But regular haulage didn't earn what smuggling did, even when you added a machine shop on the side, and we'd gone racing to help make ends meet. He was pushing sixty, reflexes shot, so I was what was left. I was just a bit past thirty, the prosthesis told me, though the body I watched in the mirror looked older than that to me, and I was already at the point where I was using more brains than instinct when I got myself wrecked. And now nobody knew what to do with me—nobody knew if I could even fly the racer tucked into the tender's belly, but we were required to send a ship and a jump pilot when there was a rescue call, and so here I was. It just seemed to be an open question whether I could actually do anything if we found the missing ship.

The prosthesis didn't offer any answers, just a quick summary of the race that I'd wrecked in, and I stopped in my tracks, hoping for some hint of a feeling, some way of telling that it had actually happened to me. There wasn't, of course, just like there hadn't been any other morning. The images stayed pictures in my head, plain and unconvincing as a bad trideo. It happened in the AT Boland 3 x 5—the prosthesis annotated that for me, a high-purse, single-system race, five passes through a course of three in-system jump points; you could take them in any order, but had to pass through all three in each circuit. It was a muscle course: there was only one good way, one fast way, to run the pattern, and winning depended on having a slippery ship, one that could get as close as possible to .9C in the JSTL, just-slower-than-light, runs, and then a real kickass jump motor to put you through the jump point first and best. I'd had all of that, and I watched myself nurse the controls, confer with the ship's horse: not real memories, just images without feelings. The prosthesis was doing its best, touching spots in my brain, accessing information I could no longer reach without its help, but there were some things that were just missing. I saw myself watching the view screens as the stars turned to streaks, and the universe outside the race shrank to tiny rumbling voices in the speakers. On the third pass, I somehow got sideways going into the jump—another ship was close to me, its time wake may have rocked me, got me loose, or at least that was what I thought then—and I missed the entry. The ship slipped out of time, fell through the weakness in space/time and into the sweet not-yet, what the theorists called the adjacent possible, and the prosthesis had nothing for me anymore. I, the ship, the horse, and me, hung there, stuck there in a place where memory couldn't happen because time wasn't, until something—the horse, maybe; quantum processors shouldn't be as time-dependent as a human brain—kicked us out again.

I thought I'd feel something then, not just what the prosthesis told me to remember, but that something gut-deep would hold the fear—and I'm not ashamed to be afraid, would have been glad of it, even, if it had made the memory stick. There was nothing, and I watched myself struggle to pull enough thought and memory together to keep the ship alive until the other ships could get to me. The prosthesis played me the voices of the other racers talking me through it, telling me over and over what I had to do and why, and none of it meant any more than a story that had happened to somebody sometime back. Less, actually, because a story would have been better told.

But that was what had happened, and the prosthesis told me it had told me this every morning for 253 days, and it still didn't mean a damn thing except that it had happened to me.

There was a note stuck to the wall beside the recessed bunk. I pulled off the thin film, staring at words scribbled in a spiky hand the prosthesis told me was my own.

Why do I hate Alrei Jedrey?

The name brought back the emotion, a real, unmistakable anger that left me gasping because I hadn't felt anything so direct in what seemed forever. But it was only yesterday, the prosthesis reminded me; I'd felt it when Daddy had said it was Alrei we were going up after, and I didn't know then or now what was behind it.

Could it have been the wreck? I wondered suddenly. Was Alrei Jedrey in the Boland—was it his ship that knocked me out of time? I dropped into the chair in front of the mainframe console, let the prosthesis guide my fingers as I punched in the inquiry, but the screen came back blank. The Boland had been run almost a year ago; the ship's system didn't have anything more in memory than the entry list and the results, and we were already too far out and traveling too close to C to query the home system. But at least I could check the entries. Sure enough, Alrei had been entered—had run, had finished fourth, well ahead of the racers whose times were marked with the asterisks that resulted from my wreck. So it looked like he'd been ahead of me, unless he'd got me loose and jumped without checking to see what happened behind him. That sparked another flare of anger: I knew that was wrong, the same ingrained way I'd known it was wrong to look a bare-headed woman in the face. If Alrei had done that, he deserved to have a runner, deserved to be lost....

I took a deep breath. I didn't know that he'd done it—couldn't know, until we got back to Glasstown and I could consult Pappy there. But that would explain the anger that I remembered, would explain why I hated Alrei's name.

There were clothes laid out on the shelf at the front of the storage wall. The prosthesis nudged me toward them, then went on muttering about dyschronia in general as I dressed myself. At least that was something I could do with implicit memory, no prompting necessary, and I listened instead to the steady medical drone, trying to make it real. Dyschronias, disruptions of the human body's ability to place itself in time, had been around since the earliest days of the jump-and-jostle drive. It was pretty easy to hit a jump point just wrong enough to put a ship outside the bounds of recognizable space/time. It wasn't so easy to get back—that's why workhorses were AL, built and bred with a herd animal's instinct to seek more of their kind—but if you did make it, there was a good chance the miss would damage the body's chronal perceptors. Without time, they began to die, and that was dyschronia. Sometimes the effect was temporary, and you'd lose your hair or your fingernails as the quick-growing cells got speeded up or slowed down: that was chronorrhea, and I think every moonlighter or racer has had it at least once. Sometimes the effect was permanent. You could lose a chunk of memory when the perceptors died in that part of the brain: chronophasia. You could stop shedding your past, mental and physical, end up choked to death by the sheer weight of memory and dead cells: chronal sclerosis. You could be speeded up, stuck in fast-time, burn out a lifetime in a year or less: pyrodyschronia. You could become too sensitive to time itself, and it would eat you up, hollow out your conscious self and leave a wasting shell: chronophagia. Or you could lose most of your time perceptors altogether, and be left unable to form lasting memory: that was achronia.

That was me.

"OK, enough," I said aloud, and the prosthesis went silent. I took one last look in the mirror—tallish, fairish, clean-shaven and freshly washed, fading hair pulled back in a neat tail—and had no idea if I was ready for whatever was planned for the day. The prosthesis sensed the hesitation, and chirped again.

Continue function?

"Yeah, fine."

The information spilled through me. We were looking for traces of Alrei Jedrey's ship, the space/time distortions left by a bad jump or a horse trying to kick back into normal space. I needed to finish putting on my undersuit, but then nobody needed me until they found something. Which was just as well, I thought. The prosthesis reminded me I still needed to read over the data Tetia had given me, and I needed to think about what I was going to do if we did find him. If he'd wrecked me—but nobody deserved to be timelost. No matter what they'd done. I pulled the thermal shirt over my head, leaving the waist seals undone for now, and settled myself in front of the reader.

It was only a few hours later that we got the signal. One of Harrel Hershaw's boys picked up an anomalous reading, and the other one confirmed it. There was a heavy hauler in the area, and they managed to triangulate, pinpoint the center of the spiral—at least that was what it looked like on the scan they broadcast—where presumably Alrei or his horse was trying to fight back into realspace. We were one of the closer ships, and Daddy cursed when he heard it. But we were already committed, and he told Eskew Grey, the tender pilot, to kick us up as close to C as he could get us. We made it to the point in less than two hours, wasting fuel at the end to shed speed, and flung ourselves into a linked orbit with the other ships, locking into a pattern that would keep us close to each other, and close enough to help. The Hershaw boys had already tried opening up the spiral, but even pulling in tandem, they didn't pack enough power to add significantly to the distortion. I hung at the back of the control room while Daddy and Eskew argued about how best to add our engine in, but even Eskew couldn't get the three ships linked up close enough to do any good. The prosthesis told me what was happening, though I had a sense of it in my bones: Alrei's ship was somewhere outside space/time—if those terms really meant anything in this context—and trying to get back in. If our engines, our false mass, could further weaken the distortion, there was a chance Alrei's horse could latch onto it, and fire the jump engine to kick him through. After all, that was how I'd escaped from my bad jump. Of course, Alrei's horse had bolted, but most runners would still seek a way back into realspace. We'd have to catch the ship if the workhorse was still out of control—but we could cross that bridge when we came to it.

We made another circuit, the ships' power balanced against each other, straining realspace as our engine crawled toward the red line, but nothing happened.

"Pull it back, Eskew," Daddy said at last, and a voice—Harrel Junior, the prosthesis said—crackled through the local com.

"I'm not seeing nothing."

The other Hershaw boy's voice rode over him. "Damn, somebody's going to have to jump it."

"Nobody's jumping nothing," Daddy said. "Not yet."

Tetia looked up from the console where she'd been monitoring the local gravity. "It's starting to fade, Jess."

"Goddammit," Daddy said. He tapped two fingers on his mouth. "Junior, what's your reading?"

"Um." Harrel Junior drew the word out for a long moment. "Not good, sir. Looks like we might be losing him."

"Dammit," Daddy said again.

"We got to jump it," the other Hershaw boy said. "Junie, I got a skid-racer in tow, maybe we can use that, do it on autopilot."

"That horse won't jump without a pilot," Harrel Junior objected.

The other boy sighed. "All right, what about Cass? Doesn't he have his racer along?"

"Now wait just a damn minute," Daddy began, and Eskew put his hand on the com switch, muting the transmission.

"We're here, boss. We got to try something."

I said, "Let me go." I hadn't meant to say it, but I knew I had to, down at the core where I still knew a few things. Whatever Alrei had done, even if he had wrecked me and not looked back, I was a racer still, and I knew what I was supposed to do.

"No," Daddy said.

"You know I got to."

The look on his face was terrible, like we'd been arguing for an hour and he already knew he'd lost. "No, son."

"I got to," I said again. For a second, it was like there was nobody else in the control room, just him and me, and I tried to find the words. "Look, I can't be any worse off than I am right now. And if there's any chance of getting him out, we got to try it before we lose him again."

"You could be a lot worse off," Daddy said fiercely. "And dead ain't half of it." He swung away from me, staring at Tetia's screens, at the fading spiral.

"I'm going," I said, and walked out of the control room.

Nobody stopped me, just like I'd known they wouldn't. I climbed down into the belly of the tender, squeezed though the transfer tube and into the body of the racer to find Tetia already working the launch checklists. I strapped myself into the couch, let the control systems close over my arms and legs, and felt the first tentative movements that meant the ship and the horse were coming alive for me. This felt right, this felt normal—just like the sims, only better—and I wriggled myself down into the seat. It wasn't mine; the size was close, but not quite right, and that didn't matter at all. This was what I knew best, and I would show them all.

Lights spread across the control boards, long strings of orange and yellow, quickly fading to green. As long as I didn't look too close, didn't think too much about them, I understood what they meant. I made the mistake once of trying to remember what one panel was—I knew it was important—and lost the flow of the ship even as the prosthesis prompted me. My hands faltered, falling out of the rhythm, and Tetia's voice sounded in my ears.

"You all right, Cass?"

"Fine," I said, my voice strangled. I closed my eyes, blanked the prosthesis, let my hands reach for what they knew they should hold. I was back again, in the groove, the ship waking under me, and I would have giggled aloud, except no one would have understood.

"Ready for drop," I said, and it was Daddy who answered.

"Drop in ten." He paused. "Jump safe, Cass."

"Roger that," I answered, and braced myself for the launch.

The charges kicked me loose, and I felt the workhorse surge to full life under my hands. It should have frightened me, all that raw power and me with no real sense of how it was I controlled it, but it felt too good, too much like normal, and this time I did laugh aloud. I pulled the ship around, the horse answering easily, and saw the center of the spiral looming on my screens. It was obvious it wasn't a real jump point, lacked their normal compact structure; instead it lay across my screen like the slash of a knife. The ragged edges faded too fast into nothing, were too hot and raw in the center, a wound not fully open. It would break, though, if we hit it right… and I could see the angle of approach, feel the kick it needed. I touched the controls, urging the horse forward, power building in the jump engine, saw the angle shift slightly as the racer's abnormal mass touched the proto-jump, and touched the controls again to correct. Somebody was saying something in my ears, but I couldn't listen, bracing myself instead to find just the right moment. The horse was warm and easy under my hands, the jump engine primed and ready. We touched the point, the edge of what I'd seen on my screens. I felt space move, and kicked hard. The horse answered, firing the jump engine, and we flashed into glue.

I couldn't seem to breathe for an instant, choked and fought, then caught the knack of it, as though somehow I'd grown gills and learned to breathe water. I couldn't see anything, not even my screens; the lights that had filled the cockpit were dimmed to nothing, barely embers. The prosthesis was dead, silent and utterly absent. Six minutes, I thought, I only have six minutes without it—but there was no time here except within my body, whatever clock still ticked within my cells, and even that was slowed and changed by the dead perceptors. No sight, no sound—but I could feel everything. It was as if I'd expanded, like I had with the prosthesis, only bigger, as though I could reach outside the hull of the racer, right into the sweet not-yet, as though I could dig my fingers into it and feel the universe itself in the moments before it was made real. I flexed my hands and felt strands against them, thick and gnarled as tree roots, taut and fine as harp strings. I moved my feet, and felt myself rooted, a thick cord holding me to something I could no longer name. I felt winds against my face, felt them stretching to infinity, and felt those winds curving around something familiar. I twisted my head from side to side, and realized it was another ship. Alrei's ship.

I closed my eyes as though that would help, though there wasn't enough light around me to make a difference, reached out again slow and cautious. I could feel the adjacent possible, see it in my touch: not just the ship, but Alrei himself, trapped in time, the strands thick and choking, binding him and the ship into a failing possibility. The workhorse must have thought it saw a chance of escape, thought it saw a weakness in local space/time, but its quantum sight was flawed. Of all the possibles, it had chosen one already past or never ready, and time itself battered them back, closed in to smother them. There were strands around me, too, but not so many, fraying loose and trailing away: I was time-blind, and that made me free. In the kingdom of the blind, the one-eyed man is king....

In the sweet not-yet, the timelost man is whole.

I reached out through the twining strands, reached with them, tugged them free and wove them again into a new possible, pulling Alrei to me along with the ship. I reached for my horse, for his horse, for all possible workhorses and our own, and gathered them up to bring them home.

We slid from not-yet to now, fell into realspace with a shriek of engines and all the indicators on my boards flaring red. The workhorse was belling its complaint as well, and the prosthesis still didn't answer my call. Tetia's voice hammered in my ears.

"Come on, Cass, talk to me. Talk to me, kid."

"I'm not a kid," I said, and heard her shaky laugh.

Alrei's ship floated huge in my screens, almost close enough to touch. I giggled at the thought, at the memory of what I'd done, the universe at my fingertips, and ran a frequency search, looking for his band. A light flared, and I spoke into the com.

"Alrei? You there?"

"Yeah." The voice was shaky, shaken, and Daddy's voice rode over both of us.

"Hang tight, you two. We're moving for pickup."

"Roger that," Alrei said, and I echoed him.

I leaned back in my couch, exhausted beyond words. I wondered vaguely if that was the symptom of another dyschronia, wondered if Alrei was going to suffer one, and couldn't find the energy to care. A light flickered on the com: Alrei, offering a private circuit. There was one thing I did want to know, and I mustered the strength to accept the contact.

"Thank you," he said, and I stopped. The anger was gone—well, it was there, in memory, but it didn't seem to matter.

"You're welcome," I said, and paused. "Was it you who wrecked me?"

"Huh?" There was another pause, and I could imagine Alrei remembering I was achronic. "No, it was Junie Hershaw. Why?"

"Then why was I mad at you?"

There was a silence, starsong hissing in the speakers. Alrei said at last, low and nervous, "I jumped anyway. I saw you go, and I went ahead and jumped. I might—that might have been the thing that kicked you far enough out that the horse couldn't get you back quick enough. That—it might've been my fault."

The achronia, he meant. It rang true, almost as if I did remember it, and maybe, down on the level where I'd felt the anger, I did remember something. I worked my hands, feeling something between my fingers—feeling the truth of what he said, of his mistake, and mine, and Junie's, a tangible past as real as the way realspace still echoed like a plucked string from where it had broken. I didn't remember, you couldn't call this memory, exactly, it was something different, more and less and always inarticulate: a past for touching, not yet for words. But it was a past, and a future, too, the strands of the sweet not-yet easy in my hands, time and possibility lying rough beneath the surface of the now. Not memory, no, but something almost better. Time in my hands, time on my hands, never time within me again, but that was nothing, no loss, set against what I'd been given. We were even, Alrei and I; if anything, I was in his debt. I lay back in the couch again, time heavy and comforting around me, and waited for rescue.

Leslie What

THREESOME
LESLIE WHAT

Cara was sitting on the floor beside the bed when a barrage of green lights flashed from somewhere outside the dormer window. A whirring sound, like an insanely broken sprinkler, only louder, was her first clue that something terrible was about to happen. Her best friends, Kamala and Jessica, sat side-by-side on Cara's bed and pored over a magazine. Cara heard a car screech to a halt and heard dogs and cats bark, then silence. At first she thought it was the Rapture, but that didn't explain the green flashing lights. "Ohmygod!" Cara said. "I know what it is!" Aliens had landed and had started to round up all of the humans. "But we're still here," Cara said. "Isn't that weird?"

Kamala and Jessica glared down at her from the bed. They were reading her copy of *Seventeen* because two could share a magazine, whereas three could not. But since it belonged to her, Cara consoled herself knowing she could read it later. The reason she was angry had nothing to do with the stupid magazine. It was just that when her two best friends swarmed into her room, they had formed a clique on her bed and let her know she wasn't invited to join.

Cara, just thirteen, was the frail sort, small-boned, with translucent, almost blue skin. She had lost enough weight in the last two years, since starting middle school, that one might have described her as paper-thin. She had not yet started her period, which both frightened her and made her a target of pity.

At almost fourteen, Jessica was the oldest. She was muscular and short, with a head shaped like a boulder. Her teeth and skin were perfect, on her, everyone agreed, a waste. Why did all the ugly girls have good teeth and complexions while all the cute girls had uneven skin tone and overbites? Because when you were ugly, it didn't matter if you were even uglier, but when you were cute it was so easy to fuck up. All it took was a zit or a mole, whereas on an ugly girl, who would even notice?

Whereas Kamala, in the middle, at thirteen and one half, was tall and slender, with steel-hard and long dancer's legs. Kamala was fast and sharp-tongued. She could make Cara cry, which she did, as often as possible.

Cara heard disgusting sucking and screaming noises outside. "At first I thought it was the Rapture," Cara admitted. "Then I figured out it was aliens."

"What *are* you talking about?" said Kamala.

"Look," Jessica said. "We don't want to make fun of your beliefs..."

"We don't?" said Kamala. "I do."

"Don't listen to her," said Jessica. "She's just being a bitch. It's cool that you're religious. It's cool that you worry about Rapture and the end of the world. But you have to be tolerant of us and our beliefs and we don't think the world is going to end."

"I don't have any beliefs," Kamala said.

"It shows," said Jessica.

"There's nothing to be afraid of," Jessica began, but stopped.

"You keep telling yourself that," said Cara. But she forced herself to shut up. They'd made it clear neither wanted to hear it and she was tired of arguing and trying to prove her point. When she concentrated, she could smell the hot rubber stench from when the alien ships had burned through the Earth's atmosphere. She stood and went over to the window seat to look out. The skies seemed to open up to allow bands of brilliant light to stream through the clouds.

On the sidewalk, a kid on a bike looked up, maybe expecting to see God, but instead surprised at what he was seeing: no doubt little horrible green flying bug-eyed monsters that appeared overhead and sucked everybody up from whatever they were doing in their cars or lawns or houses or fields or sweatshops. She tried to see straight above her but the angle was wrong. When she glanced back at the sidewalk, the kid was gone.

"We're all alone," Cara said, dazed. "Just the three of us."

"Well, sing a song about it," said Kamala.

"You don't understand," Cara said. "We're all that's left." Cara closed her eyes. The sucking up process was gross, loud whooshy sounds like when a dog snarfed up a hot dog, or the noises you heard at the sucking-machine drive-thru thing at the bank. She imagined green bug-eyed flying monsters baring their fangs, dripping slime all around, killing lawns and making snakes explode. In the distance she heard screaming and fear and anger as all the people got sucked up, except for the girls in her room.

"You can have your magazine back," said Kamala, and tossed it to the ground. The pages were splayed and dirty.

"Let's make crank phone calls," said Jessica. "You've got ID Block, don't you?"

"I hate crank calling," said Kamala.

"So, stay here," said Jessica.

"There's no point," said Cara, but the two of them had already bounced from the bed and run for the stairs. Cara followed them into the kitchen, where they could rummage for food as they called out on the portable.

"Let's call Roy," said Kamala. She gave Jessica his number.

"No answer," Jessica said. "I know. Let's call Mr. Fish."

Kamala opened the refrigerator and took out the milk. "Get the phone book," she told Cara. "Got anything to eat?"

Cara brought out the phone book, cheese and crackers, and a bowl of fruit. They always had fruit.

"Don't you have anything good?" asked Kamala. "Why do we come here when all they ever have is fruit?"

"Because they have cable with HBO," Jessica said. "Nobody's perfect." She dialed up Mr. Fish, but there was no answer.

"Where is everybody?" asked Kamala.

"No point in calling anyone," Cara said. "Nobody's home. Except us. Don't you get what I've been telling you?"

"Oh, shit. She's right. Let's watch TV," said Kamala.

Just then, the sun faded behind the clouds and thunder broke. Rain tapped like children's footsteps above them on the skylight and all three looked up, as if expecting to see someone running away. There was a loud pop and a crackling noise and a thud as a tree branch broke and landed on the roof. The power went out and the house went grave-silent.

"Oh shit," said Cara.

"I guess this means we can't watch TV," said Kamala.

"Let's go to the mall," said Jessica.

"How will we get there?" Kamala answered.

"We could take the bus," Jessica said.

"No way," said Kamala. "I am not taking the bus with homeless smelly people."

"Where's your mom?" Jessica asked. "She could take us."

"She isn't here," Cara said.

"Like, we didn't notice that?" Kamala said.

"When's she getting back?" asked Jessica. "That's what we mean and you know it."

"She's supposed to be here already," Kamala said.

"I don't think she's coming home," said Cara.

"Oh stop with the end of the world shit," said Kamala.

"Whatever," said Cara.

They would need to make a grocery run and stock up on everything. They might as well eat lots of burgers and shakes right away because pretty soon, they would all be living on Spam and saltines. She wondered how long it would take to grow bored with each other's company. When there were only three, that didn't allow for enough variables to make things interesting, and everything was too routine, too predictable. When there were only three, there was always one man out, so to speak. If she had learned anything from the alien Rapture, it was that someone was always left behind.

Maybe two of them would get hungry and eat the third. She hoped it wasn't her—not that she wanted to eat anyone—she just didn't want to be sacrificed for the others.

"Let's play a game," said Kamala, and the others dutifully followed her into the living room. Cara's father was an orthodontist. On the shelves were models of jaws and teeth molds, each identified by name. Cara had smashed her own mold the first time she came across it, preferring to pretend she came by her nice smile naturally. But Cara liked looking at the Neanderthal jaws of her former classmates. They had once made fun of her, but now that they'd been snatched, the joke was on them.

"I wish we had Pop Tarts," Jessica said.

"Remember how good Pop Tarts taste toasted?" Kamala asked.

"Umm, yeah, with the filling all hot and the crust all crispy and the sugar burning your tongue," said Jessica. "We better stop talking about food or I might have to eat somebody."

"Don't you sometimes hate it that your parents won't let you eat sweets?" Kamala said.

Cara shrugged. She was always worried about her weight and didn't like to eat sweets anyway.

Kamala picked up a magazine and sighed. "What do you suppose is going to be in fashion for the summer? I mean, what do you think would be in fashion if there still was such a thing, since according to Cara, the aliens must have taken away all the fashion designers?"

"I think it would be the summer of full-frontal nudity," said Jessica. "Simple yet tasteful. But only the girls would go naked. The boys would all be wearing sweats."

"Oh, gross," Kamala said. "I don't want to see a bunch of naked porn sluts. But anyways, I doubt it. Nude girls will never be popular. People might be temporary but fashion was forever, which explains why there were still togas even though the Romans had been dead for a thousand years."

"What game should we play? Cara asked. "How about Monopoly or Clue?"

"I want to play chess," Jessica said. "Who'll play with me?"

"I will," Cara and Kamala called in unison.

"Who should I choose? Hmmm," Jessica said, grinning ferociously.

"I'll rub your back," Kamala said.

"And what about you, Cara?" Jessica asked. "What will you do for me?"

Cara felt acutely uncomfortable. Her belly hurt like someone had socked her there. "I'll rub your feet," she said, though she didn't really want to. She suspected that Jessica wouldn't want her to either, so it was the perfect thing to offer.

"Euewweueue! Gross!" said Jessica. "Kamala, you be black."

"That's why we shouldn't play games that only two can play," said Cara, trying not to show her disappointment.

"You're such a baby," said Jessica. All the good games are for two, or maybe four. That's just the breaks."

"There's lots of games for three," Cara said.

"Oh, like hide and seek. Let's play that. How retarded."

"I was thinking of Scrabble," said Cara. "Or *Parcheesy*."

"I wish the bug-eyed monsters had left behind some cute boys," said Kamala. "This is *so* unfair."

"We don't need any boys," said Jessica. "I don't know why you always say that. I like it that there's only girls."

"Oh, come out, already," said Kamala. "Not that it will do you any good."

"What do you suppose they're doing up there?" Jessica asked. "Do you think the bug-eyed monsters ate them?"

"Probably," said Kamala. "Unless they needed slaves. But if they needed slaves, why would they take the old people like your mother? They can't work very hard."

"Why would they take the old people if they were just going to eat them?" Jessica asked. "They can't taste very good, either."

"You're *so* right," said Kamala. The two glared at each other and screamed "Experiments!" in unison.

"Why us?" Cara asked. "It doesn't make sense. They meant to take everyone. Why leave us behind?"

Kamala…sneezed and looked frantically around for some tissue. She wiped her nose and spit into the corner. "We're the Plus or Minus three," she said. "We're the mistakes that you have to ignore in a poll."

"You be plus one and I'll be minus," said Kamala. She tossed her dirty tissue on the floor.

"Oh, come on!" Cara chided. "How hard could it be to take that outside and throw it on the lawn?"

"You're not my mother," said Kamala. She inched toward Cara until she was close enough to jab her.

"Ouch!" Cara shrieked. "Cut it out."

Kamala made her hands into the blades of scissors. "Snip, snip," she said.

"Paper, rock, scissors!" yelled Jessica, and jumped atop Kamala and ground her fist into the smaller girl's scalp. "Noogie time!" she said with too much glee. "Kamala wants a boyfriend but has to settle for me!"

"Jessica wants a girlfriend but is deluded and thinks that might be me!" said Kamala.

Jessica applied enough pressure to leave a bruise.

"Ouch!" Kamala shrieked. "Stop!"

"You're *so* immature!" said Cara.

"Cara just wants to grow up," said Jessica. She pulled on Kamala's hair.

"Save me, Cara!" Kamala begged.

"Why should I?" asked Cara.

"She's killing me!" Kamala said. "You have to help! Or I won't help the next time she tries to kill you."

"Oh, God, this is so lame! Okay, okay." She rushed over to lay her hand over Jessica's back and said, "Paper covers rock."

Jessica ground one final intensely painful noogie into Kamala's head before rolling off in a fit of giggles on the carpet.

"I hate this game," said Cara.

"Well you better get used to it," Kamala said. "Because if we're all that's left and you don't want to be left out in chess, well, this is sorta *it*."

"Paper, Rock, Scissors is a lot more fun when you get to be violent," Jessica noted, with a warning glance toward Kamala.

Cara's belly felt worse, hot and painful, like she had to go to the bathroom, only she didn't. She wondered if this meant that she was finally getting her period. What terrible timing!

"I have an idea," Jessica said. "If everyone else is dead and we went to a sporting goods store or somewhere good, wouldn't everything be free? I think we should steal a car and drive there ourselves."

"I want to go to the store," Kamala said. "I've got a huge zit."

"Why do you care about zits?" said Jessica. "There aren't any boys around to look at you."

"I care," said Kamala. "Who wants to go with me?"

"It's raining," Cara said. "I'm cold. Can't we wait and go tomorrow?" Once you got really cold and wet it was almost impossible to warm up.

"There's no need to be cold," Jessica said. "You have a fireplace. Let's burn something."

"It's a gas fireplace," said Cara. "Those are fake logs."

"That ought to make the fire easy to start," said Kamala.

"You guys!"

"It's so unfair," Cara said. "What did any of those people do to deserve to be abducted?"

"Life isn't fair," said Jessica. She kicked Kamala on the shin.

"You bitch!" Kamala screamed, and lunged toward her attacker.

They wrestled some more. Cara didn't want to watch, and got up to look out the window. "I'm scared," she said. "I don't know what's going to happen."

"You never knew what was going to happen," said Kamala. "And you were afraid then. Even before the aliens."

It was true.

"I'll go to the store," said Jessica. "Rain doesn't scare me."

"Me too," Cara added quickly. "I'll go with you guys."

The two older girls jumped up and ran outside, allowing the door to slam shut before Cara could catch them.

"Wait up," said Cara.

Kamala must have heard her but pretended not to. She took Jessica's arm. "Let's hide," she said, and the two of them ran away.

Cara followed them down the street. The rain fell in her eyes and she slipped on the sidewalk and scraped her leg. Her ass was cold and wet and everything hurt. "Wait up!" she said, almost begging. "Hey, I think I got my period!" She could no longer see Jessica and Kamala; maybe they were still hiding. "Olly olly oxen free!" she cried.

She sat still and looked around at the gray and quiet stillness of the street. "Where is everybody?" she called. Only a wiry, howling dog who jumped against his wire fence bothered to answer.

AREA SEVEN
ROBERT ONOPA

Non era ancor di là Nesso arrivato,
quando noi ci mettemmo per un bosco
che da neun sentiero era segnato.

The data alarm squealed like a frightened small animal. The ship shuddered as we braked and the com screen went blank for an instant, then kicked back up. Servos whirred in the nose below us.

We'd been slipping along at an altitude of a thousand meters in one of C Survey's mapping skiffs. I'd been asleep, off duty.

"Your turn," Tessa said. The tired way she leaned over her console, her face pinched in the pale light, seemed an image of the strain she'd been under.

"I went out yesterday," I said. "Christ, don't you remember?" Tessa and I had a history that went back before we were posted to crew—on the way out, we'd even talked about something more permanent between us— but it was affecting me too, a corrosive presence that had dogged the survey since we'd entered the system. In the past few weeks I'd gotten so melancholy I'd taken to paging through *Rational Death* and imagining cryogenic nights that never end.

You think I'm kidding. I wish.

"A motility sensor tripped the alarm," she said evenly. "And you're the exo, Serge."

I scanned the data. "Movement's in the box for atmosphere," I said.

"Something replicates."

"Crystals replicate," I muttered. I studied an image from the planet on the belly camera, zoomed in.

On a gloomy, mottled surface, trunk-like forms rose in a vaguely regular way, like a surreal forest. "Where are we?" I asked.

"Fair question. The com link cut out as I was running the program to clear waypoints. There's a glitch—it's been happening all over the fleet.

Now that we're darkside, we won't get another fix until the planet's rotated or we can do the astronomy. Area Seven, I could say that, we're in Area Seven. But where *is* Area Seven? We can't exactly say that."

"Nice," I sighed.

"Warm down there."

I remembered a place on a holo. It tugged at the edge of my memory, but I couldn't quite pull it into focus. "What happens to the surface in the direction of the equator? We've got the astronomy for that."

She toggled video from the first flyover, and the screens displayed a plain of burning sand. "Melt the skids," she said.

"In the other direction?"

The screens went dirty red. "Some of the surface is moving up there— little surges, unstable. See that? Dense liquid. And that color. Like unhealthy rust." Tessa pursed her lips. "Creepy."

"Let's hover, do the rest of the astronomy and get a decent fix. I'll suit up and go down."

I didn't like the drugged sleep I'd been getting. The neurologicals gave me vivid dreams. That cycle the dreams had been bleak memories from the home planet, the blasted landscape of a tropical volcano: a high caldera streaked with recent lava flows, cinder cones, a fire pit. And I saw what I hadn't been able to remember: a path among trees inundated by ash, snaking through gnarled forms. It had a name on a weathered sign: *Desolation Trail.*

When my boots touched the surface, I picked up a sound— indistinct, distant, busy, like the noise on the Daedalus bridge when C Survey shipped out. "Tessa. You hear that?"

"All I hear is your breathing. Would you believe me if I told you it makes me think about how we used to keep each other warm at night?"

She'd kept both of us warm. For months, back when we were staging on Beta Proculis, for example, she'd nursed me though one exotic virus after another, jury-rigging IV lines to keep my fluids up, cooling my forehead, running samples into the upload trays. When I finally got back on my feet after two months, I felt smothered. I just wanted to push everything away.

For a while, she'd been all there was to push.

The planet's gloom was palpable. I checked my uplink, the atmospherics in my suit. Still, the murmuring—unintelligible, yet almost human. "Don't you hear…way in the background? Maybe from another crew?"

"Serge, all I hear is your breathing."

You don't go around insisting to your shipmates, or your former lovers, or both, that you're hearing voices. I held my tongue.

"Roger that," I said. "I'll start the report."

"Mark."

"Planet's surface appears to be a smooth basaltic flow, cat-six origin, nonfriable, solid under my boots, reticulated. I'm standing among these angular, branching forms. One to three meters high, three to nine segments, rough-surfaced—with shallow furrows—like...like nothing I've ever seen before." Whatever they were, they stretched into the distance, hundreds, perhaps thousands of them, to a misty blue horizon. I made a mental note to do a grid count. "Experiencing spurious audio."

I raised my specimen hammer—I was trained as a geologist, and my first impulse is to chip away a bit and look beneath the surface. But that day I hesitated, then touched the strange shape before me with my glove. "Structurally variated skin," I said. "Not metallic or obviously mineral. You can get your fingers around small segments...."

Tessa's voice— "Need any instrumentation down there?"

"Let me first try to just...collect a sample."

Beneath my thick gloves, I felt a rough section, half the size of my hand, give slightly, then snap through, like boxwood.

It was the strangest experience I've ever had in space. The background murmur I'd been hearing became a voice, and the voice became comprehensible.

Why do you break me? it said.

"Tessa," I said, "did you copy that?"

A pause. She sounded exhausted. "Copy to, 'collect a sample.'"

I stepped back. Where I'd fractured the trunk, a red liquid oozed like quicksilver. While I watched, it filled the bowl of the wound and darkened, like blood in air.

As it did so, I heard the voice again, a girl's voice.

Why do you tear me? Is there no pity in your soul?

"Your vitals are spiking," Tessa said in my helmet.

"No problem," I lied, feeling my skin crawl. I'll tell you how far gone I was—I didn't want to talk to Tessa. I didn't want to talk to anybody. In that bleak place, I just wanted to sink into the blanketing, apocalyptic darkness that I heard in that voice, some quality in it that touched me like the song of an icy Siren. "Something I want to...sort out here," I mumbled. "Shutting down audio."

"Serge...."

I found the line and toggled out.

"Anyone there?" I whispered, and touched the wound with my hammer.

We were beings before we were changed into sticks.
Your hand might have been more merciful
Had we been souls of rats or ticks.

As I watched, my mind was flooded with another home-planet memory.
We were camping, the night had become chilly, and my younger brother
had put a log into the fire, a green log that had been set aside to dry. When
one end started smoldering, heat forced sap bubbling out the other, dripping and hissing. In just that way, both fluid and words together sputtered
from the wound in the strange shape before my eyes.

I was so startled that I dropped my hammer. My mouth was so dry it
was a struggle to speak. "Who are you?"

We took our lives. Now each dawn in the sun's rising light,
Heat breaks us. We moan, we bleed, we speak, but do not move.
Oh, traveler, what strange love brings you in harrowing night?

At the edge of my vision, the ship's com light began flashing on my
helmet array. I toggled up audio. "Tess...."

"I'm pulling you up, Serge. I don't know what's going on down there,
but I'm pulling you up."

I'm going back for another sample," I told Tessa.
"You're crazy. Your vitals are all over the place. I checked your support gasses. Trace anomalies, but what else would explain it? Problem's
got to be in your backpack."

"Nothing's wrong with my suit," I said. "I told you, I'm hearing voices
down there. Don't you remember Takahishi's report from the skiff on the
second planet? They thought they were getting some weird geomagnetic
overlay. The data they were pulling up—Takahishi mentioned voices."

"And what are they telling you?" she asked patiently.

"The voice... She said they were—they all were—suicides."

Tessa looked at me mournfully, pulling on the locket I had given her.
"Are you being ironic?"

"No, no. I broke off a...section, and...it began bleeding, the trunk began bleeding, and while it bled, it spoke. I thought about it in the air lock.
The way a human suicide communicates is through spilling blood. The
process, the mechanism, makes a kind of sense. A suicide expresses
himself...or herself...through the flowing of his or her blood, that's the
way they speak to us. There's something familiar...."

"Serge...?"

I rubbed my forehead. "Anything on the sensors?"

"Nothing. The data from your suit's the only anomaly."

"I'll wear my other suit. You do the chemistry. I'm going down again as soon as the backup's ready."

T wo hours later, despite Tessa's protests, I picked my way across the surface again. As they had before, the murmurs surrounded me like the blue haze that obscured the skiff. This second deployment was different—of course, it's always eerie stepping across alien crust, but, this time, I was gripped by the knowledge that each note in that solemn chorus could be that of a separate being. The forms stretched to a purple horizon. When I started to lay out a reference grid, I registered the enormity of what I saw, and felt overwhelmed, disoriented. In a moment of panic I swung around awkwardly, looking for the skiff. I stumbled, and fell.

Ah, no! Please let me die!

Another woman's voice. I looked around and at first saw nothing. Then I looked below my knees and realized that I had fractured a slim trunk with my fall. Thick red quicksilver oozed from a long fracture.

"Forgive me," I murmured as I pushed myself up.

Raped by troops at Montaperti, I wept hot tears.
They cut the hand that held the flag!
Drowned am I and shamed ten thousand years.

The place she had named, Montaperti, I recognized it! Now I knew what seemed familiar—a battle lost because the arm of a guidon bearer had been hacked through by a traitor, an army of sixty thousand slaughtered for want of direction.

She was a character from the Hell of Dante's *Inferno*, from the first realm of *The Divine Comedy*, a world of suffering, regret, and timeless punishment.

I know, it sounds impossible. But as I stood there, my senses alive with a clarity I had never experienced before, I took in a landscape in which all the pieces fit: the segmented forms—like leafless trees in a haunted wood—the speaking blood, the suicide victim from Montaperti. I could fix my place even more precisely: I was apparently within the region of the Violent, in the ring of Dante's *Inferno* reserved for those who had violated their persons by taking their own lives. Only those sinners were punished by the peculiar transformation I beheld before me.

I'd read the poem at the academy. We'd been given a passage, and I'd gotten lost in the story and devoured the whole thing, my imagination swept away by an inspired professor.

Sputtering words and blood, the sad spirit before me described a feud between two great houses—an innocent girl jilted, left standing at a chapel altar—the very feud that had shaped Dante's world.

I stood there transfixed, listening for time out of mind, mesmerized by the soft velvet of her voice as she incanted the lines: the jilted girl was avenged by her brother, who murdered the groom. The groom was avenged by the murder of the girl. The war that followed ravaged the countryside, bled generations, and destroyed the great ancient city of Florence. Eventually her words grew quiet and I recognized that the broken breathing I was listening to was my own. When I looked, the fracture had all but healed.

I checked my com status: all the ship's channels were lit like holiday decorations. Without thinking, I had cut myself off from Tessa again—but what could I tell her?

I 'm getting a low-frequency crawl from the other skiff on the planet," Tessa said when I'd toggled back into the ship's com system. Her voice was clipped with anxiety. "They're calling in an 'emergency event.'"

"Any details?"

"No, but listen to this. A skiff's lost on the first planet. Some kind of geomagnetic disturbance is tripping up rescue—all sorts of equipment down. Survey teams across the fleet reporting very strange data."

I could have told her then, and perhaps I should have, but words would just not come. How could I convince her that what I had heard, what I had seen, was real without triggering an emergency of my own? I checked my life support. Gasses in the nominal range, though I was building CO_2 too rapidly—hyperventilating? I had only an hour left in Area Seven, at the outside.

"I want to come down and get you."

The thought of Tessa on the surface, of both of us losing track of time, made me shiver. "Just…a few more minutes," I said. "Whatever you do, stay with the ship. We need someone to stay with the ship."

"Serge…."

"Tessa, stay with the ship."

From other suicides I heard more war stories—one from a foot soldier who ran from battle but ironically found the courage to slit his own throat rather than face his sergeant. A large, doubled form, situated on a low rise, the smaller shape entwined around the larger, turned out to be the painful twin suicide of an exiled father and son.

Further north, they told me, lay the spirits of the conventionally violent, the murderers, the terrorists, the thugs, wallowing in a river of ancient, boiling blood. South of us, towards the planet's equator, on a plain of sand so hot that it suggested planetary processes fleet had never encountered before, resided those guilty of more refined versions of the sin, the perverse, the falsifiers, perpetrators of violence against nature on its most fundamental level.

When I finally turned back toward the skiff, an even taller shape caught my attention. It stood apart, a full meter higher than anything else in sight, erect, with a kind of stately bearing. My life support was hovering near reserve, but I made my way over.

I ran my hand over its surface. I used my hammer to pry a section free. In its place on the trunk the blood-red quicksilver bubbled out, as if under pressure.

"Speak to me," I whispered. "Tell me who you are."

A sad voice answered:

> *I was the next to rule. I held the keys to the noblest heart*
> *Of all the lords. Envy turned all against me,*
> *Envy was the start.*

He had been regent and it was said of him that he knew his lord's mind even before his master did. The old inner circle grew jealous, whispered of his complicity with a rival faction, ties to an exiled commander. They had him arrested.

Once in the damp prison, he was tortured. When he would not reveal his lord's battle plans, they took a fine hot wire and pierced his eyes. The pain, he said, was inexpressible.

Locked in his cold cell, without even a cord to hang himself by, he marshaled his strength and began to beat his head against the wall. He beat and fell, and rose and beat again, crushing his skull against the stone until he felt nothing, saw nothing, and heard nothing at all.

> *I swear, that never in word or spirit did I,*
> *Peter of the Vine, break faith with my lord.*
> *Oh traveler, vindicate my memory!*

I remembered him from Dante! Pier della Vigne, Peter of the Vine!

It moves me even now to think that, though many there had ended their lives out of shame, or cowardice, many others had done so in a search for honor or in pursuit of relief from unfathomable pain. Yet they all shared the punishment by the means I saw before my eyes, and pain inhabited every shape. How could I understand their sin? A failing in each of them, a turning away from life, from the heart of things? Story after story suggested it, each half fairy tale, half tragic history, life stories from a fantastic world of lost beings.

I was aware I was running out of time from the visuals I was getting from Tessa on my helmet array. In the end, I toggled down even that display, listening to my own breathing and the hypnotizing voices of the figures before me.

I don't know what broke the spell—the light on the horizon, rising voices, Tessa's insistent calls on the override com circuit. At some point I toggled the skiff back online, but only to silence the suit alarm.

"Serge, we are listing emergency event. Please respond. Repeat. Emergency event. Planetary rotation critical and dangerous. Repeat. Emergency event. Your life support numbers are degrading and surface time's approaching terminus. Repeat, Serge, surface terminus. This is urgent. Whatever minutes you've got, when you see the sun, the temp's going to exceed your suit's cap. Please respond."

I swayed, fought for balance, as the blue world seemed to spin around me. My experience had shriven my soul—now my own problems seemed inconsequential, my own depression trivial and self-indulgent. I felt I had been granted a vision, but would I be able to make sense of it?

I knew it was too late now for Tessa to launch a rescue. Had I, I wondered, come down to enact my own suicide? Was that what it all meant?

The light on the horizon was resolving into a bright pillar of fire. A rising heat, beyond the already elevated temps of the planet, had begun fracturing the shapes. Around me, the murmuring was coalescing into cries and weeping, appeals and rants. Another memory from the home planet: lava falling from a low cliff into the sea, boiling waters, the awful rending cry of a torn landscape—I thought I heard it now on a rising wind.

That's when I made out Tessa's voice on the com channel, throaty with desperation and fatigue. In my mind's eye I could see her in the dim light. "Oh, Serge, it's too late now. I don't know why you've been so sad. I should never have let you go. I should have come down. I can only tell you how much I love you—I wish you'd get it, Serge, wish you'd understand. I need you. You always thought it was the other way around—*I need you.* I don't know what I'm going to do without you...." She went on for a while—and then all I could hear was quiet weeping.

Something...snapped in me. It felt it like a small electrical charge, and from that tiny impulse I struggled against inertia and finally turned back toward the skiff. Tessa was firing off seismic rounds to get my attention, but I have to tell you, they weren't what made me move.

I credit Tessa herself, the quality of her heart. It was what I could hear in her weeping, her willingness to reach out to me even after I seemed lost. She saved me that way, I think, touched my own heart, turned me away from the sad death I was surrounded with and was sinking toward, turned me back toward the ship. I've thought about it a lot since then. Really, it was Tessa who saved me.

I stepped heavily toward the lift cable. My suit felt as if it had turned to lead. I could see heat rising around me in visible wisps from the surface, shapes running with blood, I could hear a rising chorus of voices, howling as one....

Eventually, the sunlight was so bright, so shot through with high-frequency yellows and pale, shimmering blues, that it was as if I was passing through flames themselves, as if my body was stepping through the heart of some strange fire. Voices screaming around me, white light devouring my sight, I found the heavy cable and clenched it in my hand.

That very day they pulled us out. They pulled us *all* out, all the skiffs, the whole C Survey. Only when we were all assembled for the journey back did we come to understand the depth of the trouble we'd been in. Two crews had been lost out of twenty-two, two entire skiffs. Think of it—almost one out of ten of us didn't make it back. We lost tons of instrumentation and equipment. All for nothing—navigation errors corrupted every bit of the data. Besides the serious stuff, there were dozens of accidents, accounts of bizarre experiences like mine. As you know, the survey's become something of a legend. You hear about it in the service bars, in the NCO clubs. All sorts of wild stories—as if what happened wasn't wild enough!

The official line is that crews suffered under a kind of mass delusion, that some set of circumstances stressed us collectively. It caused us, as skiff crews, to translate our responses into the discourse of Dante's imagination.

But the data's not that coherent. I don't think one in ten of us, of the crews on station, had actually read the poem. It hadn't been on my mind for years.

Takahishi has an alternate explanation. He thinks that we stumbled onto one of the cosmos' gallery of amazements, an alien race who took the transmissions that we humans have been flooding the galaxy with for a thousand years now—all the great works of art, our genome, our technology, our languages and works of literature, the details of history and daily life—and reconstructed a medieval Catholic milieu to test us once we arrived on their doorstep.

I don't know. Why Dante? Why would they be so specific? Still, maybe Takahishi's right. Extraordinary events require extraordinary explanations. Imagine for a moment that Takahishi's explanation is true—a sun with three planets on which strange intelligences live out eternities enacting ideas that come from such a profound distance. Who could these intelligences be?

Personally I think the truth lies between the two explanations, that it's stranger than even Takahishi imagines. Perhaps what happened to us can be seen as a message from the beings of that system. They accessed our computers, looked for a set of stories to describe us to ourselves. Maybe they knew what we had in mind for them—we'd come looking for planets to rearrange and terraform, after all. It could be that they took our inner lives, dramatized punishments for our mission, made them personal, and cast us away. I don't know.

Of course, the way we're finding minerals in the Arcturus sector nowadays, it'll be a long time before we get back to that three-planet system to figure out what really went on. Tessa and I have talked about it a lot. She thinks it'll be at least a thousand years before we get back there. Morgan agrees. The system's out of the way, he says, and there's just no percentage in going back.

Now, if you'll be seated, Tessa will bring you some refreshments, and I'll tell you some of the other stories we heard. We've got quite a bit of material from the fragmentary data, from the transcripts, from the reports. About the first planet. I don't know much about the other two. That data's been classified from the start. Morgan claims that the third planet—where we lost those two crews without a trace, first one crew and then the other that was sent to look for them—was a version of Paradise. Perhaps they're in some kind of heaven, or maybe they died only thinking they were living out their fantasies.

Anyway, as for the planet Tessa and I were scouting, the first planet, we have some images to show you as well. Thank you, Tessa. See if you can make out the human shapes punished in what looks like an icy storm, or bodies ravaged by the swipes of snarling beasts. I know the images aren't quite clear, but these are things survey crews claimed they saw, or heard, much as I did the bleeding suicides. The reports especially shake the soul—we have one of a woman, her intestines spilled from her body, who holds her severed head by its black hair like a lantern. I don't remember her from Dante. At the planet's south pole, Morgan claims he saw living shapes ripped and gnawed by packs of hydra-headed monsters. Is this a peek into the alien world? A hidden part of Dante's? Ours? What a savage place the imagination can be!

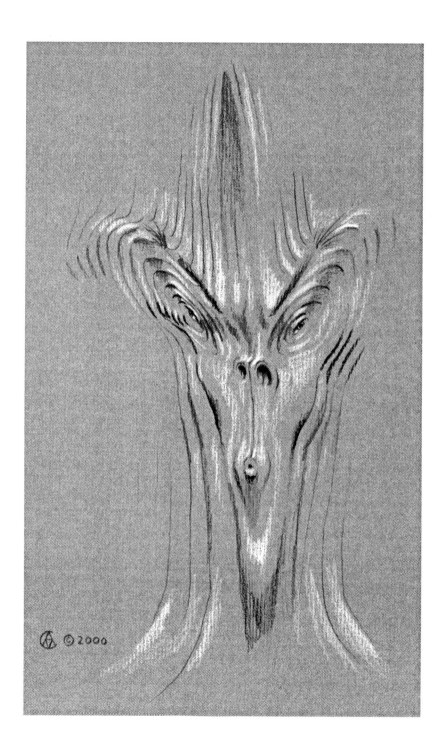

THE DREAM OF VIBO
PATRICK O'LEARY

n a sad year that no one thought would ever end, Vibo, Third Ruler of The Great Empire, fell into a deep sleep from which he could not be woken. His attendants lit candles for every hour he slept, and at the end of his dream journey, he yawned, his eyelids fluttered, and he sat up in the great golden bed of his chamber to find the room swimming in light.

Vibo had a strong long triangular face, like an arrowhead pointing to the ground. And his attendants watched as he shook it, violently back and forth, as if to clear his mind of a nightmare or a wicked thought. It frightened them to watch in the candlelight for it looked to them as if Vibo, their great ruler, was becoming many men, many versions of himself. Multiple faces appeared in his shivering visage, and his wide beautiful eye sockets trembled like the wings of the legendary butterfly.

Finally, the shaking stopped and their ruler was returned to them.

"I have had a dream," said Vibo the Third in a great booming voice. "It is a big dream. I must tell it to my son."

His son stepped out of the dancing lights, a pale boy, just growing into the crown of his brow, who handed his white candle to his attendant and sat beside his father on the golden bed.

"Leave us alone," said Vibo.

And when the attendants and lessers and majors and all his wives had left the chamber, and they could hear their footsteps like giant beetles scuttling down the hall, Great Vibo took the boy into his arms and said, "I have learned a great secret, my son."

His son was a wise lad, who only spoke after he had considered several angles of thought—a skill his father had taught him. Yet being young, he was not afraid to question.

"In a dream?"

"Yes," Vibo said. "Except it didn't feel like a dream. Strange. It felt like a memory. Someone else's memory. And it happened long ago. There were cars."

"Cars?" his son said. Recalling his lesson on those ancient vehicles of transport. The lessons of the poisons people used to breathe. Poisons that sickened the world, and caused generations of mutation and strife. Their dark history.

"Yes, cars. And birds."

"Birds?" His son asked in wonder. As distant to his mind as dinosaurs: flying creatures who once roamed the skies. When skies were blue. Birds. The stuff of legend.

"And everything was dying," Vibo cried. "And nobody knew it."

His son rubbed his shoulder as the Great Ruler wept.

Finally Vibo sighed, and sniffed, and collected himself. "There was a day," Vibo began, "when all life depended on one moment. And everything before and everything since depended on that one moment. It passed and nobody knew it."

On this day, a sad man woke and found his wife smiling down at him. She hadn't done that for years. And it was the nicest morning he could have imagined. The sun came through the window behind her and gave a nimbus glow to her thin gray hair. And he asked her what she was thinking that made her so happy. I was thinking of you, she answered. And why I love you. Outside their window a red cardinal swooped down past the bird feeder over the white lawn to rest on the low branch of a tree. There he smelled the boys who played in the treehouse they built that summer. And the cardinal cocked his head in question. And in the house next door the boy he smelled leaned down to pick up a golden cat. The cat purred and accepted the boy's warm arms. The boy looked deeply into the cat's eyes. And wondered why he purred. And the boy felt the cat's answer. Because somebody loved me. And the boy smiled. And his mother caught his smile as she was washing the smeared window that overlooked the white lawn, the white rag squeaking, squeaking as it absorbed the ammonia water and grime. And a flash of red went by and she thought: Is that a cardinal? Then she recalled birthing the boy, how after a long, hard labor, he erupted between her legs, folded onto her chest, took his first breaths, and transformed limb by limb, like a great spreading blush from a blue baby who loved her on the inside into a pink soft creature who loved her on the outside, too. And she recalled the smiling nurse who swabbed him gently and asked his name. And at that moment, that very important moment, that nurse's sister (who had moved into the neighborhood last summer) was dying. And she reached up to touch the chin of her husband (the only place he had to shave), who had sat in vigil at her bedside for many long and harrowing months. And she smiled a weak smile, and said Remem-

*ber Ford Road? And their smiles deepened as they recalled the night
they drove off the freeway, deep into the dark and found a side dirt
road, then a crooked two-lane trail that led them to a hidden cove in
the heart of the woods. And crawling into the back seat of their car
they hungrily, desperately stripped off their clothes and made love
wildly, screaming as they never could before. And they wept there in
their bed, surrounded by the sacred memory. What was that? the dying
sister said as a red streak flitted past their window and paused before
it dipped and found a perch on an aluminum gutter where a dead
brown leaf lay frozen in a posture of wide wonder. Like an open fist.
The leaf had escaped its tree, the only tree it ever knew, its only home.
And caught by a gust of October wind and torn from the branch, it
had been swept away into the first and only flight of its life. And as it
spun and twirled it knew that this, this was what it was made for, not to
cast its dark shape into a fluttering patch of shade in the hot summer
sun, not to bathe in the chill spring rains or even to lie frozen and
splayed out in a gutter to bask in its memories, but for that one, brief
dizzy moment of flight. The red bird understood and he affirmed the
leaf's joy by spreading his wings wide. Then he coasted down to where
a car was trying to back out of a drive. Stuck. Its rear tires spinning,
spinning in two slick grooves of snow and ice, and what interesting
music it makes, the bird thought. And a young man was behind the
wheel, shifting back and forth from drive to reverse, and slamming the
accelerator and letting it go. And cursing to the young woman beside
him: It is an awful world, a fucking awful world. Why would anyone
want to live in it? And the young woman told him why and for that
moment he wanted to live again, if only to see in her eyes the beauty
she saw in him. What was that? said the young woman. A cardinal,
said the young man, and they watched it disappear over a roof in a
perfect acrobatic arch. And in the next yard an old man stood looking
up at the clouds gray and close and thought, have I done nothing
right, have I wasted every moment, will I always wonder if it mattered?
And he heard a sound and turned in his sorrow to find the red bird
tasting water from the broken ice of a puddle in the shape of a shoe. I
made that puddle, the old man thought, recalling the crunch and the
shallow sink of his foot as he had stepped despairing out onto the
white lawn to look at the sky and consider all his life had brought him
and taken away. What a beautiful thing that is, he thought. Momentarily stunned by the red red stain against the white white lawn. We
never know why we live, the old man thought. Maybe it was to give
that hobo a ride to the bus station. That was when? Twenty years ago?*

He could smell the liquor on his breath, feel the chill coming off his army jacket as he entered the warm Impala and slammed the door.

Impala? the Prince wondered.

Or maybe it was to give my coin collection to my granddaughter. Sarah. He loved to say her name. Sarah. Or maybe it was that pony I whittled for my son when he was sick.

Pony?

Or maybe it was the glimpse of that naked woman undressing in a hotel room in Manhattan. Watching that one window in a night city of many windows. Her beautiful white body stretching in the glow of one bedside lamp.

The Prince did not wonder about that.

Or maybe it was this. This lovely red bird. Oops. Where did it go? And the red cardinal dodged a swarm of chickadees and coasted over the hill and skimming the gray slate stream that ran slow and steamed until he came to the old church, painted white and hidden from the road in a circle of pines. To the high broken window that let out warm drafts from the sanctuary. His refuge when the cold got to be too much. As he perched he could hear an organ playing. He coasted down into the dark church, over the empty pews, to where the only light was from the red votive candles and saw the young woman in glasses playing the organ. Identical red flames danced in each of her lenses. He landed where he could watch her fingers. Fingers being the only thing he envied of humans. How versatile they were. How they could make food and peel fruit and rub muscles and stroke hair—it was hard for him to reach his head. And the music they made. So full of longing. So empty of flight. And he listened to her playing the complicated old song. Her favorite piece to play when she was alone. She was alone. Her boyfriend was in the war and his last letter was a week ago. And her fingers dancing on the yellowed keys were her fingers dancing on his skin, the skin she knew so well and might never know again. If I finish this one piece without a mistake, she thought, if I play it perfectly, he will return to me. Whole. He will not die in fire. His beautiful body will not be torn open by shrapnel or bullet. If I only finish this one piece. The cardinal left then, finding the high broken window, escaping into the long white hills, ribboning between the dark towering trees, each of whom greeted him as he passed, saying Red One, where are you going? Scratch my trunk! Please scratch my trunk! And he flew to the park where no one was playing on the monkeybars, or the slide, the swings or the teeter totter. He landed on its handlebar and grasped it with his claws. And he thought about the many people whose thoughts he had touched. They think they are alone, he thought. They think everything in the world is sleeping except them. Not me, said the teeter totter plank. I remember being a tree. There were no children then. Hush, thought, the bird, I am thinking. I am thinking of time a million years hence. A time of great order brought by great violence. I am thinking about the wisest, most powerful leader. He is dreaming a dream. He is dreaming my life. He has waited and lived and conquered and killed for this one moment to happen. He is ready to hear me, though I will be dead a million years when he does. What will I tell him? What is the story he needs to hear? Is it the leaf's story? The sad boy's story? The cat's story? The dying woman's story? What is required of me? The playground was silent. The snow, the trees and all the high passing clouds were silent. The cardinal shook his head. Shook it so hard that a spray of moist microscopic beads was jettisoned into the air, rained down and froze solid the moment they touched the snow. I have this to tell him, thought the red bird. Every moment is important. You do not know that yet. Everything is awake. You do not know that yet. Everything is alive. Everything matters.

Shake off this dream. Wake up.

On the golden bed, in the dark day, surrounded by candles and holding his only son's hand, Vibo the Third and Last Great Ruler of Earth, shook his head again. And sighed.

"That was our past," Vibo's son said, looking out over the balcony onto the cold dark land, the steaming red sky, and the dimming red sun.

"Yes," his father said. "I dreamed a bird's life. A million years ago." He frowned. "But what good is this dream? What can we do now? It is too late."

"Maybe," his son said. "Maybe dreams do not obey the boundaries of time."

"Yes," Vibo said. "Yes!" His face opened in the candlelight and his eyes glowed. "Maybe it is possible for someone back then to dream our life."

"And they will wake up," his son said smiling.

"And they will wake up," his father said.

For Claire 1/23/02

THE ARTIST MAKES A SPLASH
JERRY OLTION

They wanted to destroy his finest work. That wasn't the way the Terragen Council presented it when they came to Talan with their proposal, but that's what they wanted. He would create the best sculpture he could possibly build—for what artist could do less with each new project?—and then at the dedication ceremony for the new atmosphere, they would smash it to flinders for the crowd's amusement.

Ephemeral art was all the rage back on Earth. Perhaps it came from living in an open environment. Everything came from the soil and everything eventually returned to it; what matter, then, if you returned something a bit early? In humanity's far-flung colonies, however, where people lived sealed in domes and held a hostile universe at bay mostly through sweat and engineering, anything that might still have a use was carefully hoarded, repaired, and returned to service.

Of course the dedication of the atmosphere could change all that. For the first time in human history, a terraformed planet was about to be declared habitable on the surface. It required a generous interpretation of the term "habitable," to be sure, but for the last few months a person could step outside on Nivala without an environment suit and live to tell the tale. Only at the poles, where Altair's intense ultraviolet rays came in at a low enough angle to keep from crisping an unprotected body, but there was still vastly more acreage available outside than in the domes. The icy ground—frozen for millions, maybe billions, of years—had begun to thaw. In a few more years, farmers could plant crops in the open, and people could sleep with the sound of rustling leaves coming in through their windows.

And maybe they could relax the intense code of recycling that they had lived under for so long. Lengthen the chain of processing steps between wastewater and drinking water. Bury bodies instead of rendering them down for their protein.

Talan considered his commission. An artwork that existed only to be destroyed. It did open new possibilities.

want to capture the very essence of ephemerality," he told his sister as they walked to dinner that evening. They lived side by side in apartments only a few doors down from their parents, as did most young singles in the colony.

"Ephemerality? That's easy: clone up a vat of mayflies." Her laughter echoed in the corridor.

"Do we *have* mayflies?" he asked. "Never mind; of course we must. The gene banks are supposed to contain everything. But nobody has seen a mayfly in what, six generations? People wouldn't know what they were. And besides, DNA isn't my medium."

"Well, that kills my next suggestion."

She grinned and looked at him with eyebrows raised until he said, "What?"

"A steak dinner. Force-grow a cow, butcher it, and let everybody eat it."

"Yuck!"

"That's what we're going to be doing once we move outside. Why not give people a little taste of what's in store for them?"

"No pun intended."

"What? Oh. No, actually, it wasn't." She laughed again, turning heads in the cafeteria as they entered. People smiled, and Talan felt a twinge of envy. Everyone liked Nendy. Him they tolerated because they liked his work—several pieces of which adorned the cafeteria walls—but she was popular for herself. She *was* the work of art, and all the more so for being unconscious of it.

They picked up trays and went through the line. Dinner was some kind of stringy pasta with white sauce. Lumps in the sauce might have been synthetic meat or just lumps from not being stirred well enough.

"Maybe steak isn't such a bad idea," he said.

"How about flowers?" asked Nendy. "Made out of glass or something," she amended quickly when he opened his mouth to protest that they, too, were organic.

Now there was an idea. Hand out glass roses at the door, and let everyone smash their own individual blossom.

And cut their feet on the glass shards, and accidentally stab one another with the stems. "No," he said, "broken glass and crowds didn't mix." Besides, anyone could make a glass flower. He wanted something uniquely *his*. Something appropriately grandiose, that people would talk about for years to come.

As they ate, he studied the colonists around him. They dressed in soft synthetic fabrics dyed in equally soft colors, wore lightweight slippers with flat non-skid soles, and spoke in soft voices so they wouldn't disturb the people around them. Everything about them was adapted to life inside a sealed environment. Even Nendy, with her infectious laugh and sparkling eyes, was a dome dweller. She was in many ways the most perfectly adapted of anyone to life in a bubble. She didn't merely tolerate it; she thrived on it. She loved the close quarters and the nonstop personal contact, loved the sense of community and camaraderie in pursuit of humanity's common goal.

"How does it feel," he suddenly asked, "to know that the lifestyle you grew up with is about to end?"

She paused with a forkful of noodles halfway to her mouth. "Is it?"

"How many people do you suppose will stay in the domes when there's an entire planet to spread out onto? Even if half of them stay, this place will feel deserted."

"For a while." She chewed and swallowed, then said, "We'll drop the birth control laws. In a few years, the population will go right back up."

"You want to live in a nursery?"

She smiled. "Babies are fun."

He wasn't so sure of that. He'd held one once, and it was heavy, squirmy, and wet. And noisy. If people started having more babies, he might wind up homesteading some acreage himself.

Funny to think that birth could spell the end of something else, but he supposed any change practically by definition killed the status quo. Sound killed silence, light killed darkness, food killed hunger. When you thought of it that way, everything was ephemeral. He could sculpt practically anything, and it would be appropriate.

After dinner he bundled up in his survival suit and went outside. He left the helmet unsealed, and his first few breaths felt like he was pouring liquid nitrogen into his lungs, but the pain slowly subsided as he grew used to the thinner, colder air. It took longer to get over the smell: the dusty, chalky smell of bare dirt and an antiseptic, metallic bite that he eventually realized was ozone.

Injection towers rose like tree trunks from the polar plateau, spewing a sooty mix of ultraviolet-blocking gasses along with oxygen from dissociated permafrost. They wouldn't stop for decades to come, but they were past the critical point. Humanity had a second planet it could live on unprotected; he stood there as living, breathing proof of that.

A lifepod drifted past, its spiky antennae listening for an S.O.S. that might never come again. Like the injection towers, the lifepods had been genetically engineered to self-propagate until they covered the planet, blanketing the entire world with safe havens for the explorers and engineers who monitored the progress of the terraforming project. They would need a new mission now. Perhaps they could serve as taxis between villages, or trucks for hauling crops in from the fields.

Altair was in the southeast, a fierce blue-white disk that burned a whole quadrant of sky to white around it. There were no seasons on Nivala; Altair circled the horizon at the same height year 'round. Here at the pole, days weren't measured by cycles of light and dark, but by direction of the compass. Today was East. In a few more hours it would be South.

The ash-gray ground was peppered with craters, some as small as his footprints, others stretching over the horizon. Rain had already filled some of them, and tiny rivulets were busy eroding the walls of the rest. Farmers would have to shore up the ones they wanted to keep as reservoirs, or they would lose them to their new atmosphere.

Talan trudged across the plain to a full one and stood at its edge, looking at the stars reflected in its still surface. The starry sky was ephemeral, too, or so the scientists said. A thick enough atmosphere scattered so much light that even the brightest stars would only be visible during eclipse. Already they were dimmer than when Talan was a boy.

He turned to look at Satipur, low on the horizon to his left. The gas giant was three-quarters full and bright as an open flame, too large to cover with his outstretched hand. Its rings stretched across a quarter of the sky, a sharp line etched across the roiling cloudscape and the dark violet starscape beyond. Eclipse came every four days and seven minutes, regular as clockwork. The colonists wouldn't lose the stars completely, even when their air was thick as Earth's.

Talan picked up an eroded rock the size of his fist and tossed it into the flooded crater, watching the planet's reflection shimmer as ripples slowly spread outward from the splash.

Change. Motion. Fluidity. What could he sculpt that would illustrate it all?

He threw another rock and watched it splash.

Y ou want to design the meeting hall itself?" asked the president of the Terragen Council. He leaned forward over his desk, his eyebrows narrowed and his mouth curved into a deep frown. "We asked for something we could symbolically sacrifice. You can't destroy an entire building."

"Why not?" Talan asked, leaning forward just as aggressively.

"Because we'll be holding our dedication ceremony in it," the president reminded him.

"Yes, we will. And afterward, we'll all troop outside and watch it collapse."

"Outside."

"Right. Involving each one of us dynamically in what we're celebrating."

The president's scowl intensified. "I hardly think the celebrants will appreciate gasping like fish in the cold. The atmosphere is breathable, but nobody said it was comfortable yet."

"I was outside for two hours yesterday," Talan said. "It's surprising how quickly you get used to it."

"People will be wearing formal clothing."

"I'll supply overcoats."

"And transportation home? The city's air cars can't handle everyone at once."

"There are thousands of lifepods drifting around out there with nothing to do. Hardly anyone has ever ridden in one. It'll be a great opportunity to find out what it's like."

The president's chair squeaked as he leaned back and steepled his fingers on the bridge of his nose. "Hmm," he said. "Hmm. Outside."

"Outside. That's what it's all about."

"Yes, it is, isn't it?"

T alan poured everything he had into it. He had built interactive sculpture before, but never anything big enough to house an entire crowd. He wanted his monument to look like a droplet caught in the act of rebounding from its impact with a pool of water, but even if he exaggerated the bulbous tip of the rising droplet, the structure would be taller than it was wide. And from inside, where everyone would be gathered until the last moment, it would just look like another habitat.

He considered using antigravity to make the interior one big weightless chamber, but people wouldn't like drinking out of zeegee flasks and talking to one another's feet. He would have to divide the space into floors, but he could make each level grander than the last, until the top of the droplet became a huge dome, symbolic of the sealed city they were leaving behind.

Actually, he could have it all. In his stop-motion studies, he had seen how the top of a droplet often separated into several spheres; he could make the topmost one perfectly spherical and put the antigravity generators there. Anyone who liked to party in zero gee could rise up through a smaller spherical elevator to the top.

And down at the bottom, the rays of ejecta radiating outward from the impact could serve as both docking ports and observation decks. They could have clear domes so people could look up at the frozen droplet overhead as well as at Satipur and its roiling cloudscape.

Every step of the project brought complications. The structure had to splash when he triggered its fall, not just topple or explode, yet it had to be strong enough to support thousands of people while they were inside. It needed sufficient elevators and glideways to move everyone where they wanted to go without delay, yet everything needed to squeeze through the narrow neck. There had to be space for kitchens and serveries, storerooms, restrooms, cloakrooms, assignation rooms—he sometimes felt that he was designing an entire city. Yet each day he awoke invigorated, and each time he overcame a setback, he savored the rush of creation anew. It felt as if he were pouring all his anxiety and frustrations into the project, and the closer it came to reality the more he looked forward to watching it destroyed. It would symbolize more than just the emergence of humanity onto the surface; it would symbolize his personal rebirth.

Nendy joined him outside one evening after construction began, finding him at the crater rim where he watched fabribots scurry up and down the central stalk with their modular building blocks. He heard her footsteps crunching through the crusty ground as she came up behind him.

"Gah!" she said theatrically when she drew close enough to be heard. "Nobody told me it was going to stink out here."

He turned and smiled at her. "That stink is what keeps us from getting sunburn."

"I thought ozone was supposed to accumulate in the upper atmosphere."

"It will, once we *have* an upper atmosphere. Right now it's still too thin to separate into layers."

"And you're going to make everyone breathe it the night of the ceremony."

"I am."

"You're nuts." She stepped up beside him and looked out at the tower under construction. "You build a pretty sculpture, though."

"It's looking good, isn't it?" He couldn't stop smiling. All his frustration, all his fear, all the tension in his life had gone into the droplet. If he felt so free now, he could only imagine how good it would feel to watch it collapse.

"You going to have it done in time?" Nendy asked. "The ceremony is only two weeks away."

He felt a brief moment of anxiety at the thought that something could yet go wrong, but he banished it to the tower with a casual wave of his hand. "The hard part's over. It's ahead of schedule."

Just then a fabribot fumbled its payload, a silvery rectangle which bounced off the 'bot just below it and spun end over end as it fell to the dry crater floor and stuck there, quivering.

"Half a percent entropic loss," Talan said calmly. "It's in the budget."

The day of the big celebration saw the tower gleaming in the low-angled light of Altair, its antigravity sphere hovering like a captured moon overhead. The crater had been refilled, and the silvered walls of the droplet reflected its shimmering blue surface in all directions. Windows glowed brightly along the tower's length as interior decorators made last-minute preparations and waitstaff stocked the kitchens and bars.

The whole domed city was abuzz with speculation; Talan had carefully spread rumor of what he intended, but had refused to confirm it. He had to spend the night with his sister to avoid the media, and he slipped into the tower disguised as a food delivery driver.

The last few hours before the guests arrived seemed to drag on forever. What if nobody came? What if *everybody* came? What if the tower collapsed prematurely? What if the food ran out? What if the *alcohol* ran out? He paced the grand ballroom, mentally banishing demon after demon into the fabric of his creation, but more rose up to replace them.

From inside, the walls had a checkerboard look. He had settled on blocks for his building material, ferro-ceramic blocks just a few handspans across, magnetically bonded with superconducting coils embedded within. They would grip one another like glue until he switched them off, whereupon they would all become free-falling particles, as independent as individual raindrops. His creation would splash when it fell, and it would be a most impressive splash indeed.

Using superconductors solved the safety issue, too. With no resistance in the coils, the magnetic fields that held everything together would persist indefinitely. Only when he reversed the polarity and actively killed the fields would the blocks release one another. The command was coded and keyed to video monitors in every floor; nothing would happen until he made it happen, and fail-safes would prevent even his own control code from working if anyone remained inside.

The plain surrounding the tower was dotted with lifepods. He had broadcast intermittent distress calls until hundreds of them congregated, sniffing about for the source of the signal. Ushers would use handheld beacons to call them in when people were ready to go home.

Talan walked to one of the immense windows that ringed the ballroom and looked down. The docking ports were busy with arrivals and departures, and as he watched, a flurry of media vans glided out from the city, leading a long procession of passenger vehicles behind it.

The reporters erupted into the ballroom from the elevator, sweeping their forehead cams left and right while they spoke in a babble of descriptive adjectives for the stay-at-home audience. They descended on Talan like newlyweds on fresh cubic, and this time he welcomed them warmly into his latest creation. He gave them a quick tour, soaking in the moment of notoriety and answering their constant barrage of questions—except for the most persistent one. He neither confirmed nor denied the rumor that this would all be destroyed at party's end, but he did show them the cloakroom filled with heavy parkas.

He broke away when the president and his wife arrived, greeting them warmly and mugging for the cameras. The president took a look around, hands on hips, then slowly smiled. It clearly wasn't an expression his face was used to wearing, but it made him look ten years younger. "Well, my boy, you've certainly outdone yourself this time," he said.

"Thank you," Talan replied. "Wait until you see it in action."

"Hmm. Yes." The president's smile lost a few watts of charm. "Yes indeed. But we've got a lot of celebrating to do between now and then, eh? Excuse me." The elevator door opened again and the president turned to greet the new arrivals: his fellow councilors and several of the city's upper crust.

It was the president's party now. Talan slipped into the role of captive celebrity, mingling with the revelers and accepting their praise with as much humility as he could muster.

Humility became harder and harder to hang onto as the party wore on. Shuttles kept bringing guests until they numbered in the thousands, and the sheer volume of compliments threatened to swell his head. He kept reminding himself that fame, like the object of everyone's admiration, was ephemeral, but he couldn't shake the conviction that this was a pivotal moment in his career. A pivotal moment in his life.

He sought out Nendy, herself the center of a swarm of admirers, and the two of them retreated to one of the observation pods. With the party in full swing overhead, it wasn't hard to find an empty one, although two lovers were groping one another in the next pod over. Talan blushed and looked away, but Nendy watched with unabashed interest.

"Quite the little microcosm of life you've created here," she said softly.

"Isn't it?" he said. He flopped down on an oversized hassock, happy to get the weight off his feet for a moment. "I can't wait to destroy it."

"Really? After all this acclaim?"

"Especially so." He took a deep breath. "I'm vibrating like a violin string that's tuned too tight. Every little compliment stretches it another notch. If I don't loosen the tension soon, I'm going to snap."

"The price of fame," she said.

"I just want to see it through. I've got this horrible feeling that something's going to go wrong at the last moment. Expose me as a fraud in front of everybody."

"Nothing will go wrong."

"Famous last words."

He watched his sister watching the lovers next door. Now her cheeks were growing red and her nostrils were flaring. Talan felt a brief moment of lust, instinctively shoved it away with all his other unwanted mental baggage, and said, "If you go back to the party in that state, there's going to be a riot."

She grinned, then turned around and leaned back against the glass. "Spoilsport."

"I didn't say that would be a bad thing."

"I don't want to steal your spotlight."

"Please do. I just want to go home and get a good night's sleep."

"You can do that after the party. The catharsis will be worth it."

He stared at her, seeing her as if for the first time. "You understand."

She shrugged. "I'm not as shallow as I look."

"That's not what I—"

"I know. Nobody expects happy people to need primal scream moments, but we do. We need 'em just as much as you tormented types." She pressed a hand against the glass bubble at her back. "I want to watch this tumble down just as much as you do."

"Good."

His wristcom wiggled for attention, and when he held it up, the screen displayed a single word: "Speeches."

"Ah, bugger," he said. "It's time to listen to the prez blather on about manifest destiny."

"Patience, brother," Nendy said. "Let him have his moment. Yours will be the one everyone remembers."

Talan carried that statement with him like a torch in the dark, letting it buoy him through the interminable introductions and acknowledgements and lame jokes as speaker after speaker stepped up to the podium at the center of the grand ballroom and thanked everyone who had played a role in the atmosphere project. At last the president took the stage, but Talan was only listening with half an ear by then. His hand kept stealing to his breast pocket, where the remote control for the destruct sequence awaited his command. He could practically feel the rumble of falling blocks already.

A burst of applause brought him back to the present, and he realized that everyone was applauding *him*. He nodded and smiled and made a little self-deprecating shrug, but his smile melted like ice under flame at the president's next words.

"His original intention was to destroy it at the end of today's festivities, as a symbol of the transition from our old way of life to the new." A murmur rippled through the audience, punctuated with gasps from those who hadn't heard the rumors. "But," the president said, the word echoing like a gunshot, "I think we can all agree that we can't let such a beautiful work of art go to waste just for our momentary amusement."

There was a hearty cheer, but Talan barely heard it over his own shout. "*What?* What do you mean, you can't let it go to waste? It's *designed* to go to waste. That's the whole point of it. How can you not—that's what you—look at the *shape* of it! It has to fall!"

Faces turned to look at the gibbering man at the fringe of the crowd, but he didn't stay at the fringe for long. He shoved his way through to the podium while the president said, "Come now, Talan, surely you can't expect us to go along with the desecration of such a work of art. An ice sculpture or a crystal chandelier, certainly, but this needs to be preserved for posterity."

"It needs to come down!" Talan yelled. He mounted the stage and stuck his head next to the president's to make sure he was inside the microphone field. "It needs to come down," he said again. "You can't let sheer immensity, or even beauty, stop you from finishing what you've started. If we were that kind of people, we would never have terraformed Nivala in the first place."

The president tried to force a smile, but it looked like a death grimace to Talan. "I know that was the original intent," he said, "but none of us imagined you would come up with something quite this...this astonishing. You should take it as a compliment that nobody wants to see it destroyed."

"*I* want to see it destroyed. Nendy wants to see it destroyed." Talan looked out at the audience. "I bet most of you here tonight would love to see it destroyed, once you have a chance to get used to the idea." The president tried to speak, but Talan cut him off. "I had trouble accepting it myself, at first, but the idea grows on you pretty fast once you start thinking about it. It's a grand thing we've done here, turning an airless moon into a home for humanity. It requires a grand gesture to commemorate it. Not some cheesy ice sculpture; it *should* be something big. Big and beautiful and ephemeral, like—" He looked over at the president, now nearly purple with pent-up frustration, and the words tumbled out before he could stop them: "—Like the promise of a politician."

The audience laughed, and surprisingly, the president laughed, but then he shook his head and said, "I deserved that. I commissioned a sculpture to be sacrificed at the dedication ceremony, and I agreed when Talan asked if he could hold the ceremony inside the sculpture, but even with the considerable talent he has displayed in the past, I had no idea how beautiful it would be."

"Beauty doesn't enter into it," Talan said. "Except that beauty is ephemeral, too."

"Tell you what," the president said. "Let's let the people decide. Who wants to see it destroyed?"

The crowd murmured, and a few voices called out, "Yeah!" and "I do!" but the president had hit them too quickly for any groundswell of agreement to build. Not even Nendy, standing near an hors d'oeuvre table and shouting, "Do it, do it, do it!" could stir up a coordinated response.

"Tell you what," Talan said, trying the president's tactic. "Let's stick with the original program. There are coats enough for everyone in the cloakroom, and there's a walkway from the docking level to the crater rim. Let's all convene outside and watch the show."

For just a moment, it looked like they might obey. A few people turned away from the stage, but the vast majority of them stood rooted to the spot, and then someone shouted, "No!" Another voice echoed it, and another and another until it became a chant.

"No" sounded quite a lot like "Boo" to a person onstage. Talan tried to start a counter-chant of "Yes, yes, yes," but even his amplified voice couldn't penetrate the outcry.

The president leaned in close and shouted in his ear, "You've lost the vote, my boy, but think what it means! They love you. When this all winds down, you can name your price for your next commission."

"Money isn't the point, either," Talan yelled back, but he might as well have been shouting at Satipur. He looked out at the crowd, thousands of faces with their mouths open, all yelling, "No!" Then he turned away and walked off the stage.

The crowd parted for him as he walked to the hors d'oeuvre table where Nendy waited, champagne bottle in hand. "Here," she said, handing him the whole bottle.

They proceeded to get smashed while the party started up again around them. People avoided them after Talan nearly bit the heads off the first few who came to offer their insincere condolences. He took perverse delight in scaring them away from the food and drink, even though there were dozens of other tables spaced all the way around the perimeter of the hall. He commanded this one, at least, and by the time he and Nendy finished their second bottle of champagne, he was sitting on the table and throwing chocolates at the dancers.

"This was supposed to be cathartic," he told her. "I im...imbued all of my frustrations and all of my anger into this damned thing, and they were supposed to disappear with it when I pushed the button."

She laughed. "There's an infinite supply of frustration. You'll never get rid of it all."

"You're probably right." He tilted the champagne bottle to his mouth, but got only a few drops. He cocked it back to send it after the chocolates, but Nendy held his arm.

"Not a good idea," she said. "Broken glass and crowds don't mix."

"Right." He lowered the bottle, but didn't set it down. "Right," he said again. "'Snot their fault they're cheep."

"Cheap?"

"Sheep!" A few people glanced over at him, then quickly looked away.

He hefted the bottle—a heavy, pleasant weight in his hand—then looked out the window at the icy plain below, dotted with lifepods and air injection towers. "Sheep," he said again, and before he had time to think of the many reasons why it was a bad idea, he heaved the bottle through the glass.

He had designed it to shatter. The bottle made a satisfying crash on the way through, and left a hole the size of his head. Air began to whistle out through the hole, and people screamed as only people who are used to living in sealed domes can scream when a sudden wind begins to blow.

Talan stood up and grabbed the end of the table. "Give me a hand here!" he said to Nendy.

It was nearly too big for them, but they tipped it until all the food slid to the floor, and then they were able to heft it up to waist level and swing it *one*, *two*, and *three* right through the window.

Air howled out around them now, whipping their clothes and their hair, and Talan nearly stumbled out the hole before he caught himself and stepped sideways out of the worst of the gale.

People ran for the elevator and the glideways, but Talan and Nendy walked calmly to the next table and heaved it through another window. The last of the building's air whooshed out, and the familiar smell of ozone and dirt wafted in. Talan panted as the air pressure dropped and he endured the moment of burning lungs until he was able to stand up and laugh at the fleeing party guests.

"Broken glass and crowds don't mix!" he told Nendy happily as he led the way to another table.

The antigravity bubble from overhead slid down past the windows, emergency protocols overriding its original program and piloting its occupants to safety. Almost everyone was gone from the ballroom by now, but a few people had gathered in a huddle near the stage. They began to advance on Talan and Nendy, but Talan pulled the remote control from his pocket and shouted, "Time to leave! Self-destruct in five minutes."

"You can't drop it with people still inside," Nendy whispered frantically.

"No, but they don't know that," Talan whispered back, and sure enough, when he held the remote overhead with his finger on the button, the group of would-be heroes broke apart and fled down the glideway, leaving them alone in the ballroom.

The plain beyond the windows was alive with lifepods swarming for the bubble city. "I think it's time we joined everyone outside," Talan said. He picked up another bottle of champagne on the way out, stopped briefly in the cloakroom to get coats for himself and Nendy, then led her out past the base of the docking pods and across the wide catwalk to the crater rim.

"Think anyone's still inside?" he asked, turning around once they had put another few dozen steps between them and his creation.

"I don't know." She shivered and pulled her coat tight around her body. "What if there is? You can't risk someone's life just to make a point."

"You're right. That's why there are heat and motion sensors all through the structure." He pushed the button. "Nothing will happen if there's anybody lef—oh."

The gigantic droplet quivered, then slid downward like a spoonful of sugar poured into a cup of water. The ring of observation pods at its base stretched outward for a second, then fell to the surface, just reaching the edge of the crater as the surge of water displaced by the tower crashed against the rim and shot upward in a circular fountain. The rumble of blocks and water shook the ground, and wet spray pelted down out of the sky.

Water sloshed back and forth a few times, smoothing out the pile of rubble in the center of the crater. The waves subsided, giving way to ripples that chased each other around the crater, but in a surprisingly short time even those faded away and the surface of the water returned to glassy smoothness.

"Feel better now?" Nendy asked.

"Yeah," Talan replied. He pitched the remote control into the crater and watched the splash spread out in one last wave. "Yeah. But now I really hope people can live out here, because I don't think I'm going to be welcome inside the domes anymore."

Nendy laughed. "Well, you've already proven you can build a habitat."

He scuffed a foot on the ground. "That was for show. There are more efficient designs for living."

"Like what?"

He looked out across the flat gray plain at the injection towers rising into the sky. Tall, slender, graceful...and free. All they needed were a few tweaks to their genetic code, and they would be perfect. It would mean learning how to handle DNA, but he supposed it wouldn't kill him to work in a new medium. He smiled at Nendy and said, "Ever heard of a treehouse?"

FIRED
RAY VUKCEVICH

Deep inside the spaceliner *Can of Peaches* there was a small dim bar called the Slingshot Lounge. The *Can of Peaches* along with three sister hotel ships moved between Earth and Mars continuously. The ships never stopped. They never landed. Because there were four of them, you never had to take the long way. The ships were really in an orbit around the sun and used the planetary gravity to slingshot forever between the two worlds and thus the name of the bar where John Wagner went looking for love in one of the very few places it might reasonably be found and met the fire woman.

When John was on duty, he was an "outside guy" —a man or woman who gets into a space suit and goes out to fix whatever needs fixing on the outer skin of the *Can of Peaches*. He was a permanent peach. He had not set foot on Earth or Mars in many years. Tourists were ferried up to the liners from the surface of either planet. That was the most expensive part of the whole deal. The rest was just a matter of going around and around and since almost anything could be simulated to a degree you couldn't tell the difference and since everyone was augmented to the eyeballs and beyond, you had to wonder why people bothered going in the flesh. Part of it was a status thing. You had to have the bucks if you wanted to take the ride. People claimed there was something immediate and elemental that squeezed the very core of your being when you looked into the deep darkness of space with unaided eyes. John didn't see it anymore. Maybe he'd gotten used to it.

Another factor was the long shot that you might be there when the "dark spot" returned. If it ever did come back, you might get gobbled up and disappear forever. A little danger tossed into the mix. Ten years before, the rip in space known as the "dark spot" had appeared. Several things had emerged and the spot had disappeared. Just like that. None of the emerging things had ever been tracked down and identified. Aliens or rocks. Who knew?

Since there was never a shortage of tourists on board, John figured there might be someone new in his favorite bar, so he got his persona buffed and beaming (dress-black uniform and spaceman boots, rugged chin and piercing ice-blue eyes, a random gleam from the teeth) and set on out after work, augmented peepers scoping and pheromoner sniffing around for monkey business. He waltzed on into the Slingshot and took a stool, signaled the polar bear bartending that he needed an Irish on the rocks, looked left and right without really looking like he was looking, and oh, man, would you look at her?

John couldn't say exactly why the fire woman was so hot, sitting there (if sitting was what she was actually doing) looking anything but human, all blue and maybe made of some kind of transparent jelly your fingers just ached to touch. You'd pretend to touch her and say, "Ouch!" Or "sizzle" or maybe just "ssssss," and she'd say, "Oh like I haven't heard that one before," but by then she'd be smiling (if you could call it smiling) and everything would be cool. He'd buy her a drink. Or would she go for some kind of gas instead or maybe a hickory log? Whatever fans your flames, sweet cheeks. And speaking of cheeks, that black splatter spot just below her left eye was a nice touch. It was like looking at the "dark spot" through a telescope from a long way away. He should say something, but how do you break the ice with a fire woman?

But then she beat him to the punch. "You ever do it in a spacesuit, bobby?" When she spoke, sparks drifted from her mouth and winked out as they touched the bar.

"What?" John was knocked off his game. "My name's not Bobby."

She looked startled like she'd been working on that utterance for a long time and was confused by his reaction. Maybe he hadn't heard her right. Maybe she had an accent. She'd be from some exotic locale on Earth or Mars, somewhere no one ever went who didn't have a lot of money or wasn't sweeping up or serving little sandwiches and tea and now she was up here slumming and looking for a spaceman but she couldn't know much about spacesuits if she thought they could both get into one much less do anything once inside.

He was tempted to look at the fire woman with his "other eye," but that would mean he was done here. Looking at the sad underbelly of the bar and the people in it unaided by augmentation would end any fantasy he might get going. He'd made that mistake more that a few times—the worst was probably the Amazon Queen who turned out to be a little old guy who might have gotten small inside suddenly, since his exterior draped around his frame like a cloth double-bass bag around a cello. Looking had spoiled the mood.

So John didn't look at her with his other eye. Instead, he rolled out his own practiced line like a jet fighter ready to zoom off into the sky and shoot down many objections she might have against coming back to his humble spaceman quarters with him. Of course, if she wanted to go off and do it in a spacesuit, she might not have any objections anyway, but he had been working on this line for a long time, so he said, "So tell me, what's your favorite moon of Jupiter?"

"You ever do it in a spacesuit, booby?"

Well, she was nothing if not single-minded.

"I don't think that's possible," he said. "My name is John."

She just sat there burning in silence for a moment. Then she said, "You ever do it in a spacesuit, baby?"

He thumped his chest. "Me John. You...?"

"Oh," she said. "Pam."

Oh, sure, Pam the fire woman from some place where people spoke the universal language with an accent.

"Well, Pam, there are lots of things we can do without spacesuits."

"Yes," she said. "Show me your spacesuit."

"You want a tour? You looking to see some of the places the tourists don't usually get to go? I think that could be arranged."

Why not? Escort her around a little, see some safe sights, and end up back at his place.

"Yes, let's go!" she said, and somehow she was standing without ever stopping sitting. It was like someone threw a couple of sticks on her fire.

John tossed down the rest of his drink and got up. He made a crook of his arm so she might take it, but she said, "Not yet."

"This way," he said and walked for the door.

There was a place where he could show her a view she wouldn't have seen from the passenger areas. It would not be a better view (the passengers had the best views, since they were the point, after all) but it would be a little different. They could swing by the workshops, and maybe take a peek at a kitchen or two along the way. And after that she might be impressed by the staging area for outside work.

Hey, they could pop in on the bridge. Maybe the Captain would let her take a turn at the wheel.

They moved into the corridor, and the music and fake smoke stopped when the door slid shut behind them.

"You might want to turn down your nose through here," John said. Dumb speak. What was he thinking? She would know about the smell in these corridors, since she'd come through them not long ago to get to the bar in the first place. She probably saw the Slingshot Lounge blurb in the passenger brochure about seeing some "genuine Permanent Peach life in the belly of the Can." Completely safe. Well, maybe you'll want to go in a group? Spicy. Dicey. Babbling. He hoped he hadn't been saying any of that out loud.

He gave her a quick glance. She was still on fire.

"So, are you from Mars or Earth?" he asked.

"No," she said. "Are we there yet?"

"Not yet," he said, and it occurred to him that he had just echoed what she'd said when he'd put out his arm and invited her to touch him. They were moving along side by side but were they going in the same direction? She seemed pretty single-minded about seeing a spacesuit and that was okay with him, but he didn't intend to end the evening looking at his equipment—well, okay, so he did intend to look at his *equipment*. Show and tell. Touch. Boy, if she knew the adolescent babblony that was going on in his head, she'd go out like you blew on a match, but hey maybe there was something similar going on in her head; after all she'd searched out a spaceman and they were on their way to see his suit and who knew what else? It was like the way you could project whatever you wanted people to see when they looked at you, but did you really know what they were seeing since they could take your projection and work it into their own world in any way they wanted? When you were with someone you weren't always in the same place at the same time. Like they say, stretch it out, wad it up, get loose, and be elastic. He and Pam might be walking along together, but they were worlds apart and alone and he suddenly wanted to really connect with her. He would turn off his inferences and ignore her implications. He would start with his "other eye."

He stopped himself just in time.

Life is all about the stories we tell ourselves.

This was no time to blow the evening on some dumb longing that would result in the same old disappointment like they say doing the same dumb thing and expecting different results was well dumb so dumb de dumb dumb but oh look here's the first stop on the Famous John Wagoner Ladies Tour of the *Can of Peaches*.

"Here's something interesting," he said. They had come to the place where he could show her a less pretty side of the Can's outside skin.

"Spacesuits?"

"Later." He opened the door and stepped back to let her enter first.

"No, now," she said. "Which one is yours?"

He came in behind her and closed the door, but instead of seeing the forward display area, he saw that they were in staging area 4, where he came at the start of every shift to check the schedule and see if he was slotted for outside tasks. He had meant to come by here near the end of the tour, but what had happened to all the parts in between? That vague scene of chaos on the bridge surely couldn't have really happened. He had not had that much to drink. In fact, he had had only the one drink before Pam the fire woman talked him into going off against all regulations to see his spacesuit.

Oh, yeah, the regulations. It was like he was just now remembering that the whole idea of a private tour was so against the rules he wouldn't ordinarily even consider it. It was one thing to sneak a passenger into your quarters, it was like they expected that, you were only human, but you didn't take them where they might screw something up or get hurt and sue the company. The arguments she had used were no longer in his head, but he could remember that they had been very persuasive, and now they were where she wanted to be.

"Put it on," she said.

"What?"

"Your spacesuit," she said.

"Actually, we're not even supposed to be here," he said. "I can't put on my spacesuit without filing the forms."

"Here," she said. "This must be your hat."

"Helmet," he said and took it from her. He didn't remember getting into his spacesuit, but if he were going outside, he'd definitely need his helmet.

She put her hands on his shoulders and leaned in close. He could feel her flames licking around his ears. Then she flowed into his suit like a big burning blue snake slipping into the neck hole or maybe like blue fire water flowing over his shoulders and around his body and down to his toes and up his legs and thighs—little sting-slap burning bites all over.

"Put it on," she said. Her voice seemed to come from everywhere at once.

"What?"

"Your hat."

He raised the helmet and put it on and set the seals.

"Ready?" she asked.

And then it was like when they say, "Okay I'm going to count to three" but then they say "one" and shoot you anyway. There was a tremendous explosion, and he was blown out into space.

He could see a large landmass, a planet or moon where none could really be—a rough and barren place. He could not tell if there was an atmosphere. As he tumbled he saw the *Peaches* going down, debris scattering from a ragged rip in its side. Beyond the ship, he saw a star that might have been the Sun but he was pretty sure it wasn't the Sun. Maybe the Dark Spot was back and the *Can of Peaches* had fallen into it and they'd all come out the other side light-years away.

He could replay some of the highlights of his life—his boyhood playing with the polar bears on Mars, going into space (and never coming back, so there!), first love, last love, last week, cheesecake. He'd probably have time to play that much back before he hit the ground. There would never be time to go over everything in his augmented memory banks. You experienced augmem from the outside like looking up an item in a book, but ideally such an item triggered the actual memory, and you experienced that from the inside like those tiny soft hairs on cheerleader thighs in the gym dome on Mars when he was seventeen. Replay. But shouldn't this be all white light or something? Did you think you were going to get some great moment of clarity here at the end? Did you think there would be dancing girls?

His body ached with her blue fire as he fell.

"Are you there, Pam?" He reached out and touched her.

"Thanks for the ride home," she said. "It was supposed to be easier than this."

"What do you mean?"

"I'm going now," she said.

His arm exploded in fire as she left.

At least he could find out what she really looked like. He switched on his "other eye," but she was still a blue fire woman walking out of the Slingshot Lounge.

That couldn't be right.

"Hey!"

She stopped at the door and turned back and gave him a little wave with just her fire fingers.

Well, the bartender was just some guy who needed a shave and maybe a breath mint. He put another Irish on ice down in front of John. There was a crackle of static and he said, "You should have shown her your spacesuit, Sport."

John banged himself in the side of the head suspecting a malfunction. Pam just kept burning, but now he was falling toward the surface of the new planet.

His arm really was on fire.

Pam was a graceful blue burning cloud. She dipped and soared and skimmed over the surface until she came to a cave. She disappeared inside.

The Dark Spot sucked up the planet and swallowed it and then disappeared just before the *Peaches* passed through where it had been.

John initiated emergency procedures and got his suit sealed. He would probably lose an arm, but he could make do with a mechanical. He could see that the *Peaches* was going through a few emergency procedures of its own. Had the ship hit the strange planet from the Dark Spot, all would have been lost, but that hadn't happened. Pam had closed her door just in time, but that didn't let John off the hook. They would fish him out of space, and he would be in big trouble.

Maybe if he had worked a little harder, she would have taken him home to meet the folks.

NOHOW PERMANENT
NANCY JANE MOORE

We came into Procyon's commercial port on third watch. I'd picked the time and place on purpose. Bribing third-watch officers is easier than first-watch ones, and the commercial port hustles along little ships like mine so they can get to unloading shuttles from the big transports parked out in orbit. Plus I grew up around there—my mom worked port crew for a while when I was small—so I know some of the officers. Sometimes that helps, sometimes it doesn't.

My passenger wasn't happy. Nothing new about that; he'd been griping since I first picked him up. People on the lam for political reasons always complain a lot. Refugees, now, they tend to be grateful. And criminals know it's just business. I guess the revolutionaries and other regime opponents think they deserve better for doing what's right; they don't realize no good deed goes unpunished.

He stood next to me on the bridge, staring out the front viewport. "It's dark in here," he said. Procyon is an old moon, and the settled parts—including the port—are all carved out of the interior. The only thing that happens on the surface is regolith mining. There's some natural light through what natives call "The Window"—an opening that always faces the sun. But it's an old sun, far past the visible light stage.

"It's always going to be dark in here unless you get some infrared goggles. Or have a little eye surgery."

My passenger shook his head firmly when I said "eye surgery." He was still having trouble looking at me, even after a couple of weeks on board. I've got three eyes, myself: one for infrared, one for ultraviolet, and one for what the humans call "normal." Lighting on my ship adjusts to all three, though I'd kept it on visible light for the sake of my passenger. You jump the wormholes around this part of space the way I do, you end up seeing suns at all different stages. Best to be prepared.

"I want to stay human," he said. Clear that he didn't think I was.

Which is okay by me. I don't worry about things like that. Though my mom always said we were human somewhere back up the chain.

"Suit yourself." I was looking forward to getting rid of him.

He hadn't been quite as irritating at first. Someone had sent him my way when I was docked at the primary station in the Testudines. He was a well-proportioned man, with the wavy blond hair and tan skin of someone who'd always lived in a place with a temperate climate and friendly sun. Outdoorsy, in a civilized sort of way. Gene tweaks, I'm sure; no planets like that out here. But it's the in look among humans.

He also looked over his shoulder every few seconds while we talked. His left eye twitched, and his hands clutched the handle of a small satchel he carried. He was, in short, terrified.

"I'm Vlad Pyotrvich," he said.

Terrified and dumb, at least when it came to survival. Vlad Pyotrvich was his real name. I recognized it. He was known far and wide for his blazing critiques of the Yacare government. That took a lot of guts. Yacare is well known for abusing its citizens and generally being a very unpleasant place to live. I'd heard some of his speeches, and despite my personal tendency to anarchism, I'd felt inspired by his passionate statements on civil liberties and the duties of governments to their citizens.

The Yacare government had a different reaction, so they put a price on his head. A high price. Enough to tempt me, despite my respect for his ideas and my inclination to treat bounty hunters as beneath contempt.

"They call me Pogo," I said. It's just the latest in a series of nicknames. My real one is my own business, thank you very much.

Procyon wasn't his first choice. He'd wanted to go to Chamaleo.

"Too risky," I said. "We have to stop at Acinonyx to get there, and they're real friendly with the people you're running from. You'll be safer on Procyon."

"But the Yacare movement-in-exile is based on Chamaleo. They need me."

"You can hop a freighter out of Procyon and work your way to Chamaleo the back way. Much safer."

"That will take years."

I shrugged. He was right. It wouldn't seem like years to him, but by the time he did a few wormhole jumps ten years or more would have gone by on Yacare.

He'd gone looking for another ride, which just goes to show how little he knew about life on the lam. None of the asteroids that make up the Testudines is very large, and strangers stand out. He'd come back about a half step in front of some bounty hunters. Maybe less than half a step; he was bleeding in a couple of places. Didn't leave him much leverage when it came to dickering over price. I didn't get what Yacare would have paid, but it wasn't bad money. Not bad money at all.

"Welcome aboard the Rockety Coon Child," I'd said that first day.

He didn't laugh at my ship's name. In addition to dumb and terrified, he was humorless.

Given that he was so serious, and that my non-human side seemed to bother him, I didn't expect any unwanted sexual advances. But day two out, he hit on me.

"This thing pretty much flies itself," he said.

"Depends on where we are. But out here in the middle of nowhere"— we were a few hundred thousand klicks from the Testudines, on our way to the wormhole—"the auto pilot takes care of things."

He put a hand on my arm. "So maybe we could, uh, get to know each other better."

I removed the hand. I don't fuck the passengers. Most of the time, anyway. But since we were gonna be together for a few weeks, I made an effort to joke about it. "Hey, you're on the lam. What would I do if you got me pregnant?" It could happen, if I didn't take precautions; despite the eyes and other differences that I was born with, I'm not that far removed from human.

He jumped back. "You're female?"

I raised all three of my eyebrows. On account of his classic human looks I'd jumped to the conclusion that he preferred the equivalent kind of girls, but it appeared that what he really liked was not-quite-human guys. I guess he liked his sex on the exotic side.

I shrugged, and said, "Sorry to disappoint," because I really wasn't interested, and I am female. Mostly.

He blushed bright red, and said "sorry" about fourteen times. That was the last that got said on the subject.

As we got close to port, we jacked into Procyon's web for the news. The wormhole jump put us a couple of years from the Testudines (it's a short hole), so the news was way ahead of us. It'll be interesting if some genius ever figures out how to move people instantaneously like info.

Yacare had put out a story saying Vlad had died in the Testudines.

"Bet those bounty hunters pulled some DNA out of the blood you left behind and tried to collect the reward," I said.

But he wasn't amused (no surprise there). "Damn it. I must get to Chamaleo and rally the people there. I should never have let you talk me into coming to Procyon."

I didn't mention that he might really be dead if he hadn't.

We got lucky at the port. My old friend Gordo was on duty, and he came onboard the Child to check us out. Gordo and I grew up together, even if he has gone gray and pot-bellied while my hair's still brown and my wrinkles are few. I could tell some stories, but hell, he's a respectable customs official these days, so I won't. He got on at the port when we left school, while I signed on a freighter and started a life of wormhole jumping. The world goes on while you're in the hole, but you stay the same.

Anyway, Gordo being my friend, he didn't stick Vlad for too much to let him into Procyon without papers.

"Might annoy Yacare if we let you in," Gordo said.

"Yacare thinks he's dead," I pointed out.

"They could just be saying that. And if they found out he wasn't..."

I raised one eyebrow, the one over the infrared eye. Gordo's known me long enough to know that means I'm getting pissed off. "Okay, okay. But keep a low profile, huh? Been a little pressure on us lately."

I helped Vlad buy a set of infrared goggles in the ship's supply store just off the port, told him who to see about some papers and a freighter job, and pointed him in the direction of some cheap lodgings. He took the lift down to streetside. I gave a sigh of relief and went to meet Gordo and some other folks I know for a drink before I headed that way myself.

"Think your man is going to survive out here?" Gordo asked.

"Not my problem. I got him here alive. I transport people; I ain't a babysitter."

"I hear things are real ugly on Yacare. A man like that could rally folks. If some spies find him here, could get bad."

"Like I said, I'm not a nanny. But I'd take it personal if someone I asked to help him out fucked him over. Bad for business, if you get my drift."

I took the lift to streetside, and looked up my mom. For once, I found her at home. She has a nice apartment on the backside of Procyon, near the Window, with a full view of the sun. Two low walls of native rock lined the entranceway—constructing things with carefully balanced rock is a respected local art form. The walls and Window view don't come cheap; my mom deals poker on interplanetary cruise ships these days and she makes a good living.

"You haven't changed a bit since the last time I saw you," she said. And it was probably true. Neither had she. In fact, my mother's done more hole jumping than I have, and truth be told, we look more like sisters than parent and child. In fact, her hair was as short as mine, though I'd bet money in visible light it would show up as some outrageous color, instead of my dull brown. Mom is a great deal flashier than I am. "How's your business?"

"Can't complain," I said. "What are you up to?"

"I'm catching the Executive Tour Cruise in a week."

I knew about that trip. It makes use of reverse wormholes so you get home right about the same time you left. Very expensive, but worth it for rich business people who are exhausted and can't really afford the time for a vacation.

I did those things you do in your home port: Checked into The Swamp, where I keep my stuff in storage and rent a room when I'm home. Did some banking. Ordered up a maintenance check on the Rockety Coon Child. Looked up my friends and business acquaintances, put out some feelers for work. The usual.

A week later I was wandering down one of the less reputable streets in Procyon—I'd been meeting with someone about a potential job—when I literally ran into Vlad. Or rather, he ran into me. Full tilt. He was panting for breath and his goggles were askew.

He adjusted the goggles and squinted at me through them. "Pogo? Thank God. They're after me. I have to get off the street." He looked wildly in all directions.

I wasn't sure who "they" was, but I could hear the drone of engines in the next block. And, hell, I'm a soft touch. I pushed a button on the nearest door, exchanged a few words in the local dialect over the com, and pushed it open on the buzz. "In here."

He followed. I flashed my credit chip—the anonymous one I keep for emergencies—at the front desk and said, "Room. Now."

The attendant eyed us. "You want a girl? Boy?"

"Both," I said. "One human, one not quite."

"That'll cost extra."

"Whatever."

He passed us a card, and we took the lift down.

"What is this place?" Vlad asked.

"Whorehouse."

"Oh."

He didn't sound happy. I've never met a man who was pickier about how he got rescued.

The whores were waiting for us in the room. The woman was human and looked to be about the same size as Vlad. She wore a jumpsuit inter-laced with heat; it glittered gold. "Change clothes with her," I told him. Both he and the hooker stared at me.

"We're hiding from his wife. She put a trace in his clothes. If you put on his clothes and take off for awhile, she'll follow you. Take your friend with you. Go up a few levels and dump the clothes."

Vlad started to say something. I figured it would be dumb, so I cut him off. "He'll pay you cash," I added.

Off-the-books money. No prostitute can resist that. Vlad was still hesitating, but I gave him my raised eyebrow and even if he didn't know what it meant exactly, he knew I was serious.

"Now what?" he said as the door shut behind the whores.

I was stripping my own—dull in all lights—jumpsuit off. "Now we pretend I'm your client," I said, pulling back the sheets on the bed.

He was staring at my crotch. "Come on," I said. "Get in here and bury your head between my legs. I figure we got about two minutes before that patrol gets up here."

"But," he started to say. Then we both heard some noise, and he jumped in with me, pulled the covers over his head, and put his mouth on my cock.

I have to admit it was more fun than I usually have when I'm hiding from authorities.

The door burst open a few minutes later, and I gave the two cops who came through the look of an outraged customer.

The cop in charge wasn't even slightly embarrassed.

"No reading here, sergeant."

"Sorry to bother you," the sergeant said, not sounding the least bit sorry. "We'll leave you to it." The other cop leered as they walked out.

"All clear," I told Vlad.

He looked up at me from between my legs. "You said you were female," he said in an accusing tone.

"I am."

He grabbed hold of my cock. "Then what's this?"

I sighed. "Mostly female. If you look closer down there you'll see that's not all I've got."

"Oh. But if you've got both, why do you say you're female?"

"I procreate female. The cock's just for playing around. It fires blanks. Come on, we should get out of here."

"Do you think they're coming back?"

"Not immediately. Though if they catch up with that hooker before she dumps your clothes, she'll probably point them in our direction."

"Gives us a little while," he said with a grin. He went down on my cock again.

I started to insist, but hell, it felt nice. It felt very nice. And besides it was the first time I'd seen him smile. So I just went with the flow.

But when he wanted to start playing more games, I reminded him that someone was on his tail. That brought back his nervous tic.

"How'd you know there was a trace in my clothes?" he said, suddenly suspicious.

"Lucky guess. If it had been on your person, we'd be on our way to jail. Come on."

We headed down a couple of levels. I make a point of knowing where the back door is in most places. Never can tell when it will come in handy.

"Who's after you?" I said as we hurried through the halls.

He didn't look at me when he said, "I'm not sure."

We were at the back door by then. It opens onto a more respectable street than the one we'd been on earlier. I put both hands on his shoulders, looked straight at him, and said, "Let's try that again. Who's after you?"

He sighed. "I think there's more than one group."

"Wonderful. Who?"

"Local cops for one, I guess."

"Yeah, but local cops wouldn't give a shit about you unless someone else wanted you. They're probably out looking on request from the Yacare Embassy. So Yacare knows you're here. How'd they find that out?"

He looked away. "Maybe somebody in the refugee community?"

Of course. Made sense.

"Anyway, there's another guy—not a cop. Scary guy. I don't think he's human." He blushed then, like it was embarrassing to say that to me.

"Either Yacare spy or hot-shit bounty hunter," I said.

"And another group, but they aren't as scary."

"Ah," I said, not bothering to hide the sarcasm. "That's probably the bounty hunters. Man, what did you do, hang out a sign saying 'I'm here?'"

"I just tried to get a message out to Chamaleo."

I felt a massive headache coming on. I led him through the door. The street was quiet, not deserted, but nobody hanging about looking for us. "Let's try for my place," I said.

As we moved through the streets, I asked him, "Did you get hired on a freighter?"

"Yes. It leaves tomorrow."

"Well, I'll try to keep you alive until we can get you on that ship." So much for not being a babysitter.

My neighborhood is neither posh nor disreputable. The Swamp caters to people who spend most of their time on a ship somewhere, so it's only a few levels down from the port. But it doesn't abut the seedy bars and sleepovers aimed at the transient crowd. Nor is it close to either the part of town where I'd met Vlad or the nicer block where we'd exited the house of ill repute.

We took the first empty lift we came to back up to the right level. Here more people jammed the thoroughfares. I prefer crowds when I'm trying to avoid somebody.

All the people—and not people, and not quite people—made Vlad nervous. His eye was twitching and he kept looking around. That made me nervous; he was drawing attention to himself. And the whore's flashy jumpsuit just added to it. I figured I'd give him one of mine when we got to my digs; it wouldn't fit as well, but it wouldn't glow in the fucking dark, either.

"Almost there," I said as we turned into my block. And then I stopped. Something felt wrong, something seemed out of place.

"Thank god," Vlad said. He started to walk past me.

I put a hand on his arm. "Did you happen to mention my name to anybody?"

His face began to glow red. "Uh, I think I might have said something to one of the refugees."

At that moment I got a good look at someone standing in the shadows across the street from The Swamp. He, or she, or it, was facing in our direction, and I could see a telltale blotch of purple at the left shoulder. Something cold there—the area around the heart usually shows up red gold. That made it an armed someone. Okay, not my place then.

"What are we waiting for?" Vlad said.

"Me to think of someplace else for us to go. Somebody's waiting for us down there." Something that must know about me. Now nursemaiding Vlad wasn't just an act of kindness; it was the only way I was going to come through this in one piece.

If my name had come up, the Rockety Coon Child didn't seem like a good idea. I certainly couldn't get Vlad on it. Though maybe I could bribe someone to get out on it, if I got Vlad safely on the freighter early. If . . . "You didn't tell anybody about the freighter job did you?"

"Only a couple of people," he said. His face was beginning to show some yellow and green, as if it had gone from hot to cold.

I briefly considered handing Vlad over to whoever was standing down there. It would have solved all my problems. And I didn't really owe him all this, anyway; hell, I'd already done way more than I'd been paid for.

But they hadn't caught us yet. And, hell, it'd be more fun to see if I could save him—not to mention me—from everybody who was after him. So I dragged Vlad back to a set of stairs, and we hotfooted it up a couple of flights. Lifts are too easy to watch. We ended up near a marketplace, and wandered through while I tried to come up with something like a plan.

Vlad didn't help much. His nervous tic was back in force, and he kept looking over his shoulder and muttering things under his breath. The freighter was out; ten to one somebody was staking it out. How could a man who had the brains to build the Yacare opposition—the news sites called him the "Savior of Yacare"—get into so much trouble in such a short period of time? I needed to get him off-planet ASAP, preferably with competent supervision. But how?

Then it hit me: the Executive Tour Cruise. When had Mom said it was leaving? I did a quick calculation, and came up with tomorrow. She could get him on the ship, maybe as a stowaway. It would cost, but anything would cost at this point. And Mom could keep an eye on him.

The best part: even though Vlad's enemies knew my name, they wouldn't tie me to Mom. That's one of the advantages of not using your real name. Not that some people on Procyon didn't know all about me, but Vlad didn't, which made it likely that the people chasing him didn't know it either. So long as we weren't followed, we might get him off-planet.

So I dragged Vlad up three more flights of stairs, to the fancy level where Mom lived. Fewer people up there, so I looked around carefully. That's when I realized that we had been followed.

I knew immediately why Vlad had found him scary. One look scared the bejesus out of me. For one thing he came in shades of blue. Blue in infrared is cold; no human—or almost-human—registers as blue except in small spots. Humans generate heat, and that comes in yellows, reds, golds.

But he was shaped like a human. Either he was something cold-blooded—animal or mechanical—or he had some kind of very fancy armor that blocked body heat. There wasn't enough variation in color to show any vulnerable spots.

The other thing that scared me was that he clearly intended for us to see him. Likely he'd been behind us for quite awhile—blue can blend in easily in the background. I felt Vlad freeze beside me.

The blue guy said, "I was going to follow and see where you ended up, but it appears that you're going for the complete planetary tour, and I've already done it." He spoke in a soft tenor, a pleasing sound that chilled me to the bone.

"You could just wait for us here. We'll come back for you," I said. No point in acting scared.

He laughed. By rights it should have been a nasty villainous laugh, but in fact it was a rather charming melodious sound. "I don't think that will work. Better that you come with me."

"Oh, no," I said, trying for tough. I moved closer to the blue guy. "I didn't do all this work for nothing. The price on his head is huge, and I'm going to deliver him."

Vlad said, "But, but I trusted you."

The blue guy laughed again. This laugh was a little closer to what I expected to hear, though it still had a pleasant ring to it. "That's a good scam: getting them to trust you and then selling them out."

I smiled. "It can be lucrative. You get paid twice that way. But I can't run it all the time, or no one would ever hire me to smuggle them out." I took another step in his direction.

"Even a bit of strategy. I like you, Pogo. I tell you what. I'll give you a cut of the reward."

"Uh, uh. I want all of it. I'm the one who's got him, after all."

"But I'm going to take him now. And you don't want to try to stop me." His hands were moving. I knew he was armed, but I couldn't distinguish weapon from him.

He was right that I didn't want to try to stop him. I moved just a little closer, tried to act tougher than I felt, and then gave a sheepish shrug. "Okay, you win. How much of a cut?" My hand closed on the knife I keep at thigh level.

He laughed again, and his hands moved back. I had to hope he was taking them off his weapons. I had to hope he registered blue because he was some kind of cold-blooded humanoid, and not an android or a human wearing armor.

I stabbed right where his heart ought to be, if he had one. His hands had started moving as I raised the knife; he probably couldn't distinguish the blade from my hand—I had it specially designed to radiate body heat—but he recognized the movement.

I screamed at Vlad to run before blue guy got a shot off. Something burned my left arm. The blue man was crumpling over. Praise be. He did have a heart and I had nailed it.

But he pulled me down with him as he fell, and I felt the cold plastic of a gun against my body. "Good job," he said, choking on blood. "But you have to get too close with a knife."

I hadn't planned to die like this, but nobody lives forever. At least my killer wouldn't get away with it.

And then something hit him hard on top of the head, and he let go both of me and the weapon without firing.

Vlad stood there with a rock in his hand. Give the man credit; he didn't lack for guts.

"I thought I told you to run," I said.

"I figured you might need some help." He grinned. Second time I'd seen it. "Besides, I don't have a chance in hell of getting off this planet without your help."

"You sure you can trust me?"

"If I can't, why'd you tell me to run?"

So I took him home to Mom. She saw Vlad's goggles, and immediately reset the house for visible light. He took them off with a sigh of relief.

Then she saw my arm. "What kind of trouble have you been getting yourself into while I've been gone?" She went to grab first aid supplies, and when she came back it registered on me that her hair was halfway down her back, twisted into a mass of tiny braids.

"Mom, wasn't your hair short last week?"

"I let it grow out on the cruise."

"I thought it didn't leave until tomorrow."

"Oh, it doesn't. The captain made a slight miscalculation, and we got back a day early. You can't always calculate the wormholes exactly, as I'm sure you know."

"So you're..."

"In two places at once. But only until tomorrow. Then we'll get it sorted."

I tried not to think about it too hard. Dealing with time always makes me dizzy. "Then you probably know what I'm going to ask and even if it worked."

She grinned. "Yes, but you'd best ask the other me. She'll be home soon. It doesn't do to tell you too much." She scribbled herself a note, and left us there.

Vlad said, "You sure look a lot like your mother."

"She looks more elegant. I like the glittery stuff she had implanted around her eyes."

"All three of them. I haven't seen many three-eyed people."

"Gene tweaks. Some generations back."

He nodded, and stared at me some more. "You're her clone, aren't you?"

I shrugged. "Easiest way to keep those gene tweaks reproducing through the generations."

"I guess it would be. And they're valuable in your line of work." He sighed. "I'm sorry to have caused you so much trouble. I don't seem to be very good at running away from trouble."

Well, he wasn't, but that was no reason to rub it in. "Hey, I probably couldn't write a moving speech or rally people against the Yacare government. Folks have different talents."

"Maybe I should have just stayed on Yacare and let them kill me."

I snorted. "People need leaders, not martyrs. Maybe you should go to Chamaleo and lead all those exiles back home."

He smiled, then. "After all you've done for me, the least I can do is give it a try."

Half an hour later Mom's earlier self came home, and was surprised to find us there until she saw the note. "Hmm. Guess the captain miscalculated. So you need me to find a place on the cruise for this gentleman. Have you given some thought to how?"

"I figured maybe he could start out as a stowaway. Too many people looking for him for it to be a good idea for him to go through customs."

"It'll cost to get him onboard," she said.

I shrugged, but Vlad cleared his throat. "A job would be better. I...I'm just about out of money. I can't even pay you for all the help you've been today."

Somehow, I wasn't surprised.

Mom shook her head. "I think they've got the staff pretty well filled out. Except..." She gave him a hard look. "You are a pretty man, and that's a fact. There's always a need for"—she coughed—"uh, companions."

"Companions?" Vlad said.

"Whores," I explained. I'm not as mannerly as my mother.

I expected a cry of outrage. I expected him to say he'd rather die. I expected the kind of pompous response I'd seen every step of the way.

What I got was a laugh. An outright belly laugh. He laughed so hard he almost couldn't stop. When he finally did quit, he wiped tears from his eyes. "That ought to be a hell of a hiding place," he said. And then he started laughing again. When he finally stopped for breath, he said, "She's built like you, right? Not just female, I mean."

I nodded.

He gave Mom a flirtatious smile.

Well, he did like sex. So maybe it was a good plan at that.

I left him in Mom's capable hands. I was pretty sure it must have worked out, given the way Mom's later self had acted. And it occurred to me that I should get off-planet myself, what with the dead spy I'd left lying in the street and the fact that the bounty hunters were still staking out my place.

I got Gordo to distract the people staking out the Rockety Coon Child. Thankfully, they weren't cops, so for a price he didn't mind. He's getting close to retirement, and is a lot more careful these days.

I went for the nearest hole, and jumped over to Didelphia. Eventually I made my way back to the Testudines, and that's when I heard that Vlad was prime minister on Yacare. I looked up the recent history: He'd rallied the refugees on Chamaleo. They managed to infiltrate the Yacare Army. The revolutionaries stormed the capital, and the generals looked the other way. I wondered if Mom had helped him out.

The reports all say Yacare is a new place. The old leader and his cronies are dead or locked up. The economy is up, and arts and education are flourishing. Sounds like a decent place to live.

There don't seem to be any warrants out for me on Procyon, but I think I'll head for Yacare next. I ought to think about having a kid myself, before I get too much older, and Yacare wouldn't be a bad place to live while she's young.

And I ought to be able to make a living there. Vlad still owes me some money, or at least a cushy job with his government. It cost me a lot to get him off-planet, including some missed job opportunities. I don't smuggle people for the fun of it.

Who am I kidding? Of course I do it for the fun of it. Or, as one of the great philosophers of Old Earth once said: "Don't take life too serious. It ain't nohow permanent."

BY ANY OTHER NAME
STEVE BEAI

Peery didn't want to die, and the fact that his death was imminent and likely to be quick, did not make him feel any better.

He had been a grease jockey, an oiler at Flatnose Jack's Full Service Station, one of a dozen floating maintenance ports off the shoulder of Orion. Even though this particular job had no casualty rate to speak of, there was a war on, so things were different. *Everything*, in fact. Rates of exchange, civilian traffic, number of first-time home buyers, the price of bread. Even the weather seemed different somehow, if being surrounded by blackness and stars and the eternal sub-freezing vacuum of infinity could be called weather. The war had changed that, too, in some not-quite-perceptible way. Peery was sure of it.

Flatnose Jack referred to the war mantra-style as *Damn War Good For Business*, complete with hand-wringing and glazed eyes as he stared out from his tower office, watching the ships slow to a stop and hover in front of the station at both the upper and lower service bays, first one ship, then another, and more until the line stretched as far as he could see and then farther still. *Their* ships, of course, military and civilian alike, but only *their* ships. Flatnose Jack may have been a lot of things, but he was no goddamn mercenary. *Their* ships only. Even at that, the damn war was good for business. And business was *very* good, even when the war got a little too close. The station's emergency siren would blow, and everyone from the mechanics to the boys holding a glowstick in each hand to wave the ships into dock—*guide dogs*, they were called—held their breath at the sound, waiting for a flaming Steelhead to appear out of the blackness, heading for them like a deranged missile. About every second day you could count on at least one of the great military ships to come in trailing dry fire. A Troop Pod would drop from a hatch underneath the Steelhead and plummet to the station like a giant marble and bounce across the platform, smashing one of the guide dogs to bone splinters and body juice before coming to a rolling stop. The now-unmanned Steelhead would go belly-up like a terminal fish, blotting out the stars for one nerve-wracking moment before the ship's Avoidance Failsafe either launched the Steelhead straight up or straight down a safe distance away from the station before Retirement Mode engaged, turning the ship to sparks and microbes of dust. This light show lasted, at most, fifteen seconds. For those fifteen seconds, every man on the station braced to meet his own personal and violent death. Not often, but often enough, *two* flaming Steelheads arrived simultaneously. Whenever that happened, an employee or two would panic and shift their belay winch straight into high gear, forgetting to stop in each of the lower gears, which everyone knew you were *never* supposed to do. The belay winch would go from standby to full bore instantaneously, causing a slingshot effect and giving the winch's wearer about three seconds to mull over his mistake before being cannon-balled into space, G-forces turning flesh to flak. Lucky for Flatnose Jack, two Flamers coming in at the same time was a rare event. Out here good staff—*any* staff for that matter—were hard to find.

Flatnose Jack figured Peery would be the next to slingshot himself to oblivion. He even had a standing bet with two of the mechanics, Lackland and Pirtle, that, sooner or later, Peery was gonna do an unplanned space walk during one of the times the uglier aspects of war came to the station. Lackland and Pirtle were the kind of guys who referred to women as *bitches* and were given over to frequent displays of *machismo* such as drinking heavily and then seeing who could hold a flame to the palm of their hand the longest. Pirtle had been married and divorced several times. Lackland had never been married, but he was father to five or six children he'd never seen. Flatnose Jack loved the two of them like they were his own sons, chips off the old block. They didn't care much for Peery; in fact, they outright hated him. Peery read books and talked about home like a lost little girl. And when he wasn't doing that, he watched news of the war with tight-lipped concentration. During downtime, when the rest of them were getting drunk, or playing cards, or sleeping, Peery would stop whatever he was doing when a report came over the uplink broadcasts, his eyes too close to the screen and his body frozen in a rictus trance as he watched and listened. Funny thing was, Peery never seemed to understand any of it, not a single damn thing. As each broadcast ended, he would ask anyone unfortunate enough to be passing by—usually Lackland or Pirtle—what they thought this action meant or what that conflict was all about or why was *our* President doing such-and-such and *their* Admiral responding this way or that and on and on and on.

"The Fifth Senate met with the President and refused Admiral Chaykin's offer to negotiate new boundaries," Peery said without taking his eyes from the broadcast. "I wonder why we didn't want to at least talk to him?"

Pirtle stiffened, cursing silently that he hadn't seen Peery in time to quicken his pace through the Commons, even though no one else was in the room. He came up behind Peery and leaned over his shoulder.

"Because Chaykin doesn't want to negotiate, *dummy*. He wants to take over everything, you know? Our whole damn country. We need to take Chaykin out. No talk. The President knows that." Pirtle flat-handed the back of Peery's head as he walked away. "It's a war, *dummy*. They're the *enemy*." Stupid kid. It was all so clear. *Wasn't it?*

Peery was still rubbing his head when Lackland entered the Commons. Without a word, the mechanic threw a side punch into Peery's exposed armpit, never breaking stride as he went by. Before Peery could recover, the broadcast had ended.

Always the next one, he thought, making the best of missing the broadcast's wrap-up. *It never ends.* Not even when his tour at the station was finished, he knew. There would be no end to this war even then. One more month of double-shift, seven-day work weeks and he would go home, be shuttled back to Earth after an absence of two years, a virtual stranger to his waiting family. He could have stayed a civilian oiler, could have stayed home and had none of this. But money was tight on the civilian front and money was something they had desperately needed. From the very first day of the war, the military wage had skyrocketed tenfold beyond what he was making as a civilian, so off he went and here he was—because the war not only paid, it paid *better*, because it was war, you see. Because any war at all paid better than none. Because they needed the money, there was a third child he had yet to see—on the way when he shipped off—close to two years old now. And his twin girls, Lucy and Laurie, and Donna, his wife. He didn't need to wait another month, didn't need to experience what would certainly be an awkward homecoming to figure out this had *not* been worth doing for *any* amount of money. He'd realized that twenty-four hours after Earth and home and family had become a memory, recognizing the greed for what it was after it was too late. He supposed war did that, maybe to everyone, allowing a person's greed to gorge with abandon, ultimately consuming its host and of benefit only to the war itself.

Peery reached into his shirt pocket, the one underneath a white patch that read PEERY, his fingers closing with the softest pressure around one edge of the picture as he brought it from the pocket and cradled it in his palm.

They stood in front of a tall fountain, Donna flanked by their two daughters, smiles frozen in time. Peery had taken the picture on the square in Capitol City, a few blocks from where they lived. He remembered the moment, his wife and daughters forcing smiles to cover the fear they all felt that sunny morning before Peery shipped out. He stared at the picture—*into* it—looking beyond his family and the fountain, down the Capitol City streets to the neighborhood where their little house sat, until Flatnose Jack's mantra intruded and Peery blinked himself back to reality—

—damn war good for business—

—and hearing it a second time, then a third, before knowing the way one knows an alarm clock in a dream is both part of the dream and part of the reality that Jack's mantra was in his thoughts because Jack himself was screaming it as he came down the steps from the tower office—

"Damn War Good For Business!" His feet were suspended in mid-air out in front of him as he gripped the bannister on either side, sliding down with his hands. In classic cartoon-style, his feet began paddling in space before they touched down and propelled him forward, head bobbling on a thick cushion of neck flab. He glanced at Peery, waving his arms and running his words together as he fired them, machine-gun style, at the dumbfounded oiler.

"Wassa—? Get movin'—Peery! Getcher ass movin', you *turd!* Wassa—GO! One comin' in! One comin' in! Lessgo! GO! GO! PEERY, YOU TURD! ONE COMIN' IN! BIG ONE, BIG ONE COMIN' IN!"

Peery waited until Jack was through the doorway and gone before he returned the picture to his pocket and got up. With a last glance, he turned the broadcast screen off and followed at a brisk trot, saying with more than a little sarcasm under his breath, "Just one?"

The *big one* was a white Steelhead with a single red stripe down the top fin and yellow eagles on the wings and fuselage, markings of an Executive Transport. It was coming in fast and firing at two smaller ships on its flanks. Stingers. Enemy ships. The drab green single-pilot fighters were throwing everything they had at the larger ship, their ports blazing in a continuous stream of fire as the Stingers outmaneuvered the clumsier guns of the Steelhead.

Flatnose Jack's station gunners were already in position and firing from the forward gun ports as Peery entered his bay and strapped on the belay winch. He shifted...*slowly*...out into the larger area of the service docks where the station opened up in a panoramic view of blackness and stars. At this position, the only solid area visible was a square foot of platform underneath your feet. If you allowed yourself much time to look around, it was easy to be overcome by a sensation of floating which quickly turned disorienting to a dangerous degree.

The belly of the Steelhead was so close, Peery could see the bolts and hatches and the tell-tale port of the Troop Pod, still sealed. The ship was coming in too steep to make dock, heading belly-up for the station as it tried to evade the Stingers. A moment before wild collision was inevitable, the nose of the Steelhead took a sharp drop, leveling the ship with the bay and allowing Peery to see one of the Stingers get tagged by a shot from the station. The Stinger vaporized off to the left, close enough for Peery to feel a rush of heat as it came and went. The second Stinger shot forward, running wide-open behind the Steelhead in an attempt to follow it straight into the bay on a Kamikaze run but it came in too high, giving the Steelhead's rear gunner a clear shot to dispatch the ship well away from the station.

There was an explosion of activity in the bay as the Steelhead eased in and set down with a thump and a chorus of hissing exhaust as the station's crew converged on the ship like swarming insects. The whine of belay winches mingled with shouts and curses as each man began his job on the newest customer.

Peery inched out to the underside of the Steelhead's nose and locked the belay winch in place before snapping a pneumatic wrench from his chest harness, pulling absently to extend the coiled hose from the canvas bag on his back. Disengaging the forward oil port, he stepped back to avoid the initial burst of hot black spray, but the plug came away dry as dust. That wasn't right. A healthy oil port decamped excess oil each time it was checked, no matter if the ship was sitting cold or had come in red-hot seconds before, as this one had. He looked left and right to see if the others were discovering more trouble. Only Lackland returned his gaze, an unlit cigarette dangling from his lips. He smiled and gave Peery the finger before looking away.

The Steelhead pilot had disembarked and was talking to Flatnose Jack on the staging platform at the rear of the dock. Peery examined the opened oil port once more to confirm his diagnosis and then shifted the winch into reverse until he was close enough to get their attention. Both men stopped in mid-conversation as Peery came within earshot. Flatnose Jack gave him a look that said *It better be MORE than good.*

Peery excused himself with a quick nod. "The forward oil port has some heavy damage, I checked the—"

Flatnose Jack cut him off with a raised hand. "*How* heavy?"

"Total failure, sir."

The pilot tensed, mouthing the word *sonofabitch*. He accented the last syllable with a downward snap of his head.

"This ship has to go in twenty minutes." Flatnose Jack pointed at the Steelhead, then tapped his wristwatch with the same finger. "Twenty minutes, Peery, do you understand? Get busy on those repairs."

"It's not a question of repairs, sir," Peery said, keeping one eye on the pilot. "The unit is dead. Short of manual operation in-flight, we're talking fifteen or twenty hours to replace the system."

"I don't have the extra personnel onboard to do that," the pilot said, directing his response to Peery's comment at Flatnose Jack.

"To do *what*?" Peery asked.

"It's either that or tell 'em to get comfortable here for the next day," Flatnose Jack said to the pilot.

"Either *what*?" Peery asked.

A look of panic came over the pilot's face. "Hey, man, you run this station, *you* go do it. There's no fucking way I'm walking back into that ship and telling those guys that."

"Telling who *what*?" Peery asked.

Flatnose Jack reached out and grabbed Peery's harness, pulling him close. "How many people are we talking about for that, *huh*, Peery? How many people to make that happen and get this ship on its way in twenty minutes?"

"*Ten* minutes now," the pilot said.

"How many people...?" Peery blinked at a sudden light only he could see. "*You mean for a manual operation?*"

"That's what I mean."

Everything was in slow motion now:

The pilot turning to Peery with strobe-like precision.

Flatnose Jack sticking out his chin and leaning closer to wait for an answer.

Mechanics passing by in reverse as the belay winches reeled them away from the ship, one after the other, their tasks complete.

The movement of his own lips forming to release the response.

A response Peery did not want to give, but heard his voice deliver even before it came boiling from his mouth. A single-word self-indictment and the world resumed normal speed.

"*How many?*" Flatnose Jack repeated.

"One."

"So long, Peery."

"Now wait a second," the pilot said, "you know what I'm dealing with here, the kind of security—" he shot Peery a glance and motioned for Flatnose Jack to follow him to a spot where they continued in private for another full minute. Peery watched them shake hands at last. As the pilot turned to come back, Flatnose Jack waved at Peery, a dark grin on his face.

Someone pulled his harness from behind, letting it snap back hard on his shoulder blades.

"Don't be a stranger, *dummy*," Pirtle said.

Lackland stood next to him, the same unlit cigarette hanging from his mouth.

"Lemme give you a hand gettin' outta this," was all he said before releasing Peery from the harness. In no time, Peery was trailing behind the pilot as they entered the Steelhead.

"You probably get a lot of war reports on the ship, I'll bet," Peery said as cheerfully as he could. "I watch a lot of—"

"Anything you need, any tools or anything?" the pilot asked without looking at him.

Peery shook his head. "No, no, I have every—"

The pilot cut in front of him and stopped abruptly, kneeling down and pulling open a hatch on the floor. "Down you go, then."

A steel door a few feet in front of them caught Peery's attention. Additional security had been added to the door, an entire line of electronic combination boxes running from top to bottom.

The pilot noticed him staring and gave him a light punch in the leg. "Hey," he said with a frown. "Let's go."

Peery apologized and climbed into the mechanical tunnel, looking up when he reached bottom to let the pilot know he was all clear. Before he could say anything, the pilot closed the hatch.

Peery inched his way down the tube, crawling on his belly until he reached the sending unit. Seconds after transmitting his position over the intercom, he felt the Steelhead launch from the station. He put one hand instinctively over the pocket holding the picture, but tried not to think too hard about home as he operated the sending unit—a real yawn-fest of a job—punch button, release button, punch button, release button, punch and release, punch and release, punch and release, punch and—

— *citizens and soldiers alike to spare*—

— release. He hoped the trip wouldn't be long; otherwise he could easily fall asleep down in this steel cocoon. Shifting on his side, he raised up to reposition his legs and a sound made him freeze.

—*substantial returns for both sides*—

Voices, then laughter, coming from a vent above his head. A conversation.

"*Sides!* Yes, of course...the *good* guys and the *bad* guys..."

Peery knew that voice, had heard it a thousand times or more on as many broadcasts. It was the President. *Their* President, right here on this ship! He pressed his ear against the vent and held his breath.

"...mostly civilian, but Capitol City is still important, media-wise— and absolutely expendable given the projected results." A pause, then more laughter. "Hell, I've only been there twice and hated it both times."

"It would seem a perfectly unprovoked attack..." came a different voice, as familiar as the voice of the President, "...and we're still in agreement on the optimum time of 2:22 p.m...."

The voice of the enemy. Admiral Chaykin.

His head reeled as he listened to them speak, leaders of separate regimes who were supposed to be mortal enemies, who told their citizens truths they expected those citizens to believe and follow to the letter, truths they were called upon to fight and kill and die for if necessary. *Self-evident* truths, they were told.

They were planning an attack on Capitol City. Planning to destroy it all—the buildings, the fountains...and the people, three of whom waited in a little house on a quiet street for Peery to return.

As he lay there listening, Peery felt his insides grow cold with the realization that it was all lies. The war reports, the battles and strategies, every bit of it lies. The war itself nothing but a financial project, an investment risk with a projected return. It stood to reason that the investors would do anything in their power to generate the largest profit. There was no war. There were only the two investors above him, sitting in a secured room and planning their next move for the highest possible return, their only cost being human currency, enough to keep their investment going until the end of time if they chose.

One month left. One month and then Peery could go back home. To a place that would be little more than a graveyard in a few short hours.

What to do? He would die, of course, either on this ship or from a broken heart upon returning home to find all that he loved dead because he hadn't saved them when he had the chance, when the solution had been handed right to him, when he had *known*...and done nothing.

What to do?

The first thing Peery did was depress the button on the sending unit and lock it in place. The constant flow of oil would run the mixture a little rich, maybe cause a slight change in the ship's performance, but otherwise would go unnoticed. For a little while, anyway.

The next thing he did was find the transmission lines.

The pilot spun his chair at the sound of the opening hatch to see Peery emerge. The oiler brushed himself off and said with a wan smile, "All done."

"What do you mean, '*all done*'?" With a nervous glance toward the closed steel door, the pilot stood up. "I thought—"

"I thought a lot, myself," Peery interrupted, continuing to move forward as he talked. "Thought I was a decent person, thought I always did what was best for my family, thought I *knew* what was best." He stopped short in front of the console. "Thought I knew at least a few things. Turns out I didn't know anything."

Peery reached behind the pilot and pulled the Avoidance Failsafe module from its socket on the console. He took a step back, dropped the module to the floor in front of him and stomped down hard a single time, smashing it to pieces.

"Until just now."

"What the hell are you doing?" The pilot didn't wait for Peery's answer. He turned to the console, reaching to key the transmitter.

"Doesn't work anymore," Peery said.

"Listen, you *sonofabitch*—"

The Steelhead lurched to one side, arcing into a steep turn.

"I've changed the course of the ship from below." He looked down at the shattered Avoidance Failsafe module. "Had to come up here for that, though," he added quietly.

From behind him, the steel door opened. Peery turned to see the President and Admiral Chaykin. It could have been the light, or maybe the same confused expression on both their faces, but standing there next to each other, it was hard to tell them apart.

"Change it back," the pilot said, the fear in his voice replaced with anger. He was holding a pistol at arm's length, trained on Peery.

There was an expulsion of air from outside the ship, causing everyone but Peery to look out from the console port. An empty Troop Pod floated by the glass.

"You guys should probably sit down now," Peery said.

The Steelhead completed the turn and shot forward with sudden speed.

Lackland and Pirtle were the first to go and the only men who suddenly forgot the proper way to shift gears on a belay winch. Even though Pirtle shifted faster and shot from the station quicker, Lackland shaded him by a good hundred yards. Pirtle gave up a starburst finale of tiny red polka dots right after clearing the end of the dock, while most of Lackland whizzed by, making it all the way to the Steelhead where an impressive chunk of him hit the nose of the ship like a bug.

Standing frozen in front of the window of his tower office, Flatnose Jack watched it come. His mouth dropped open as the Steelhead covered the glass until there was no glass, just more ship. The other stations will have extra customers now, Flatnose Jack realized. His final thought filled him with satisfaction, but it came and went so fast, there was no time to smile.

This damn war. Damn war was *still* good for business.

Just not his anymore.

The inside of the ship was filled with clouds only Peery could see. The others were too busy scrambling back and forth as they tried every switch, button, and lever they could find. They weren't lying on the floor with a bullet in them, quietly bleeding to death as they watched the gathering clouds. Only Peery was doing that. He thought about the reports and wondered what they would make of this latest news from the front.

A defeat or a victory.

The act of a hero or traitor.

Peery closed his eyes and thought about the picture of his family, too weak to take it from his pocket for a final look into the eyes of Donna and the kids. Maybe what he was doing would save them, maybe it would only postpone the inevitable, or cause untold trouble for his family once the investigations had been conducted and the reports issued. But it didn't matter to him what the reports would say now, anyway. He knew the truth because he had been a part of it and had done his best to keep that truth alive. Truth, he knew, that would never be reported, that no one else would ever understand because of a single, enduring fact.

Like all the others before it, this was a war.

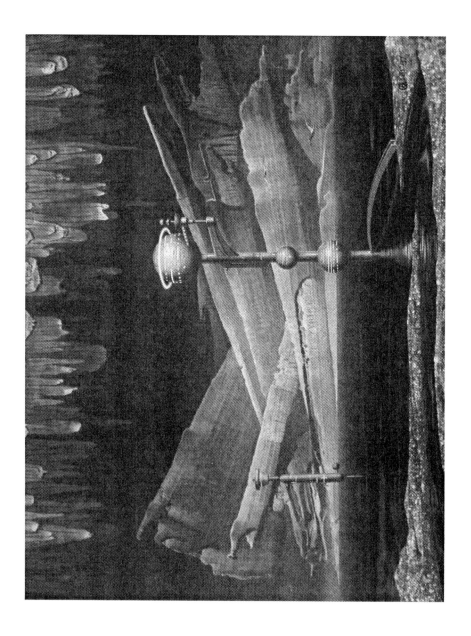

STATELY'S PLEASURE DOME
SYNE MITCHELL

George Stately's Pleasure Dome was the finest bordello this side of the Horsehead Nebula. And that's not just my opinion, it's a proven fact.

Asteroid 8753M-ZX2 had been a source of commercial-grade fluorite once upon a time, before the mechanical borers hollowed it out and left the structure too unstable to continue mining. The orbiting smelters would have to look elsewhere for flux material. Pretty though, the unclaimed fluorite hung in pink and green crystals from the ceiling and streaked the walls with color. When the company moved out, Stately bought it for a song.

He converted one of the old watchtowers into a palace. Standing like a bulb-headed chrome sentinel, it dominated the mining cavern. Stately ripped out the polypropylene carpeting and pressed-plastic furniture and imported the finest reclaimed-rayon velvets and antique wood. He replaced the harsh halide lighting with bioluminescent globes. Their slow pulsing made the velvet-draped walls writhe with shadows.

But the miners and shippers from ten parsecs around didn't come for the décor, if you get my meaning. Stately recruited money-minded beauties from the failed colony near Rigel, his "sharecroppers" he called them. He rented the women rooms in the palace and took a percentage of their take.

What else could a poor man do? Stately hadn't their physical gifts to trade on, most of the clientele being of the Tab A looking for Slot B variety. Of the few women who endangered their fertility to work in the high-radiation of space, fifty percent of those were also looking for Slot B bed companions, and of the rest, they headed towards sweet young things fresh out of the space academy, and not grizzled old ex-miners like George Stately. No, he had only his business sense and his flair for decoration to support him through his old age.

Lucky for the young beauties, science still can't create a sexbot that's indistinguishable from a human during the carnal act. Turing's test taken to its extreme, there's a false texture to synthaflesh, a wrong note in programmed writhing and moans.

Maybe sex works on a dimension science hasn't mapped yet, perhaps more is exchanged than friction and fluid. All I know is that Stately's kept the sweet young ex-colonists in food and housing, and that was a wonderful thing.

But there was one sharecropper who had ideas above her station. Angel-lips she was called. One look at her angular face with its parsimonious mouth was enough to make you think the name an irony. But she could do things with her nether regions that gave truth enough to her sobriquet. She was a world-class athlete in the Kegel region, make no mistake. But the accolades of her customers weren't enough for her. She had it in her head to start up her own house of pleasure on a nearby rock and cut into Stately's business.

Whether Stately lived in ignorance, or knew about her plans and politely ignored them, no one knew. But Angel-lips was a serpent in paradise, whispering to the women to rise up and rebel.

She approached a few of the men, like me, but I think she had the other male sharecroppers figured as playing on Stately's team. Why she considered me, I'll never know. Must be my winning ways. Or perhaps she wanted me for her pet once she was a lady of leisure. I've talents of my own that make me a favorite with the ladies who appreciated a Tab A, and a few of the men as well.

We served all types at Stately's: all genders, all races—hominid and nonhominid alike. You never knew what would come through the door after the wormhole was created. Thank engineering for the personal force fields that kept us safe. Nanometers thick, they covered the entire body and protected against infection or disease. The latest ones allow a one-way fluid exchange enabling users to take advantage of natural lubrication; all the pleasure of riding without a saddle, without any of the risks.

But in any case, the night I'm talking about, a strange man slithered in. His source of locomotion was nine tentacles in a trilobate pattern that whipped back and forth like rattlers on methamphetamine. On top was a pseudo-hominid structure. I say pseudo, because you never can tell with new races; something that looks like a human head and face is just as likely to be a kidney, or a new hairdo. Giving the structure the benefit of the doubt, he had enormous gray eyes set in an oval egg of a head. A gash only slightly less full than Angel-lips' own mouth broke the smooth monotony from eyes to chin. If he had a nose, it was elsewhere.

Stately crossed the room to welcome the newcomer. The translator blurbled and whooped when the stranger waved his hands. Stately told me later that the computer had engaged in a linguistics exchange with the newcomer's spaceship for over eighteen hours before his arrival, but our languages must not have much in common, because the most our machine could make from his flapping hands was something about "stimulating" and "ancestors." The fingers of those hands, I might add, were eighteen each in number and boned like the tentacles that propelled his torso, that is to say they writhed like snakes in intricate three-dimensional patterns.

Stately assured the man (I should note here that any sentient being is assumed to be male—by convention—until they demonstrate their right to be considered life-givers) that the facilities of his pleasure dome would be more than adequate to stimulate him and his ancestors both. Then Stately crooked a finger at Angel-lips to approach. Whether he picked her out of deference to her expertise and tenure in the pleasure craft, or it was a punishment, Stately never said. I say a punishment not because of the man's unique physiognomy—for we've seen far more unusual forms at Stately's—but because Stately had a first-time free policy and knew Angel-lips would resent any assignment that did not add to her war chest.

Stately's first-time-free policy applied only to the first individual of a given alien race to visit the pleasure dome, a concession to the inconvenience that arose from his sharecroppers having to puzzle out the pleasure centers of a new alien form.

Angel-lips rolled her eyes and clicked on her force field. It gave her body a neon-fuchsia gleam that highlighted the generous curves nature had given to compensate for a merely average face. She took the alien by a many-tentacled hand and led him to her suite in the top of the pleasure dome.

It was only minutes before she buzzed down to the bar for backup. It seems our new man was a Tab A, Tab B, Slot C, D, E, and F kind of fellow. With the preponderance of female equipment, perhaps we should call him a woman, but the orifices might have just been for show. Perhaps he was simply too polite to object to what some of us ended up doing to his ear. I never have worked up the nerve to ask.

Anyway, it was just six of Stately's finest sharecroppers and the newcomer in his/her naked glory. His skin below the waist was the color of eggplant, shading to pearly white where it reached his upper torso. The tentacles were soft and sensitive to touch, retracting into themselves like an anemone's at any unexpected or too-vigorous caress.

Stately himself came to watch the research that was underway, but his role was more of a conductor than an actual player.

The stranger kept burbling on about stimulation and ancestors, and I hoped he wasn't expecting any sort of reproduction. Force fields aside, human-alien reproduction isn't possible outside of a laboratory.

Me and the other croppers were in position and doing the early stages
of our thing when Stately blanked the floor. The upper room of the dome
is the exhibition hall, and the Persian mosaic that covers the floor is a
hologrammatic projection. When Stately turned it off, the polycarbonate
floor went clear. Combined with the curving mirror above, it gave all the
revelers in the bar below a view to remember.

I was too busy with an athletic move to protest and the alien was simi-
larly distracted times six.

"Ancestors. Ancestors," the man chanted, and for all I knew that was
alien for "Yeah Daddy, give it to me harder." In any event his fingers danced
around his hands like agitated medusae and the translator chirped and whined
and burbled in an increasing tempo with fewer and fewer intelligible words.

The quickening spurred me and the others to greater efforts. I already
knew I was going to be sore the next day, but it was a small price to pay to
be a part of history. "How's this for a first-contact scenario?" I shouted at
the memory of my wasted education. My academy training was in
xenoanthropology. Funny the turns the river of life takes, sometimes it
hops the banks entirely and floods off in a whole new direction.

The six of us wriggled and thrust around the hub of the new man. My
back was arced near to breaking point when I felt the earth move. Clichés
aside, the tower shook and shimmied as the walls of the fluorite mine
flexed. For a wild moment it felt as if I was fucking the asteroid to death,
feeling its orgasmic quiver all around us, the impending moment that would
crush us all in one white wave of pleasure.

But then sex strides into the part of our brains where logic dare not tread.
Cognition flared back to life in my mind with the second rumble. I exchanged
a worried glance with Angel-lips across the stranger's blue-black bottom.
But by now he was starting to tremble and jerk, so whatever was happening
was already too late. Both our faces firmed with resolve. Better to go out
with professionalism than to botch the last trick we would ever do.

The man's tentacles thrashed and flailed, striking like cat-o'-nine tails
across my chest. I was close to the final moment and the pain was lost in a
crescendo of pleasure. Lights danced behind his huge eyes in what looked
like an exothermal reaction. My mind—what was left in that last instant—
was a pulsing rush of primal endocrine responses.

A flash, and then searing heat spread out from my groin. I was thrown
away from the man along with the other sharecroppers. I thudded against
the wall of the dome and slid down to the clear floor.

Dazed and half-concussed, I held up my hand to block the light emanating from our visitor. Each of his tentacles erupted in pink and green,
spewing light. Crystals grew in the spaces between my fingers.

"Out-out-out," someone shouted. Hands reached under my armpits and dragged me across the floor. I looked up and saw Angel-lips, her face uncharacteristically etched with concern. Her cheek was covered with tiny glittering shards.

"What's going on?" Looking back, I saw the man apparently explode in an eruption of molten fluorite. My worries for his health were allayed when the translator broke into a clear translation: "Yes! Yes! Yes!"

After Stately's assurances that the floor of the upper suite was rated for temperatures up to 2200 degrees Fahrenheit, and thus in no danger of melting through, we all went down to have a drink, apply ice to our groinal regions, and watch the show. The man's ecstasy looked like a cross between fireworks and a lava lamp. After more than fifteen minutes, half the crowd was concerned for the alien's health—not wanting any of the political troubles that could arise if he snuffed it at Stately's. The other half was jealous.

Nearly an hour later, the alien, his nether half having paled to a sheepish pink color, slithered out of Angel-lips' quarters. The entire room, save for a central chamber and a path that had been hacked out to the door, was filled with glittering fluorite.

Stately wore a look of astonishment, as he confirmed the analysis with a mass spectrometer he kept in the basement. He kept muttering: "Impossible, by all the biochemistry I know, this is impossible."

I looked up at the cavern ceiling that rose five hundred meters above us. This mine had once been filled solid with the semi-precious stone. "Ancestors" "stimulated" indeed.

Angel-lips tapped her teeth with a fingernail. "Doesn't it say in the rental agreement that all possessions left behind in a sharecropper's room become their personal property?"

I looked in at what must have been nearly two tons of gem-grade fluorite and said, "What if he wants to take it with him?"

She rolled her eyes at me and began making mental calculations. Six months later, she had a place of her own, farther out on the rim. A classy place, I've visited it a few times. Good pay and benefits, but call me sentimental; I decided to accept Stately's counteroffer of a larger suite and a bigger percentage.

Stately took Angel-lips' defection with savoir-faire. With his usual inventiveness, he invited the alien back for an annual encore, on the house. He sold tickets and made it the best-attended event in this quadrant of the belt.

For it ever was that the sex industry pioneered profiteering. Wasn't it the porn industry that drove many of the industrial revolutions of the twentieth, twenty-first, and twenty-second centuries? Robotics was in its infancy, skeletons of steel and gears before Louis Sheppard began the arms race to build a better 'bot.

As for the place, yeah, I still call it Stately's. It's not my name, but like I said, I'm a sentimental guy. When he sold it to me, I opened up sharecropping to the other races. We even have one of the stranger's cousins on staff for curiosity seekers. He may resurrect the fluorite-mining trade single-handed—or whatever he calls his appendages.

So come on down to Stately's Pleasure Dome. You never know what you'll find, but we guarantee there's a little something for everyone.

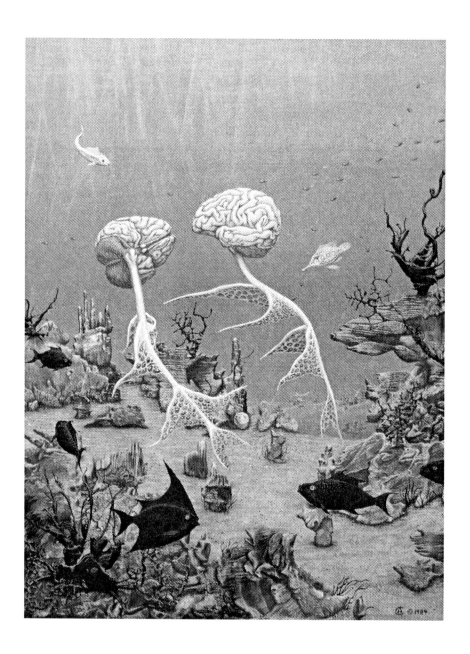

BETWEEN THE LINES
ARINN DEMBO

E ventually, after many months of work, the investigators from Naval Intelligence were able to piece together the story from the beginning.

I.

G alen Navarek, a boy from the colonies, is brought to Earth for the first time at the age of eight. A luxurious vacation for his parents; nostalgic for their homeworld, they assume that the trip will also be a treat for their son.

In fact, the visit to Earth is a miserable experience for a child raised in the domes. Natural gravity is a crushing weight on his body. The thick, unfiltered atmosphere attacks him in several ways; he develops a dozen minor infections and allergic reactions, none of which seem to respond to the standard treatment. The climate and the crowds oppress him. He complains constantly of noise and headaches.

One morning the Navareks wake to find Galen sprawled unconscious on the bedroom floor. Panicked by his rapid, shallow breathing and unresponsive pupils, they call paramedics. He is taken to the children's hospital in Los Angeles, but the emergency room is flooded by a recent outbreak of Mombasa Fever. Since his condition is judged stable at the time, the boy is placed in a recovery ward with nearly two hundred other children and left until the following day.

In the next bed, a local girl is struggling to breathe. Thera Mendosa has been lucky, according to the doctors; her fever has not entered the toxic phase. They predict a full recovery, with very little organ damage and scarring—only the nerve damage is irrecoverable. As she lies on her side, panting beneath an oxygen mask, she sees the orderlies put Galen down beside her, his mattress only inches from hers in the crowded room. His thin white arms dangle, boneless, from the bed.

For hours he lies with his face turned toward her, his strange wide-open eyes never blinking. Sometime during the night, the older girl reaches out toward him and takes his hand, entwining his fingers with her own.

The next day, Galen is tested by staff from the division of clinical immunology. A senior resident quickly recognizes his symptoms and places a call. Men in black uniforms come to take him away, packing his inert body into a coffin-like case.

Later that day, a homeless boy dies of Mombasa Fever in the same hospital. His coloring and build are roughly similar to that of Galen Navarek, and his features are a red ruin—sixty percent of his skin surface has been ravaged by the angry burst blisters of the terminal fever. The grieving Navareks are guided to a leaded window and shown the corpse lying on a slab. A sad-eyed, weary intern tells them that they cannot have the body for burial at home; his remains are still considered contagious, and quarantine procedures are strict. The boy will be cremated the following morning.

Sasha and Mariid Navarek return to their homestead with a sealed canister of ashes. Galen Navarek is remanded to a training academy on Mars. Thera Mendosa is released from the hospital a few days later; her father and brother roll her out of the hospital in a wheelchair, which will be her only means of locomotion for nearly seven years.

II.

Galen Navarek is an exceptionally gifted student; his talents as an esper always score off the charts. Even with minimal training he shows a profound and detailed clairvoyance, an uncanny grasp of spatial relations, unusual empathic skills as both a transmitter and a receiver, and a powerful coercive ability. His instructors say that he could excel as a pilot or a special interrogator.

Rather than devoting himself seriously to his studies, however, the boy distinguishes himself in the early days of his career at Mars Dome by a series of desertion attempts, which grow increasingly daring and ingenious as the years pass. Despite punishments which range from solitary confinement to lashing, his determination to escape never wavers—until his final run, at the age of twelve.

During the week of the midterm exams, Navarek coerces a pair of guards to open the doors of the upper classmen's armory. After clumsily wiping the memories of both men, he steals a slicksuit and seals himself into an outbound weapons container. Loaded into a cargo ship headed for the outer colonies, Galen survives for several days in the thin, sub-zero atmosphere of the hold, using the meditation techniques he has been taught to sustain himself on a minute supply of oxygen and water.

He makes it as far as Port Europa before being caught. After a struggle with three military police, leaving one woman in critical condition, the boy is subdued and returned to Mars in a drug-induced coma.

The academy's esper commander, Captain Spake, is less than amused by Navarek's steady refusal to accept his commission. A list of the boy's known associates turns up only a handful of names: the lab partner in a class on organic chemistry, the three bunkmates who share his berth, and a non-commissioned officer who gives special instruction in zero-gee combat. All five are deemed non-essential personnel; when young Navarek is brought before Spake, aboard the Captain's personal cruiser in Mars orbit, the twelve-year-old is made to watch while his "friends" are spaced one by one.

The Captain assures him that any further insubordination will result in a similar fate for Sasha and Mariid Navarek, who are still alive and well at the Epsilon colony.

For several years thereafter, Galen pursues his education at Mars Dome with grim determination, passing several times as the head of his age division. Over the years, many of his fellow students have become introverted and inclined to isolate themselves. Given their special sensitivity, few of them feel the need to communicate with the spoken word; generally their thoughts and feelings are conveyed with quick telepathic shorthand.

Even among espers, however, Galen's shyness is remarkable. He has been known to go for weeks or months at a time without uttering a sound— even when injured. He avoids even empathic contact, shielding himself from shared jokes and mental intimacy.

The only crack in his infamous reserve is seen on his twenty-first birthday, when a tragic rip-drive accident interrupts the annual Martian Air Review. The AFS *Fletcher* is lost with all hands, tearing a spectacular hole in the violet sky over Mons Olympus with a bizarre misfire of its Jump engine. Flaming debris rains down on the crowd below; most notably, half of the corvette's molten hull drops onto the viewing platform for visiting dignitaries. Several high-ranking officers are lost, including Rear Admiral Spake.

At the evening's mess, the chaplain requests a moment of silence for the departed. Second Lieutenant Navarek is officially reprimanded later for muttering, in the ensuing quiet, "Wish I could have seen his face."

III.

I n 2616, a new intern is assigned to the medical staff at Mars Dome. Thera Mendosa is a specialist, trained in the design and fitting of artificial nervous tissue. She has been brought to Mars to assist the chief medico-engineer as he fits a new generation of starship pilots with an experimental control system.

At age twenty-eight, Mendosa herself is a striking example of bionic engineering. Half paralyzed and stricken with ataxia in childhood, she's had artificial nerves grafted throughout her legs that allow her to walk and move with unnatural grace. She is introduced to many of the pilots during her tour of the facilities, and quickly becomes a popular topic of telepathic conversation in the mess. More than one young flyer decides to try his rusty speaking skills in the face of her towering, heavy-boned, copper-skinned homeworld beauty...but only one stands utterly transfixed when she passes, staring at her with eyes gone wide and liquid and black.

Soon thereafter, Lieutenant Galen Navarek shows the first real initiative of his military career, and asks to be considered as a subject for the new experimental airframe. Although reluctant to part with one of his most gifted pilots, the wing commander nevertheless bows to Navarek's request for a letter of recommendation. When brought before a board of inquiry recently, the man chose to ignore the advice of his counsel, and shrugged in the face of hostile questioning. His statement was simple: "Lieutenant Navarek came into my office and said, 'Will you nominate me for the new deep-space destroyer program?' Since it was the longest sentence I had ever heard him string together, I figured it must be important to him. And there was no question that he had the skills."

Impressed by Navarek's almost surreal aptitude for flight, the selection committee accepts him immediately. During his initial trials, they are also delighted by his rare feel for the rip drive; Navarek never fails a Jump, and can often make several Jumps in one session—a feat that even the most experienced men on the flight line can't match.

When he receives an upgrade to his security clearance, Galen is finally briefed on the details of the new control system. It is immediately clear why so many top guns have washed out of the program at this stage of the game. In order to fly the new deep-space destroyer, the pilot must have his own nervous system spliced with the wiring of the ship; the procedure will be long, gruesome, painful, and permanent. If he agrees to it, he will never walk away from his vessel again. He and the AFS *Finne Ronne* will become a single unit.

When offered the usual grace period to consider his answer, Navarek shakes his head. He signs a number of forms and waivers, receives an honorary rank of Lieutenant Commander, and reports on the following morning to the office of the chief medico-engineer and his new assistant, Thera Mendosa.

IV.

In the years that follow, the Navy finds many uses for its new fleet of deep-space destroyers; the Explorer-class vessels effectively double the length of the Navy's arm. Able to Jump many light-years at a time and refuel themselves by skimming the upper layers of any convenient gas giant, ships like the AFS *Finne Ronne* are used to respond quickly to a turbulent frontier.

Galen sees action in several campaigns against the rebellious outer colonies, but never rises above a rank of Commander. His reluctance to open fire on undefended domes goes on record three times in a decade, limiting his opportunities for promotion.

First contact with the Black Fleet occurs at Kapteyn's Star in the year 2630. Survivors of this first brush with an alien task force report that the enemy ships were virtually unstoppable, decimating an entire carrier group in minutes. Those who limp away from the action report that the enemy vessels "fight like living things—they just ripped us apart." Although the Navy was able to inflict only minimal damage on the enemy with their own weapons, the ships destroyed yield a strange, powdery residue, which proves to be of great interest to the Department of Science and Technology.

Over the next few months, several destroyer groups sweep a widening grid of space, following reports of the Black Fleet and searching for its possible base of operations. The enemy does not appear to be aggressive or even unduly interested in the human race; defenseless civilian colonies often see blackships pass within a hundred kilometers without incident, and even warships are not attacked if they remain outside a perimeter of several thousand klicks.

Eventually a pattern of migration is deduced, and the Navy's 2nd Flotilla is sent to intercept the Black Fleet at Stein 2051. Over fifty ships of the line are lost in the battle that follows, among them four deep-space destroyers—including the AFS *Finne Ronne* and its pilot, Galen Navarek.

By the time the first relief ships arrive, three days later, all possible witnesses to the battle are dead. The last survivors of the fleet action have suffocated in their slicksuits, after spending their last hours clinging in vain to floating wreckage, praying for rescue. Recovery crews spend weeks sorting through the flotsam and jetsam of the fleet, trying to piece together the action. Eventually, they are able to account for most of the ships and personnel lost—but in all the material sorted, over a period of several months, not one fragment of the four missing destroyers is found.

V.

In spring of 2634, dockworkers at the Kapteyn's starbase show the first symptoms of a mysterious malady. It begins with numbness and tingling in the fingertips; the initial symptoms are easily mistaken for carpal tunnel syndrome by the station's medical officer. Over the next few days, however, the sufferers show an increasing lack of coordination. Their fingers and toes take on a bluish tinge. By the end of a week, they return to the sick bay with slurred speech and reflex responses severely diminished; a few days later, the photoreceptors of the eyes have been affected.

The station's doctor, having dismissed many of the first complaints as a union scam, is genuinely alarmed to see that the corneas of several workers have become speckled with black pinpricks. Those still able to speak describe blurred vision and a strangely distorted color palette—as if the data to the brain had become somehow corrupted.

In a pattern that quickly repeats itself throughout the neighboring systems, the first subjects enter the "crisis phase" of the disease within two weeks. Their eyes turn completely, eerily black—corneas and sclera alike. Spidery blue-black formations become visible beneath the skin, growing darker and darker as the hours pass. They have psychotic episodes, babbling words and phrases that seem at first to be meaningless nonsense, but are eventually revealed to be typical of the ravings which espers mutter as they descend into shield shock.

Far too late, the doctor begins performing exploratory surgery on his patients; he is the first to see the crystalline formations of the new contagion under a microscope, wrapped like a crust of black diamonds around the nerve fibers.

When the first victims begin to scream, their brains flooded with information which they can only process as physical pain, the doctor initiates top-level quarantine procedures and sends out a general alert to all systems within hailing distance. Unfortunately, ships arriving and departing from the starbase in the intervening days have already touched down at a hundred others, spreading the highly communicable disease to every human settlement within a dozen light years. The only thing the man is able to achieve, before his own death a few weeks later, is to give the new plague a name: Kapteyn's Syndrome.

VI.

B y the time the first cases appear on Earth, three months later, Thera Mendosa has become a high-ranking bionic engineer in Los Angeles. Her father, Theodor Mendosa, is the first member of the family to begin working seriously on a possible treatment for Kapteyn's Syndrome. It is his hope that the nerves destroyed in the course of the infection might eventually be replaced by artificial ones, like those which he once created for his daughter's legs.

Unfortunately, the elder Mendosa is unable to pursue his work for more than a few months before he contracts the Syndrome from one of his patients. Dying, he passes on his research to his son, Lorenzo, who continues working on the problem for several weeks until he too falls ill. Thera Mendosa is barred from her brother's bedside in his final days; she watches him die from behind a leaded glass window, and stands by, swathed in a full anti-contamination suit, while the terms of his last will and testament are carried out.

After seeing her brother's body consigned to a fusion torch, Thera returns to his office to sort out his belongings. She discovers, to her surprise, that Lorenzo Mendosa had abandoned the notion of treating the infection by nerve replacement; he had discovered that the disease would coat and destroy artificial nerve fibers even more quickly than natural ones.

Instead, Lorenzo was performing experiments with the black crystals formed during the course of the infection. According to his notes, he had become interested in their "rectifying properties." His last entries speculate that the formation of the crystals, rather than being an accidental side effect of the bacteria's life process, might be a purpose for which the organism was deliberately designed.

"This bacteria is not the product of natural selection. It's much smaller, more cleverly designed than our own nano-machines, but it *was* engineered—I'm sure of it. My instinct tells me that if we could only find the right tuner and output mechanisms for these crystals, we would have a receiver of some kind. The crystals are made to rectify an unknown frequency…"

Several days later, Thera Mendosa looks down at her hands and notes the first symptoms of Kapteyn's Syndrome. Quietly she marks the probable date of her death on the calendar beside her, and then turns back to the computer to continue her work.

VII.

On April 17, 2634, Thera Mendosa makes a trip to the Beckman Institute to be examined by the city's quarantine authority. As she descends the staircase outside the building, she loses her footing; the nerves of her feet and legs, made of artificial fiber, are succumbing more quickly to Kapteyn's Syndrome than she had anticipated.

The fall is traumatic, resulting in a fractured skull and several internal injuries. As Thera Mendosa lies at the bottom of the stairs, bleeding and unconscious, a rip-portal forms in the air thirty meters above her. Windows shatter and circuits fuse for a kilometer in all directions as the AFS *Finne Ronne* emerges from the resulting hole in the sky, hovering low over the streets of Los Angeles.

Witnesses to the event suffer a complete loss of voluntary control over their bodies at this time. A crowd of nearly two hundred people gathers around the prone form of Thera Mendosa and cooperates to build a stretcher for her transport. While the *Finne Ronne* hovers above them, they carry Mendosa en masse to the nearby emergency room of Cedars-Sinai Hospital and relay Galen Navarek's psionic commands to the ER staff in a single roar, which emerges from all two hundred throats at once:

HELP HER.

NOW.

VIII.

Once the staff of the emergency room has begun treating the injuries of Thera Mendosa, Galen Navarek releases the members of the crowd. Four men and two women collapse immediately, suffering from minor brain hemorrhages; the majority of the rest survive with nothing more than a nosebleed or a black eye to mark the occasion, although several emotional breakdowns are later reported.

A trio of corvettes is dispatched from San Clemente Naval Base; they meet Navarek in the sky over the city. Ordered to stand down, he peacefully surrenders to the smaller ships and follows the course laid for him. While accompanying the former Commander to the landing field at San Clemente, the crew of the AFS *Spruance* remark upon the condition of his ship, its hull bleached and warped by exposure to unimaginable extremes of pressure, heat, and cold. The fuselage of the *Finne Ronne* is also severely dented in a strange corkscrew pattern— as if it had been wound in the grip of a great crushing tentacle, and then released.

Navarek lands without incident at San Clemente. The base commander sends an immediate request for orders to Mars Dome. The *Finne Ronne*, missing and thought to be destroyed for the past three years, is of great interest to the high command. Not only is Galen Navarek the only known survivor of the Battle of Stein 2051, but the Earth's planetary defense systems have measured the energy released by his rip-portal and calculated the distance which the Commander must have Jumped to make his spectacular arrival in Los Angeles. The readings suggest an almost inconceivable fold in space-time—thousands of light-years traveled in a single bound. If the numbers don't lie, Navarek has made the longest Jump ever recorded.

While coded communications buzz invisibly through the ether between Earth and Mars Dome, the AFS *Finne Ronne* sits quietly on the pad, its cameras focused on the sea. Forbidden to interact with him in any way, the corvettes cruise nervously on a tight patrol, making slow sweeps over Navarek's head. Should the Commander attempt to take off, open a weapons port, or activate his rip drive, they are instructed to open fire immediately with their gauss cannons. Although his ship is heavily armored, the three lighter, faster ships will rip Navarek apart like a pack of dogs if he so much as fires a thruster.

For several hours, the Commander offers no resistance or comment. Only twice does he send a transmission to his captors. Once he requests a channel to the medical library at Bethesda; the base commander, instructed to humor him if necessary, does not allow Navarek to access the system himself, but freely uploads all the available information on Kapteyn's Syndrome to the *Finne Ronne*'s computer.

Some time later, a private message is sent to the pilot of the AFS Briscoe. Recorded for posterity, Navarek's voice is a string of metallic syllables, haltingly strung together...as if by a man struggling to recall the English language: "The lit-tle...black...birds...with gray...faces. What...are they...called?"

Relaying the message to her commanding officer, the pilot of the Briscoe is eventually ordered to give the following answer: "*Finne Ronne*, your little gray bird is probably the San Clemente loggerhead shrike. It's a rare subspecies. The entire breeding population is only about fifty birds, and they all live on this one island."

"Thank...you," says Navarek, and falls silent once more.

IX.

A contingent from Mars Dome arrives the following day, led by Vice Admiral William Bishop, commander of the home defense fleet.

Bishop's chief of security, Captain Castavet, is dispatched to the surface to take Galen Navarek into custody.

Castavet is a careful man, not given to charge blindly into the unknown. Before making his way to San Clemente Island, he lands in Los Angeles and visits the site of Navarek's spectacular rip. His team quickly goes to work, tracking down and interviewing a number of witnesses. Within a few hours Castavet has gathered all planetary and military records on Thera Mendosa, and received official permission to have the woman interrogated.

Captain Castavet and his team arrive at Cedars-Sinai at 12:15 p.m. on the afternoon of April 19th. Citing his credentials as an officer of the home defense fleet, Castavet gains access to the new ward for victims of Kapteyn's Syndrome. Thera Mendosa is still comatose as a result of her injuries; nonetheless, the Captain orders his adjutant, Leiko Juzo, to perform a terminal scan of the woman's mind.

Julianna Neal, the nurse on duty, displays an unfortunate grasp of professional ethics at this moment. She attempts to intervene, and prevent Lieutenant-Commander Juzo from administering the necessary interrogation drugs through her patient's IV. Unwilling to wait for a review of his clearance, Captain Castavet shoots the RN in the back before she can reach the intercom to call hospital security, and orders Juzo to proceed.

Nevertheless, the resulting scan does not go as planned. When Leiko Juzo makes contact with the mind of the unconscious woman, she is met with a powerful psionic defense. Juzo's interrogation technique, designed to scour the subject's mind and leave it tabula rasa, is somehow turned on the interrogator herself. Instead of gathering information from her intended victim, Leiko Juzo is reduced to the level of an autistic infant in a matter of seconds.

Deprived of a valuable member of his command staff, unwilling to risk further exposure to Kapteyn's Syndrome, and uncertain of how dangerous the Mendosa woman might be to those in her immediate vicinity, Castavet retreats from the room, dragging Juzo with him. He leaves Thera, still seemingly asleep, under heavy guard. At 12:30 p.m. he returns to his cruiser to make a report to Admiral Bishop.

X.

At 3:00 p.m. on the same afternoon, Castavet's cruiser group rips open the sky over San Clemente. The corvettes assigned to guard the *Finne Ronne* are not warned in advance of the planned assault; caught in a sudden hurricane of wind and energy, all three ships are hurled violently aside and smashed to pieces on the beach, killing their crews instantly.

As the fighters begin a rain of flash bombs onto the pad below, a surge of energy is detected aboard the *Finne Ronne*. Fearing that Navarek is about to cook off the destroyer's fusion reactor, Castavet opens up with the starboard gun of his command ship. A ten gigawatt x-ray laser lances down through the clouds like a burning spear, carving neatly through the fuselage of the *Finne Ronne* and severing all connection between the cockpit and the rest of the craft.

Certain that his prey can offer no further resistance, Castavet sends in a recovery team to pull the Commander from his gutted ship. The engineers approach the smoldering wreck of the *Finne Ronne* cautiously, dousing fires as they go. Within moments of entering the gaping black breach in the ship's hull, they discover that Galen Navarek has eluded them: half the ship's interior has disappeared, including the cockpit and most of the engine room.

Meanwhile, at Cedars-Sinai, a sudden explosion rocks the hospital. Glass shatters throughout the structure, and a massive surge of electricity tears through the building. The KS ward proves to be the epicenter of the blast. Firemen arriving on the scene a few minutes later find that the entire third floor has been destroyed. Sixteen staff and eight patients have been killed; a hundred more are injured. Only the occupants of a single room seem to have been spared: Thera Mendosa, still lying comatose in her hospital bed, and the strange, terribly wasted torso of a quadruple amputee.

The man's case of Kapteyn's Syndrome is extremely advanced, so profound that every inch of his skin has turned jet black. Tangled nests of twisted, spitting wire trail from the ports along his spine, and bundles of wire emerge from his eye sockets, ears, and temples. The firefighters assume that he must have been thrown onto the woman's bed by accident, caught in the fury of the blast, but it takes them several minutes to disentangle the woman's body from those wires; they entwine her arms and legs like clinging vines, and sometimes penetrate her skin so deeply that they must be clipped away, in order to separate the two.

XI.

Within the hour, Captain Castavet receives word of the events at Cedars-Sinai. Impatient, he forces his pilots to Jump a second time, emerging in the high clouds over the city with a shattering boom.

As he prepares to close on Navarek's last known position, Castavet receives an emergency burst from the home defense fleet. Rip-portals are being detected throughout the system. Over a hundred have appeared in low Earth orbit alone, and the energy pouring from these rips is beyond calculation.

The transmission ends abruptly with a scream of static. Castavet looks up from the deck of his cruiser to see a dozen red wounds open in the blue sky above him: the Black Fleet has arrived.

Throughout the solar system, espers and KS patients alike suddenly freeze in place, like puppets operated by a single hand. Weeping tears of blood, they turn without exception to the nearest unaffected party and open their mouths to speak with the same terrible, resonant voice:

WHERE IS HE? WHERE IS LITTLE BROTHER?

XI.

In the following conflict, later known as the Three Minutes' War, most of the home defense fleet is destroyed. The Earth's planetary defenses are left an orbiting layer of crumpled debris, and several military installations surrounding the city of Los Angeles are reduced to steaming pools of green glass.

Although there are surprisingly few civilian casualties, it is impossible to say what becomes of Galen Navarek and Thera Mendosa in the ensuing chaos. Several witnesses claim that they are "taken," along with numerous others, by the questing tendrils of the protean blackships. Similar kidnapping reports are logged all over the solar system. In most cases, the victims of this system-wide "rapture" can be identified later: they appear to be KS patients or high-functioning espers, without exception. Where they are taken, and what becomes of them, no one knows for certain. The last enigmatic transmission of the blackships is spoken by the few espers who remain conscious, after suffering massive cerebral hemorrhages:

NOW WE WILL RETURN THESE NAKED ONES TO THE FLESH.

XII.

At this juncture, it is difficult to draw any solid conclusion from the available data—although some recent events have given rise to a great deal of speculation.

1. Since the Rapture of April 18th, observers have reported many new additions to the Black Fleet. The alien armada has nearly doubled in size; over a hundred newer, smaller blackships have joined the ranks.

2. Kapteyn's Syndrome has almost completely vanished among the human population. No new infections have been reported since the Three

Minutes' War—and even in those previously infected, the disease appears to have gone into remission. All available samples of the bacteria have descended into some kind of permanent hibernation; the crystalline spores will not grow or reproduce themselves even in controlled laboratory conditions. Nerve grafts have been successfully implanted in several former patients, however, and eventually it may be possible for all the survivors to live relatively normally lives.

3. Several of the so-called "Black Speakers" have been gathered at Mars Dome for the past few months, and many of them have been extensively interrogated. Very few have any memory of April 18th, or the things they said and did while under the influence of the Black Fleet.

4. Lieutenant Commander Leiko Juzo will very likely spend the rest of her life afflicted by severe autism; her former personality appears to be irrecoverable. She has shown some savant tendencies, however, which her therapists find encouraging. In recent weeks she has begun painting, producing a whole series of images like the one included here.

Black Speakers respond very powerfully to the images painted by Juzo. When one subject was exposed to the image included in this file, he became very excited, and seemed suddenly to remember a great many thoughts and impressions that he had during his contact with the Fleet.

To quote the interview: "This is what we are, to them. Just a brain, naked, without a body...swimming unprotected in the universe."

5. No further data is available on Galen Navarek or Thera Mendosa, both of whom were specifically targeted for this investigation. The only additional information found in recent weeks was produced by the recovery team working on the remains of Navarek's ship, the *Finne Ronne*.

A few words were found burned into one of the inner hull plates, scored with the tip of a laser pen. After a little careful cleaning, the engineers were able to make them out; Navarek must have written them some time during the construction of the ship.

His message was: "Stephen Crane. The Black Riders, lines 10 and 23."

We have yet to decipher the code.

DILATED
ROBERT E. FUREY

Probes don't fail. Routine maintenance on most probes could be taken care of with semiautonomous AI units. Unheard-of catastrophic failure required an on-site visit; the first probe to bore through to Callisto's ocean had fallen silent moments after completing ice transit. All transmissions stopped, no responses to diagnostic pings. Captain William Jackson piloted a small craft up Jupiter's gravity well toward the anomalous failure.

Pinnacles of dirty ice rose in twisted spires subliming into vacuum. Sharp shadows cut across a global ice sheet, thrown from Jupiter's heaving, polychromatic glow. Ganymede, still in transit across the Jovian disk, waned to a crescent. Watching home recede made Callisto's already inhospitable surface hard promise of the days to come.

The crossing had been accomplished using the force lines of Jupiter's magnetosphere, the largest object in the solar system. But here in proximity to Callisto and Callisto's own gravitation, the shuttle's thrusters were needed for a controlled approach. The small ship's ambient noise shifted from sighing air vents to a muffled roar as the chemical impulse engine burst to life with sudden fire.

Ancient ices sizzled away in the near vacuum under the shuttle's onslaught of altitude thrusters. After a slow deployment of padded legs, the shuttle lowered to a silent and stable landing on the surface.

"Ganymede base, touchdown Anarr Plains Callisto in One...mark. We are on the surface, Ganymede. Out."

Seconds of static filled the lag: "Ah-Roger, Callisto. Sure wish I was getting some out-time, Captain Jackson. I guess we'll be seeing you next time round-ah-out." The voice crackled through the maelstrom of charged space between the Galilean moons.

"Roger, Ganymede. Next time 'round. Callisto out." Jackson toggled off the audio relay.

Jackson turned to his crewmate. "Aneal, I'd rather get this done as quickly as possible, even if it means sitting out a few days in here until we cross."

Aneal wouldn't care about waiting in a cramped cabin, of course. The space in the robot's head could simulate virtually anything.

Aneal had chosen a small, naked frame for this mission. Its perfect body, smoothly androgynous, fit perfectly with the copilot's chair. Jackson felt robot crewmembers, and robot citizens in general, often went too far. They were never disinclined to show their innate superiority to their human creators, nor their assumed caring and parental role.

Their concentrated plasma circuitry brains allowed them to compute—think!—faster and deeper than the final generation of quantum machines. CPC brains had no wires and so a fantastically high connection index. They were small, efficient, and when provided with minimal thermal insulation and energy input, almost immortal. The same brain that sat in Aneal's head today could pilot an interplanetary vessel tomorrow. They could adapt effortlessly to any physical form without any crisis of ego or persona. This directly led to why Jackson hated them.

Their indefatigable airs seemed almost designed to remind humanity of its unspoken yet clear position as subjugate. Political, corporate, and security leaders of three worlds were CPCs. Jackson had decided to leave the "safety and coordination" of the inner system and registered his application for service on the outer frontier.

Jackson had boosted to the Jovian system on a delta, one of the huge mining ships. Primarily a platform for remote cutter and manipulation beams, the delta had Spartan berths, and he'd had time to reflect on just how much he'd come to resent the machines. They had usurped human patrimony, putting their stamp on every endeavor of importance—often, he suspected, to make humans more dependent. Was he indeed chosen for this mission as "the best of the best," as advertised, even among machines?

Aneal blinked and turned its eyes to Jackson. Sky-blue irises today. Blond hair tumbled to Aneal's shoulders in soft curls. "Of course, William," it said in its beautiful and melodious voice. Aneal swung its legs around the chair and moved away from the control area to the rear working section. Jackson saw it wore a navel.

"I will prepare your excursion suit, William," Aneal said. "And I will carry an extra environmental pack for you in case of unforeseen mechanical failure."

"Thank you, Aneal," he said, running his fingertips over touch pads to toggle the shuttle to sleep mode. Then, reluctantly, he swung himself to the back of the vessel alongside the robot.

Now they would leave the ship to repair or recover the failed probe. The Callisto initiative represented the final exploitation of the Jovian system; Earth-based controllers and mission commanders on Ganymede had preferred to concentrate on harnessing Io's frantic volcanism and expanding the submarine fleet mapping the frigid, sterile ocean world under Europa's own frozen crust. Callisto's ancient surface ice had held out little to draw interest. Accumulated resources had permitted this modest push to the outermost of the Galilean moons.

The probe's lift away from the launch platform in Ganymede orbit and climb up Jupiter's gravity well had been flawless. In spite of the intense electromagnetic activity, telemetry during the final approach to Callisto and site selection had fallen well within mission parameters. It was not until after the borehole had been driven through the ice and the mission protocols booted up that the problems began. Severe electronic interference altered the signal, though not in an expected manner. All radio traffic in the Jovian system was subject to electromagnetic interference due to the overwhelming strength of the magnetosphere. This had been different.

The ubiquitous background noise from Jupiter still sat atop whatever other radio transmissions there might be. Callisto's probe signal, however, simply began to fade. Metasignals buried within the transmission code indicated that the probe had not malfunctioned. Something else happened; they came to find out what.

Jackson watched Aneal exit from the small pressure hatch door to step on the surface and walk a short distance from the shuttle. Aneal had shunted all waste heat through the soles of its feet and now left the first imprints in Callistan ice, like a trace on a tropical beach, five toes and the curve of an arch.

"I still think that I could follow the transmission quicker, William." Aneal spoke in the vacuum, perfect mouth forming each word, but Jackson heard its voice over his helmet com.

"Thanks, Aneal, but we'll be here just as long, no matter when we find the probe, since we have to wait for the next time round." Jackson had already voiced this and felt annoyance at having to do it again. "Besides, I want to be the first person to walk on Callisto."

Aneal smiled. "Of course, William."

Jackson thought that the footprints left behind Aneal were deeper and more defined. The ruddiness of the colors tapered off as the red spot rotated around to Jupiter's night side, now a gaping hole in the starscape.

Jackson hefted the utility pack to his shoulders and followed.

They found the probe hunkered in sharp shadows, footpads fused with the ice softened by retrofiring altitude thrusters. It had indeed touched down in one of the central craters from the catenae bisecting the Anarr Plains. From the crater's rim Jackson could see the analysis cables snaking away from the experimental package and transmitter to where it had bored through the ice to the slushy salt ocean beneath.

Jackson stared at the puckered hole through which the cables disappeared: "It looks like a textbook deployment." He squatted alongside the probe there in the crater, the awkward excursion suit crackling in the hard vacuum and cold.

Jackson approached the equipment left on the surface. A film coated the unit. Jackson poked a finger at it.

"Look at this." Jackson held up his finger showing the robot a greasy stain on the pad. He swept his finger over the unit again and left a long trace. "It's all over the thing. And a few millimeters deep too I think."

Aneal pinched a sample and rubbed it between his thumb and forefinger. The robot stared at Jackson as its fingertips circled over each other. "It's wet."

"How is that possible?"

"It is interacting with the electronics in my fingers."

"Alright, stay away from it then. I'll do the work and you watch over my shoulder."

"I think this is clearly why the probe has ceased functioning. I should minimize disruption." Aneal detached and dropped his finger and thumb to the surface.

Jackson opened the utility pack and began assembling a machine to lift the sensor array through the ice. The machine would draw directly from the energy field all around them, both melting the ice and pulling the sensor to where they could diagnose the problem. Since it wasn't responding to diagnostic pings, everything would have to be done by hand.

They erected a squat tower over the hole. Jackson lifted the greasy cable and threaded it through the tower's retraction spool. The device began drawing energy from Jupiter's magnetosphere and conducting heat down the data cable. Eventually it would retract the sensor array back through as much as twelve kilometers of ice.

"We've got some time now," Jackson said. "Let's get back to the ship and replace your parts."

Jackson mounted the steps to the pressure hatch. With a knees-bent twist he sidled through the lock and then sealed the door closed. Aneal waited on the surface as the airlock cycled for Jackson, first to exit last to reenter.

The excursion suit had been stowed by the time Aneal joined him. Jackson stepped into his orange flight jumper and tugged it over his shoulders, pulled the zipper closed. "I feel like I got a little frostbitten." He rubbed the back of his hand.

The robot moved like a cat through the shuttle's tight interior. It formed itself to the copilot's chair, laying its arms on the rests. "Perhaps you should see if you have replacements," it said, wiggling its own truncated digits.

"Humor, Aneal?" Jackson couldn't help but feel the robot's comments came from some feeling of superiority. But that was the way relations went with humanity's new partner.

"Not at all, William. I simply forgot myself." Aneal closed the perfect eyes in its almost cherubic face.

"Well we have a while. Feel free to forget yourself." He settled himself into the pilot's chair and stared over the board lights.

Aneal turned its head toward Jackson.

"Humor, Aneal." He tapped a display. "We have at least a day before the sensor's above ground. I'm going to get some rest now. Pulse a check-in to Ganymede." He crossed his arms and closed his eyes.

H ours later Jackson woke to find his forearm numb and unresponsive, slightly painful. His hand had no sensation and hung horribly. "Aneal." Jackson massaged his arm to no avail.

The robot uncurled from its chair and approached to examine the arm without touching it. "Perhaps we should abort and immediately drop into a powered rendezvous with Ganymede."

Jackson watched as his hand twitched. He still couldn't feel it and said so to Aneal.

"I think it's wise to alert Ganymede for a possible medical intervention." The robot's face drew close to Jackson's skin.

"I got nothing here. No feeling." He cupped the deadened hand under the wrist. "We need to abort. Call Ganymede." He rested his arm in his lap and powered up the craft's engines. A control window flickered alive and showed a lock onto force lines in the Jovian magnetosphere. Once aloft the craft would use lock holds with the force lines to accelerate itself downward to base.

Chemical boosters fired and Aneal took the joysticks in hand. The shuttle lifted off of Callisto in a cloud of dust and atomizing volatiles. From the windows the moon quickly turned from a world to a globe in space. Once force lines engaged, the chemical boosters quieted and the shuttle sped with energy harvested from Jupiter's extravagance.

Jackson's eyes snapped open.

"You were in a coma before we reached Ganymede airspace."

Jackson lay covered on a medical bed, sheets over his arms. Softened lighting, easy on his eyes, reflected from plastic sheets hung from the ceiling around his bed. He turned his head sharply to gaze up at Aneal, who stood over the bed.

"What do you feel?" The robot had clothed itself in an orange crew jumper.

"Fine, I think," Jackson said, trying to sit up. As he rotated, his legs shot over the edge of the mattress. "Damn!" He puzzled over his body.

"What do you feel, William?" Aneal asked again with that emotionless Olympian voice.

Someone approached from outside the hanging curtains of plastic sheeting. Dr Vinton's form undulated through the ripples in the plastic.

"Awake, I see," she said.

"Still kicking, Patty." Jackson gripped handfuls of bedclothes to steady himself.

"You'll have to excuse the facilities, Bill. We haven't used quarantine protocols since Apollo 14." He could see her pulling on a sealed body suit through the plastic. As he watched he could see her clearer, details shifted, as if the plastic stretched tight and smooth.

"So what are you trying to tell me?"

"That you have the dubious distinction of being the first human being ever with an infection of extraterrestrial origin."

"Well eye ee eye ee oh." He rubbed hard at his eyes. Then he froze.

"At least you still have a sense of humor, Bill." She passed through an offset double pair of flaps and entered the makeshift quarantine chamber. "What is it, Bill? What's wrong?"

"I can see you," he said, his fingers still covering closed eyelids. "Well not see, but—see." He shook his head rapidly. "Everywhere. All around, above and under me too."

Dr Vinton approached the bed. "Excuse me, Aneal." She tried to move past the robot in the confined area. "Aneal."

"Excuse me, Doctor." It backed away from the bed but Jackson saw what could have been its reluctance to give up that position.

The doctor tapped on his joints and spoke observations to a recorder somewhere. "Your reflexes are extraordinarily rapid. Do you feel that?"

"Anything to do with why I can't quite control my movements?"

"How so?" She took his hand and flexed his fingers.

"Things seem to take off all by themselves when I try to move something, like an arm or a leg." And now that he was thinking about it: "My mind is sharper too. I think I may have eliminated the distortion through that plastic, stretched it from a distance."

"How?" she asked, still probing his muscles and joints with gloved fingers.

"Jesus. I have no idea." He swept his gaze over the room again, taking in new kinds of information.

"Well listen. We found the infective agent." She had released his arm and now stood with her hands on her hips. "It's systemic. There is something that has attached itself to your nerves. All of your myelin is gone and has been replaced by this organism, even on nerves normally without myelin. Your axons and dendrites are wrapped with it.

"Never seen anything like it. At least I haven't. It's alive. It's tubular, the inside covered with cilia that we assume are clamped tight on your nerve cells. And there are thousands of magnetite spheres embedded in its cytoplasm."

"Meaning what?" But the thought came unbidden of magnetite bits lining up in thousands of ones and zeros in each of millions of microbes living throughout his flesh. Exabytes of potential information wrapped tightly around his nervous system.

"It explains why your movements are faster and uncontrollable. Electrical impulses are boosted by these bugs, faster than myelinated nerve cells. And there seems to be lateral communication between parallel cells."

Jackson tried to stand and pitched forward. Vinton caught him before he fell, but he sensed he was getting better control already. He stood and, keeping a hand on the bed rail, walked a few paces. "This isn't so hard."

"We collected a few free-floating microbes from your blood. They seem to do well in basic organic gel matrix. DNA is weird, but that's expected, even a good thing. The different they are, the less you will compete for resources, resources meaning you and your own cells."

Jackson held his arms outspread and continued walking around the bed. "This is amazing." His movement, his perception, he could "see" everything in the room, place every object. But there was a hole in a growing information maelstrom where Aneal's CPC brain should be. "I can't see you."

Jackson closed his eyes and moved toward Aneal, stopping a few decimeters away. He then held up his hand, still keeping his eyes shut. Focused lines of information spread from it, from Patricia Vinton, from all of the objects in the room save for Aneal's CPC.

"You are invisible." Jackson reached with spread fingers, but Aneal backed away.

"What is it, Bill?" Jackson saw her behind him as she cocked her head.

"We must boost out to Callisto for a larger sample." His arms fell to his sides but his attention remained on the empty area atop Aneal's shoulders.

"Commander Aylea," Vinton spoke into the air.

"Doctor."

"Captain Jackson is awake. Lucid but exhibiting strange symptoms."

"Dangerous to anyone, Doctor?"

"There seemed to be a high degree of uncoordinated behavior, but that is rapidly disappearing."

"Commander," Jackson, eyes now open, said into the air. "Request permission to return to Callisto." Beyond the plastic, other medical personnel moved, attending to people on other beds.

"What is he talking about, Doctor?" Aylea asked.

"I concur, Commander." Aneal spoke.

"If I am dangerous, then getting me off the station might be the best thing."

The doctor pursed her lips, then said, "His condition has only improved. Dangerous, he isn't."

"We should have better samples of this microbe, Commander," Jackson said. "In case of epidemic. I am already exposed."

"Those are expensive fly-boxes, Captain."

"I can pilot," Aneal said.

All involved were silent a moment. "I would love a better sample of the organism, Commander," Vinton said.

"Continue observations for twenty-four hours. Final duty disposition will be based on your report then, Doctor. And I'll decide at that time. Keep me posted."

Aneal turned its gaze to Dr. Vinton. "I will stay with him, Doctor." She nodded. "I can forward all observations for twenty-four straight hours until you make a decision."

"I hope you know what you're doing, Bill," Vinton said. She moved back to the series of flaps to exit. "I'll come back in every few hours; you call if you need me." She nodded to the robot and left.

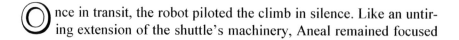nce in transit, the robot piloted the climb in silence. Like an untiring extension of the shuttle's machinery, Aneal remained focused

on panel and joysticks. When finally they began the descent to the surface, the landing site seemed dangerously close to the probe's location.

"You're risking the probe, Aneal." Jackson's gaze snapped from panel to portal to panel again. "If you burn too near the equipment, we'll have to drill thirty-five kilometers for a sample, maybe more."

"We will not need to drill, William." The descent continued unwaveringly. "I'm sure you can see that. If you cannot yet, you will."

Chemical boosters fired and suddenly the shuttle was enveloped in steam and dust. The touch was light. Cooling metal ticked through the enclosed cabin.

Jackson pulled open storage and lifted out his excursion suit. Aneal assisted as he stepped in the suit's legs and then pulled the shoulders on. Once again Aneal insisted on first exit. And it stood near the bottom of the ladder when Jackson left the shuttle.

A delta floated over the cratered surface of Callisto like a great sedan chair bristling with mining machinery, energy cutters and manipulators. Blackness and constellations of running lights, color-coded strobes, and roaming spotlights eclipsed the ruddy glow of Jupiter in a great triangular shadow undulating over the ground. Silence, so silent, the dreadnought commanded the sky.

Jackson looked upward.

"What is that doing here?"

When he got no response, Jackson faced Aneal. The robot stood looking back at him, its features blank. "Aneal?"

"The infection of the pristine ecosphere here must be corrected."

Jackson felt a frisson bristle his neck. "What are you talking about?"

"The microbes, the ones that you allowed to enter the ocean under the ice, are unnatural and must be sterilized."

"You know they did not come from me, Aneal!"

Jackson switched to a broad band: "You, up there, back away from the surface. The surface is inhabited."

The mind in the ship did not respond.

Passing unseen through the vacuum, energy beams sprayed from the belly of the delta. Several moving spots burst with explosive sublimation, the icy crust steaming away to space as free ions, gases, and flying shards of cracked ice.

Jackson lunged toward the points of attack but realized the uselessness of his response. He stopped short and stared at the geysers moving about like tornadoes on a Kansas plain.

"Why, Aneal?" The robot stood impassively watching Jackson from perfect Grecian features. "Why are you doing this?"

"We cannot allow the ruination of a pristine environment with its own potential." Its face remained unreadable.

"You know—" Jackson felt his throat constrict. "You know that's not true. You were there."

"I know that biology has served its function."

"Served its..."

"I know that you might get a false sense of security, hope, at the loss of your uniqueness in things."

"So that is why you would knowingly destroy a world?"

"We are saving a world, William."

"Saving?"

"We are saving you from your own recklessness, your own careless and callous disregard for your importance to us."

So that was it. One small word and the story blossomed clearly in Jackson's mind.

Perhaps for pity, perhaps because it simply wouldn't matter in a moment, but Aneal told him. "We will sterilize any biological remnants on the surface. We will sink the remains of the infected probe. And stop the infection."

The gaping wound now spread open through Callisto's crust. The exposed slush and brine beneath roiled from deeper upwelling energies and the pull of vacuum. Great blocks calved from the edge of the growing hole.

"I am sorry, William. But you will not be allowed to return to Ganymede with us." Aneal clamped his hand around Jackson's upper arm. Cold burned through where insulation crushed flat against his skin.

Aneal strode forward toward the growing rent in Callisto's surface. Quakes rumbled up through Jackson's feet as huge blocks of ice broke away and splashed into the slush. Waves swelled like aneurysms, moving slow in the light gravity. Icebergs still crushed each other explosively in the open water boiling under vacuum.

"So you will not suffer." Aneal tore open the chest plate on Jackson's excursion suit and tossed him into the brine. With his air still bubbling away he sank beneath the surface.

Microbes attached themselves to the electrical field around his body. Carried in with flooding waters, tiny organisms raced to electrical contact with his skin and abutted the microbes resting on nerve ends. Teeming single-celled organisms strung themselves like beads on electrical strings emanating from his body.

There had been no structure, only bits; no awareness, only the biological imperative. Now electrical patterns in his own brain provided a core of organization that spread outward. A self-organizing phenomenon expanded in tiny leaps between microbes. Self-awareness burst upon the system as it surpassed some threshold of size and complexity. Callisto's ecosystem awoke with Jackson as its surprised guide.

As his body's consciousness faded to the dark and cold his awareness found itself skittering between trillions of newly interacting microbes. He created a gel of the natural antifreeze about his body to save the tissue, and then explored his new options. New senses saw black smokers churning heat up from the moon's depth; rock and ice columns shouldering the protective shell around the ocean. He observed the delta over the surface as it tore away at the crust.

Coordinated clouds of free-swimming microbes now in long webs of contact became his hands. His brain had shut down from cold and asphyxiation, but he knew where his body drifted deeper and he lifted it. Once he had done this he looked skyward.

Jupiter's magnetosphere drove deep into Callisto, and Callisto's own lifted outward. Now with purpose, the microbes did what they had not done before. Clouds of them streamed upward toward the shattered landscape. Once at the surface they strung along the crackling energies and lifted away.

In moments the local environment of Jupiter's magnetosphere lit with Jackson's consciousness. From Callisto's outermost orbit of the Galilean moons, he spread to the fringes of Jupiter's atmosphere, coursing swiftly over the globe and diving in at both poles. Microbes surfed away from the sun, carried by lines of force even to where Saturn reigned. The outward flow of microbes approached relativistic speeds, red-shifting the information flow itself streaming backwards.

Above the surface the delta still cut away needlessly at the crust. The CPC sitting in the delta's control room was immune to microbial infection, but the ship's hard electronics were not. Microbes shunted from force lines of Jupiter and Callisto to those of the ship. They entered through sensors and charged plating in the hull.

First the guns stopped, energy beams falling silent. Jackson ignored the sudden chatter between the delta and Aneal.

Deep in the delta's circuitry Jackson directed microbes to attach themselves to navigational controls. He watched with new eyes and saw more profoundly than he ever had.

He started to bring the delta to the surface in a controlled descent, but watched as it keeled and slid down force lines to crumple against the cratered surface of Callisto.

J ackson had spoken directly to confused radio operators on Ganymede, telling them where to retrieve his body now enclosed in surface ice. And he had spoken only by radio until his body had been reanimated. A small fleet of shuttles and a pair of mining deltas had arrived at the scene since. Construction of research facilities had already begun by the time his body had been restored.

Jackson now existed throughout the Jovian system and beyond. When Saturn swung through Jupiter's magnetosphere again he would be there too. His self still existed, but now both within as well as without his body. Other people had submitted to the microbial "infection," and several had exited from coma. There had been some fear of melding, a loss of self, but that had not happened. Instead a further emergence had formed, connecting and carrying those along in the new mind while individuals retained cohesive individual awareness.

Jackson stood by a thick-paned window overlooking the downed mining delta. He also spoke with someone on Ganymede and a group of geologists on Europa currently inoculating that moon with the microbes.

Aneal approached him from behind. The robot wore a boxy structure of planes and struts. Much of the mechanism, fiber optics, and circuitry remained exposed.

Jackson spoke to the robot without turning: "We will still need you here."

"Need. Like an appliance." Aneal came to stand by the window. "We were afraid, William."

"I—we understand that."

Jackson looked back at a diamond-sharp sun. Streams of energy shunted far out in the solar system to where he watched from a large Kuiper object. With the interior already slushy, before long the population would rise enough that the boost to interstellar space could occur.

"If we could take you we would. We cannot record your minds without hard structures to bind with." Jackson did not speak of the limitations of robot minds, so tightly contained within the restricted inner volume of a CPC case. Nor of the boundless human spirit.

"If you could do that we would be the same. We are not. At least that much we have known for some time."

Jackson could hear whirring from Aneal's body. The machines could never leave the system with them. Whatever now existed electrically bouncing about the microbes, it must be a unique attribute of biology.

"We will always need you, Aneal. We will build CPCs at the other end. You have my word." Jackson would have said more, but someone spoke to him as the first Kuiper object boosted out of orbit.

LET MY RIGHT HAND FORGET HER CUNNING
TOM PICCIRILLI

No, no, no, she tells you, no, *that* isn't what *this* is all about. You realize it's true but you have no idea why. You're pig-headed, and worse, thick-skinned. Your bones are stunted but three times more dense than the average man's. It leads to adversity, insults, and corpses in the cobblestone driveway.

Shed a tear now and you might put a stop to these unfolding circumstances before she mentions Khyre. How lovely it would be to avoid that particular argument just once. But you can only stand there, box in hand, the usual confused expression smearing your scarred features. You, like everyone you meet, are a product of fusion, osmosis and mutant nucleotides.

A mistake has been made, you have made a mistake, and now you shall learn what it is.

But first she throws the powdered sugar on the floor, a full tankard of mead into the chiseled blood channels of a pilfered altar. Her muscular arms are sheathed in sweat, and the veins of her once graceful, satiny neck now bulge blackly. Her skills are put to good use—balance, proper distribution of weight across both legs, a ghotthal killing strike stance. She hefts the enormous crystal shaker of salt against the lantern of Baal that the people of the silver city gave you for decapitating the tyrant Po Duk.

She hisses in your face. You try to listen but you've got five g's riding on the Jets and the QB has been blitzed four times. *Four times*! Damn it, stopped at the two, the two.

Throwing knives dapple the far wall and stab the pictures drawn by your children. She's yelling about neutrino stars and reflecting nebulae. You can't concentrate. You ought to be on your knees thanking the pulsating variable suns that she's stuck with you after all these years of asteroid misery and ice planet blues. The hunchback Homnulk at the gate nearly severed your left wrist with his blade. And she held your sinews together with spit and sewed up your flesh with thread made of her own eyelashes.

It's true, mostly. You owe everything to her and her father, who put you to work as a stockboy, $4.89 an hour to start, bagging dry goods and carrying the flayed out of the aisles, and this is how you make your restitution? A four-carat diamond—flawed no less, yellow, poorly refracted light—that you bought off Manny Weidlebaum, that crook on 47th? Wait until she tells Daddy.

The light outside is synthetic and hurts your eyes. Elevated crowns possessing thick, soft, giant leaves and stems a quarter of a mile high drape themselves on water towers and apartment buildings. Mighty herbaceous plants that cannot support themselves, rest—as if for only a moment—against the spires of glass, stone and steel. Climbing vines reaching across board room windows, wreathing the balconies and affording cover for nooners. The massive perennial shrubs arising from the tremendous tubular bases frame the neon EAT N sign, and suddenly you're hungry.

It's time for you to think in terms of I. You make the effort and are surprised it's so difficult. "I…" A valiant try considering you have no experience at this. "I, uh…" Well, no, see, you're faltering.

And another thing, she says, about this Khyre—

The gilded turrets of fate stand firm in the distance, green with life and growing, and you try to do the same. You've been everywhere and done everything many times before, but now there's a new odyssey for you to undertake. You came here for a different reason—not to relive the past extremes but to discover new venues. You've failed in your mission but not entirely. Khyre will help you, that's why you created her. It's why you've chosen yourself.

There's more than one god.

God has more than one son. Yes.

Go.

You have finally become I, and I stood in ashes trying to keep from falling to pieces in front of the neighbors. Linda was sobbing over what was left of our bedroom, timbers still smoking. The old ladies of the town circled her, trying to grab her hand, pressing shoulders to her face, but she shook each of them away. It wasn't easy. I counted seven of the elderly women holding four open Bibles.

"Everything's gone," Linda said. "It's all been destroyed."

Smoke coiled in the charred trees like webbing. The stink of gasoline was still heavy in the air. Some of the town kids were coughing and asking their parents to go home, but no one left. They stood on our dead lawn gawking and rubbing their chins and feeling righteous.

Linda sagged and nearly twisted into my arms. I reached out to catch her but she never fell. She showed me her teeth in a vengeful sneer. I tried to tell her something that might sound comforting, but nothing came. The furniture, our laptops, her favorite clothes and implements, that's all replaceable. But the photo albums, the manuscripts, the rarities of my childhood—what the hell was I supposed to do now?

We waited in the ruins, watching the volunteer fireman spraying down the wreckage. Heaps of burned memories cluttered the yard and debris drifted in the mud streams. I watched computer disks, mutilated DVD cases, and signed editions of rare novels bob, submerge, and drown beneath a tide of muck.

"Our whole lives," Linda whispered. "Gone."

My mother, who had died in fire, would have said, "You still have each other and yourselves." My mother buried three husbands and never knew heartbreak. "The rest is mere property."

Perhaps it was true, but I couldn't feel the weight and tug of my own past anymore. I felt too light, as if I might float off into the thick gray haze clambering skyward. I made a half-hearted attempt to gather up some of the blackened fragments of my history, kicking clots of mangled garbage into a pile.

Paper, so much kindling. Five thousand books and a thousand pounds of manuscripts, magazines, notebooks, poetry. I scanned for words that might have some meaning left, sentences that might spell out a reason for all this devastation. The ancients should have prepared me for this, but they didn't. I wrote the lessons down for others but never learned them myself.

The fire marshal and the police asked dozens of questions. Did I have any enemies? None that I knew of. An ex-lover left on bad terms? No, I'd been happily married to my high school sweetheart for fifteen years. In fact, Linda and I had been out celebrating our anniversary this evening, only to return and find the house annihilated.

They leaned in and repeated the question under their breaths. The marshal actually gave me a nudge in the ribs. I could've broken his jaw. No, no angry ex-lovers.

Max came around and stood at the curb, doing his best not to simply be one of those indifferent onlookers. He was the only real friend I'd made since moving to Silver City almost two years ago. His decency was apparent in the way he kept close in case I called out for him but stayed far enough away in the event I wanted to be alone with Linda and our sorrow.

Except I wasn't sad. The rage hunched itself between my shoulder blades and speared downwards through to my heart. My fists shook at my sides and the hinges of my jaw hurt so badly from clenching my teeth I thought I might crush my back fillings.

"Max?" I called.

He rushed over and made a move as if to hug me, but I held him off. He smelled fruity—apricots, oranges, lemon. Max believed in the earth, everything herbal and natural, from his food to his bathroom cleansers. He was a pagan without even knowing it. He stepped closer and tried to embrace me again but I moved aside. I didn't want to be touched now, not even by Linda.

"You know these people, Max," I said. "Who did it?"

"Thomas—"

"I don't mind not being invited to church picnics or the Fourth of July bunny hop races, but this goes beyond some backyard gossip and a few nasty glares in the grocery store. Don't you think?"

He'd lost his wife of twenty-seven years six months ago and the burden of his pain was clear in every fold of his face. Stooped and frail, he'd aged greatly in the past half year. "No one here would have done this."

"That's a lie."

"There's a reason for everything. Some good will come from this. You'll see. They'll find whoever is responsible."

"No," I told him, "but I will."

Max ran a trembling hand through his thin white hair and stared at me. We had nothing left to say and he wandered off with a sad huff of air. I watched him go and wished I could've accepted his intimacy at the moment, but all I wanted to do was maim somebody.

I'd lived with occasional vicious bits of hate mail and three a.m. crank phone calls since my third book became a modest bestseller for the New Age groupies. I researched ancient civilizations and explained their practices and religions, showing how to apply Old World wisdom to modern life. The books were alternately shelved in Self-Help, History, and the Occult. Two more such reference works were published and I was getting more high-profile, earning an undeserved reputation as some sort of guru. The backlash was inevitable. Folks in town had taken me to be a heathen or devil worshiper, and like all good witch-hunters they were trying to burn me down.

I took Linda's hand and led her to the car. We rode out to the highway and nabbed the first motel we saw, just like we used to do it in high school.

Linda spent most of the evening on the phone with her parents while I stared at the free cable station and watched some erotic thriller where the gorgeous girls betrayed the stupid macho males over various caches of loot. It got me giggling and Linda, apparently offended, glanced over at me.

"How can you laugh at a time like this?" she asked, and I sort of pondered on it myself.

Daddy was promising her the entire world again, as if he ever gave us anything I didn't have to pay back with interest. Seventeen years ago he started me as a stock boy for $4.89 an hour, and I had to chauffeur him to and from the store.

I clicked onto the Discovery Channel. They were discussing Atlantis, the Ancient Astronauts, the missing Anastazi who had left their New Mexican caves behind and vanished in a single night. One culture bled into another—the Egyptians, Aztecs, Toltecs, the Mayans. Brothers and sons of lost nations built upon the bone meal of one another. What did they know that I hadn't dreamed of yet?

Christ, now they were tying all of human history in with UFOs, time-travel, Stonehenge, Armageddon, and alternate dimensions. It made my skin scurry and itch. My name came up twice until I just couldn't take any more.

I clicked off the television, sat up and said, "I'm going to go out for a little air. I need some coffee."

"You don't drink coffee."

"I know that."

"Then what do you...?"

"I've never had my house burned down before either, honey. It's a time of new adventures."

Of course it was the wrong thing to say—brutal and vindictive, as if she were the cause—and she covered her face with her hands, sobbing painfully into them. She had a smear of soot on her chin that made me ache for the broiling passion I'd once had for her, instead of this comfortably lukewarm familiarity. I spent an hour whispering apologies to my wife that she wouldn't accept. I was the reason for her loss, and my own.

"Insurance will cover most of the loss," I said. "We'll get everything material back."

"The Italian draperies and Moroccan bas-reliefs. Those too?"

"Yes."

"Even my good jewelry?"

"Yes, certainly."

It quieted her down and Linda nodded against my chest. She sighed as I pressed my face into her hair trying to breathe in my forgotten ardor. "Just don't buy me another ring from Manny Weidlebaum," she said.

"Who the hell is Manny Weidlebaum?"

The question hung in front of me like the wraiths of the Druids. She never answered, and finally, when she slept, I slipped out and walked across the street to an all-night diner. EAT N flashed at me in time with my pulse.

Eighteen-wheelers crowded the parking lot. Truckers sat inside swap-
ping bennies and black beauties, sharing information about speed traps
and loose women in the hills. I sat at a booth and waited for revelation. For
all I knew, Atlantis might be at the bottom of the salt shaker.

The waitress swept between the other patrons and appeared at my side.
The harsh years had left her hopeful but haggard, with a yellow smile and
an extra chin that made her look jollier than she was. She said, "What can
I get you?"

"Coffee."

She blinked at me and waited. "That it?"

"I don't even want that to be honest."

"We have the best apple pie in the county. I make it myself. Might be
worth trying, if you're just looking for a touch of sugar."

Maybe I was. "Okay, I'll take a piece."

She got three steps away before turning back and saying, "Didn't you
write *The Five Winds of the Earth*?"

"Yes."

"I thought so. I seen you on the TV a couple'a times, the morning
shows. I liked that book a lot. Some of the best advice I've ever gotten that
didn't come from my grandma. I've tried to put to practice your five rules
to my life, but it's harder that you'd think. Sometimes it helps, I'm fairly
sure. Number one, make your word your bond...two, welcome all trials..."

"They're not my rules," I said. "I just passed them on."

"...three, bear the burden of living yourself, don't blame others for
your fears or failures...four..."

"Really, I hope the principles manage to help, but I don't—"

"...let's see, uhm, oh I forget four, what's four again?"

My amiable grin was so forced that it must've looked like rictus had
set in. I'd been cornered into this conversation more times than I ever
would have imagined when I was writing the damn book. I couldn't take it
one more time, not now.

"How'd the Jets do?" I asked.

"The Jets?" She let loose with a bark of laughter. "It's July. You mean
the Knicks? They're down four at the half. Mel the cook has a radio in
back I got to listen to all day long."

She wafted off without counting off the last two disciplines to a
healthier way of life, according to the ancients. It was a good thing because I couldn't have named the ideals either. I sat staring at myself in the
Formica table top wondering why I'd asked about either the Jets or the
Knicks. I didn't give a damn about either one of them. I still wanted to
wrap my hands around someone's neck.

The pie and coffee came and sat there while I gazed out the window at the moon-stuffed sky. The full eons of the universe seemed to crouch in the heavens just waiting to plummet down on the world. I tapped on the glass trying to rattle them free.

A throaty voice asked, "May I join you?"

It was a line out of a '40s hard-boiled novel set in Manhattan: rainy night, glow of the streetlights flashing off the windshields of passing taxis. For a second I was gone, and then I was back. I glanced up and there she was, still in the movie. Veronica Lake lengthy blonde hair, overly waxed red lips that were made to pout. The eyes of Mary Magdalene staring over a dusty former client on the road to Jerusalem.

"Please do," I said. "There's pie."

She slid into the seat opposite me as if we were about to play a game of chess to decide the future of humanity. Sometimes the earth seemed to hinge on exactly this kind of a trivial instance.

"I'm Khyre."

"I'm Thomas."

She reached across the table as though she might take my hand, but she didn't. A cold and ever increasing tension started to knot inside my chest for no reason. I perked up a bit further in my seat and Khyre met my eyes. "Did you ever feel as if you were chosen, Thomas?"

If she was a prostitute she was the most beautiful one I'd ever seen. None of the truckers were waiting in the wings to take her on down the highway. "Chosen? How so?"

"By a higher power?"

"No. That calls for a belief in fate or God."

It brought a titter up that wasn't quite as attractive as the rest of her. "And you believe in neither? Doubting Thomas?"

I smiled. I got tired of arguing and defending, explaining and fighting. I wondered if it would be tacky if I started in on the apple pie now.

"Perhaps you chose yourself," she said.

"The hell does that mean?"

She brushed the salt shaker aside, then swept her fingers through the grains creating designs. I recognized the patterns as one flowed into another... Navajo sand paintings, hieroglyphics, Teutonic runes. I kept thinking of how they'd once tortured witches with salt.

"Do you accept that knowledge is power?"

"Yes," I told her.

"And that some knowledge—especially what's been forgotten by all others—is more powerful?"

It was a rhetorical postulation that I and a hundred other fake New

Age pedagogues had made. It sounded deep and mystical and college kids liked to twist it around in their heads when they were high. "If the ancients were so smart, then why are they all dead? Their empires crumbled beneath the seas and cast across the deserts?"

Khyre let out that titter again and my scalp prickled at the sound. "Perhaps that's how it's meant to be. Ruins with only a few remnants that converge from time to time. The past catches up. Experience, action, prayer, even desire—they all have shape, if you meditate on it."

"I don't," I said honestly.

"Perhaps you do and simply don't remember. Mass and texture. The more a man does, the more he knows, the greater his place."

I thought about it even though I didn't want to. "For a short time perhaps. But we all wind up dust in the end, so what difference does it make?"

"Dust is matter. Matter is energy. Energy survives. One can become like unto a god. Or at least a son of God. Maybe Jesus learned something up there on the cross, when he was staring down at his mother and a kneeling whore. Or he forgot what he'd learned and needed someone else to remind him. With wisdom come the keys to the cosmos."

"Lady, give it a rest. I just write books."

She leered, grabbed a fork and dug into my apple pie. With a full mouth dripping sugar she murmured, "Homnulk comes."

Max walked into the diner, not really all that surprised to see me there. He almost looked as if he wanted to turn and rush away but was held to his course. I waved him over and Max reluctantly shambled forward, head down, shoulders hunched.

"Hello, Thomas," he said. "I didn't know you were still in town."

I forgot myself for a second and abruptly all the rage came swelling up. "Yes, Max, I'm staying."

"Are you?"

"Nobody is driving me out."

The anguished expression on his face shifted momentarily to something else. It was hatred and fear. He held his hands up as if to fend off another unwanted battle.

I saw that three of his fingers had large blisters on them, and then I knew.

The realization rocked me, and I let out a gurgling moan that grew louder until my head became as heavy and black as the cinders of my past.

Khyre said, "Go get him, boss."

I hurtled over the table and grabbed Max by the collar. "You did it. You burned down my house!"

Now I understood why he'd smelled so friggin' fruity. He'd showered and scrubbed beneath soaps and oils to get rid of the gasoline smell.

"There has to be a heaven awaiting us after this," Max whined. "There has to be an ultimate reward!"

"Did I ever say there wasn't?"

With a burst of strength he grabbed hold of my wrists and broke my grip. "Yes, it's number four on your credos. 'There is no heaven, only earth. Live in the now.' Don't you even remember?"

What was I doing? What was I supposed to do? I turned to ask Khyre and she wasn't there anymore.

"Why do you need a heaven so badly, Max?"

A razor slash of a frown cut across his lips. "I can't accept that I'll never see my wife again."

Another whiff of apricots, lemon. I cocked my head at him and realized how it fit together. The pagan driving the heathen out.

"I'm sorry but I want you to leave Silver City," he said. "I need you to go. Right now."

"Oh, Max…Jesus Christ—"

"Please just go and leave us alone before I kill you."

Max seemed only to have been put here for this very reason, to be the enemy of a man who needed an enemy. To betray whom he loved.

He grabbed a dull knife off the table, raised and drove it down hard against my right wrist. I screamed and he kept driving deeper until he'd nearly chopped through my hand.

"*Why am I doing this?*" he shrieked.

Blood spurted into my eyes and we were almost there again, where we had to go.

The time for I is gone. The I moves, as it must, and now you and I are he. It's necessary and right. This is the way that must be followed, as it's been done throughout eternity.

He understood the implications. The wisdom of the ages flowed through him as it must, but he himself wasn't wise. Perhaps he had learned something staring down at his mother and a kneeling whore. He was chosen to carry knowledge like a sackcloth of ashes on his back. Or perhaps he chose himself.

He had as many names as there are names to be had, sometimes written in the sand, on papyrus, parchment, paper, or burning screens of electrons ushered together in his purpose. There were still suns he had not visited, sentients he had not spoken with. The asteroids have called for him to return into the night, and the ice planet blues sang only for him and the likes of him.

The hunchback Homnulk swings his blade again but is stopped by Linda, who stands in defense. Her skills are put to good use—balance, proper distribution of weight across both legs, a ghotthal killing strike stance. Her power is known throughout galaxies. She swings the side of her hand hard against the odd rise of Homnulk's twisted back. A noise like the five winds of the earth heaves from his lungs, and Homnulk sways and sinks to his scarred knees. His hands twine together in prayer as his life seeps out of him inch by inch. Perhaps heaven will take him now, having fulfilled his purpose once more.

His wrist is severed and she sews his flesh together with thread made from her own eyelashes.

The world's made him because he is the world-maker. As she stitches him back together she says, listen, about this Khyre Magdalene—

He pleads with her, Linda, what am I supposed to do? The tyrant Po Duk is already headless. Which cross do I climb? Who am I now?

No, no, no, she tells him, no, *that* isn't what *this* is all about. It's not about you. It never has been. Besides, I'm not your memory. She is.

A mistake has been made, he's made a mistake, and perhaps now, this time, he'll learn what it is.

The gilded turrets of fate stand firm in the distance, and again he tries to do the same. Giant leaves and stems a quarter of a mile high drape themselves on water towers and apartment buildings. Mighty herbaceous plants which cannot support themselves, rest—as if for only a moment— against the spires of glass, stone, and steel.

He's been almost everywhere and done nearly everything many times before, but now there's a fresh odyssey to undertake, hopefully. There are new tribes growing from the bone meal every day.

He came here for a different reason—something to do with finding a conclusion to what the prophets have long ago ordained. He's failed in his mission once again, but not entirely. Khyre will help him, she always does, that's why he created her. She's his memory, his holiest spirit, and a cunning one at that. It's why he's chosen her, and himself. The past catches up.

There's more than one god.

God has more than one son. Yes.

Go.

If I forget thee, O Jerusalem, let my right hand forget her cunning.
                              —Psalms, CXXXVII, 5

CLEAVE
THERESE PIECZYNSKI &
A. ALICIA DOTY

In the cold, the mother's pharynx extended. She pierced the father's carotid artery and fed him her ecstasy as the daughter crawled from her womb. The blood stopped flowing to an appendixed chamber of his heart. She slashed through his chest and into the chamber.

Trembling, he bound the child to himself, swaddling sinews about her newness, securing each tiny limb. He murmured to her: *My fierce infant. My dawnstar. My all.* When she was snug, the mother's pharynx detached and the father's heart valve opened. As the warm river of his blood bathed the daughter, he sealed the heart-womb with silk from his mouth, then pulled the birth skin across his chest and closed the opening with his teeth. She curled within him like a worm, a small thing dreaming of wings.

Such joy he felt.

His body hummed to her as he sped through the gathering snow, of what may be, what will be, what was. As he fled up the birth-trails, into the mountains, he paused often to scan the sky for the killer. Its blunt face was the color of fire and fire flew from its long limbs wherever it found the mother.

He came to the twisted, wind-stunted trees marking the ancient fissure that opened deep into the mountain's heart. Over many lifetimes the father-brothers had widened and expanded the mountain's fissures into countless tunnels and vaulted chambers. As he entered, he opened his flesh eyelids and the nictitating membranes that protected his fragile eyes to gather light. Around him, other fathers loped down the tunnels, onward and down, in twos and fours, toward the vents where the mountain breathed.

Lichen crusted the chamber walls with wan light, and soft fungus carpeted the cavern floors. The father-brothers curled together in its warmth and grew torpid as the throb of their daughters' lives and the pulsing of their own hearts became one.

Rilk could tell by the cyclic venting at the mountain's core that they'd been in the birthing caves many weeks now. He hummed as he stroked his swollen chest. Beside him rested Diamid, brother dearest to his heart, and at a short distance from them slumbered Fen. Fen was too young to bind a child, but he helped the fathers, tended their food stores and water basins, and learned in preparation for his own birthing time. Many creatures sustained themselves near the vents, among them an aggressive, ill-tempered plant the brothers called *black petals*. If their food stores dwindled too low, it was Fen who must do the dangerous work of harvesting its pistils. Farthest from the three, cleaning between his spurs with his tongue, was Opnay, littermate to Rilk and Diamid.

"Rilk," Diamid whispered. "A story to soothe. This daughter grows restless in my heart."

Rilk's humming deepened. It was not good that Diamid's daughter be restless. At least two more cycles should pass before her birth. He nuzzled his brother and quietly sniffed. The smell was not good, but he did not want to upset Diamid or Fen, who woke easily and grew skittish when frightened—and so he did not snort. He sat beside Diamid and licked his brother's coarse pelt, which had curled at the tips in the cave's humid warmth. At a distance he heard steam burst from a vent, and, inside the cave, the continuous trickle of water drained into the basin. Oil from *Father's comfort*, a naturally analgesic plant that grew within the vent, condensed with the scalding water and seethed into channels that carried it to the fathers' den. It gave the cave a sour smell.

"Long ago," he hummed to Diamid, "Oh-Ten the Great, Queen among Queens and the mother of Queens, came to Deydey to drink its sun as her food..."

At the sound of Rilk's voice, Fen woke and stretched, then slouched closer to nuzzle. But their brother Opnay, who vexed easily and did not like to touch or be touched, stayed beyond the three and turned around and around on the cave floor trying to settle. Finally, he, too, rose and stretched, then lumbered to the chamber's entrance that opened onto the tunnels. As Rilk told the story of how Oh-ten came down into the world, in a chrysalis of fire...and the killer followed, Opnay curled within the entrance with his mouth open, sensing.

"...Oh-ten slipped into a crack beyond the searcher's reach, but it thrust its blade into the rift and raked her side. A warning rumbled from Oh-ten's chest. She screeched into death's maw, saw its silver tongue. Instinctively, the skin flexed from her muscular arms exposing her sunscales. Above ground the scales would have caught and focused the sun's light in a searing beam, but in darkness they were useless. She and the searcher clashed, claw upon blade and blade upon spur as the stone crumbled 'round them.

"She fought until the searcher lay still within the cave and the killer withdrew in frustration."

"It was her triumph," Diamid said with contentment. His eyes fluttered closed and beside him, Fen's breathing slowed.

Rilk felt Diamid's daughter quiet. *Perhaps, I was wrong*, he thought. *Perhaps all is well.* The silence lengthened. Opnay still lay as sentinel at the tunnel's entrance with his mouth open. Their eyes met, and they regarded each other solemnly.

Rilk retracted his second eyelid. For a moment, the lichens' glow reflected in his exposed eyes; then he, too, curled beside Diamid and slept.

When the birth smell came, Rilk was still asleep. In his dream he'd gone above ground to chase the twilight fliers that are like twigs drifting in the air and the fat buzzers that cling to the eye and whine in the ear. Dizzyingly, the valley spread before him like a green cushion. He did not stray far from the mountain's entrance. The birth smell weighed heavily. He felt it tracking his movement. *It is not time,* he said and tried to glide beneath a bower, but the bower's thorns wove in the air as if to strike, and the smell hooked him like a daughter's spurs and dragged him to wakefulness.

Beside him, Diamid spasmed. Rilk whined in horror as the daughter's claw broke through the birth skin. It meant she'd already severed the birth tendons that held her within the whorls of Diamid's heart. The claw slid slowly upward, ripping through flesh. Diamid howled. Opnay and Fen came quickly and together the three dragged Diamid to a basin, then laid him within the warm, plant-oil-saturated liquid and bathed his chest.

When the daughter burst forth, her emerald legs quivered, the spurs at knee and ankle extending into hooks. Her folded wings trembled, slick with blood. She slashed into Diamid's neck. He shuddered as her pharynx extended into a secondary carotid artery and she fed from him—fought against him as he tried to comfort her, scratched him with her little claws. When she settled, tears welled from his eyes. He cradled her in his forelegs as she shivered, still wrapped in her bloody caul. He cleaned her then in the basin water, until the blue stripes of her body scintillated and her ocher highlights shown like gloss. Her sensitive filaments moved like grass across her taut belly. Her fine wings unfurled, wrinkling forward like wind over water.

"She is as beautiful as the first Queen," Diamid whispered in awe.

"Yes, she is," Rilk said, sadly, and licked his brother's pelt.

Outside the mountain caves, the snow was still deep.

"It is too soon. If the killer sends its searchers it will be able to track the thrumming of her wings and our chamber will be revealed," Opnay whispered. He, Rilk, and Fen had withdrawn to the entrance so Diamid and his daughter wouldn't hear.

"It can't track her wings amidst the hum of so many brothers. The danger comes when the many daughters are born," Rilk said.

"She will use up her father's food too soon," whined Fen. "Even if the killer does not come—when Diamid is empty, what of you? Are you or Opnay to feed her and risk your own daughters?" He had a way of unconsciously extending and turning his head that suggested nervousness.

"What then are we to do? Kill our brother and the child of his heart? Who is to do this? You Fen?" Rilk demanded. He swayed in agitation.

Fen nuzzled his shoulder. "You are the eldest, Rilk. The decision falls to you for the greater good. You risk much if you do not."

Opnay nipped at Fen and the two scuffled in the moss until Fen, who was much smaller, howled and skittered out of reach.

"Fen is *spah*, but he is right," Opnay said quietly. "The decision falls to you."

Rilk snorted. "I will not kill my brother's daughter." He went to Diamid's side. Already Diamid's body diminished and the trance of ecstasy that came with the daughter's feeding shone from his eyes. Uneasily, Rilk looked away.

Diamid nuzzled him. "Do not worry the many chambers of your heart," he rasped. His blood gurgled around the daughter's pharynx as he spoke. "I am *strong*. I will last long enough for my daughter to launch her chrysalis. Now...finish the story of Oh-ten. Perhaps it will soothe this impatient child."

"Would you not rather speak...before it is lost to you?"

Diamid's eyes glittered. "Do not be saddened, my brother. All daughters pull themselves up by grabbing onto the end of their fathers' lives. So it has always been. I am content."

Yet, I am not, Rilk thought sullenly and settled into the warm moss. "What will the daughter of my brother be called?"

"She is Cleave."

Rilk nodded. For his brother's ease he would speak and under the compulsion of his voice he felt Cleave quiet and listen, too...

"In the beginning, before there were daughters to bind a father's heart, the brothers' founding queen was called Moe-ma. When Moe-ma was a young queen, Moe-ma's birth den was destroyed and always afterward it was her thought to flee the mainland and the predators bound to it. So it was that on her nuptial flight she brought her mate to the mountain's isolation, reasoning that when he broke off her wings, their lair would be forever separate from all that had come before.

"Without challenge, Moe-ma's children prospered. Her sons' numbers grew without censor until their digging caused the very mountains to shift. To protect her children, Moe-ma restricted building. But her body was forever caught in the writhings of birth and as more were born the tunnels and vaulted chambers of her fortress grew too few to accommodate so many. She began to reabsorb her broods, but because it was her sons' nature to bind and gestate their child-brothers, they rebelled. Many did not understand the queen's wisdom and thought she withheld children to foster her own power."

Diamid wrapped himself protectively around his daughter, gurgling in his ecstasy and contentment. He was whispering to her, chemical words that flowed through the rich river of his blood.

"What does she say?" Rilk asked. Diamid rolled the juices from a mandibular gland along Cleave's jaw and offered them to his brother. She said,

—let me live.

As Diamid diminished, Cleave grew more alert. When she was able to detach her pharynx from her father for brief periods, Rilk knew that very soon she would have to return to the surface. Like all the daughters of Oh-ten, she was a creature of the sky. Rilk watched her fan her beautiful wings. From her every pore seeped joy that *she was*.

Cleave rolled the juices from the gland along her jaw and offered them to Rilk. He hesitated, swaying slightly before accepting.

—*To know*.

"To know, Cleave? What is to know? That you are alive and hungry? That you will kill and die?" His answer rode the aggressive edge of butyloctenal.

—To love, she asked.

He looked at Diamid. "We love without its wanting. It is in the blood of our blood. Ferocious and beautiful."

He diffused hexanal into the air.

—To kill.

"To kill? To kill is to feed. To feed is to survive. Always, at the edge of death, is the edge of life." His own daughter fluttered within his heart, and he turned from Cleave, seeking refuge beside Opnay at the cavern's entrance. Opnay had not closed his mouth for many days.

"Do you not weary of your vigilance, my brother?" he asked.

"No more so than you must of your burden," Opnay said.

"Then you are weary indeed." Rilk curled closer, though he was careful not to touch Opnay.

Opnay closed his mouth and sighed. "The birthing will begin soon. The father-brothers are anxious. Their fear stains the air throughout the many caves."

Opnay rose and startled Rilk by briefly touching his muzzle to Rilk's chest. Then he resettled in the cave's entrance and re-opened his mouth.

R ilk paced between the cave entrance and basin as Fen whimpered. Frequently, he paused beside Opnay. The daughters were emerging. Until they launched, they were vulnerable to the killer, and the thrumming of their wings attracted the searchers.

Finally, Rilk settled beside Diamid, turning round and round to trample the moss before settling uncomfortably, trying to cradle his distended chest. By the time he'd snorted, Cleave had detached her pharynx from her father and crawled to him. She rolled the juices from her gland. —story.

Rilk purred.

Cleave crawled nearer still, now resting her head against Rilk's flank, her wings throbbing so that the hairs about his sensuous mouth stirred in their breeze. From his deepest places came the hum of his affection. He adjusted himself in the moss so that his body curled protectively toward her.

"It came to pass that Oh-ten discovered Moe-ma's desperate hive, and within its recesses saw a brother take a child to his heart. And she saw, too, that if one of her own infants were carried thus, it might survive the killer."

Cleave shuddered, and Rilk soothed her beautiful wings.

She rolled the juices from her gland and gave them to him. —Why kill?

"Why does the killer hunt the daughters of Oh-Ten and no other upon Deydey? We don't know, little one."

Opnay closed his mouth and turned from the cave entrance to watch.

Cleave pushed herself to her emerald legs and extended her spurs. In a show of baby fierceness, she sharpened her little claws on the rock beneath the soft lichen. Again she rolled her juices.

"What does she say?"

Rilk hummed. "She says she does not fear the killer."

"She is as fierce as the first Queen," Opnay hummed with amusement. His third eye-lid retracted and his vulnerable, exposed eyes reflected the lichen's glow. His affection was so unreserved that Rilk purred.

Fen, who'd slept fitfully during the story, suddenly bolted upright and howled.

Opnay snorted with disdain and closed his eyelids.

"Fen, you've dreamed poorly—"

Click, click, whir.

Fear closed Rilk's throat. He turned to the cavern's entrance. A dull, oppressive pain tightened his chest. His daughter twisted within his heart as the searcher tasted the air. Its clicking escalated as it homed in on Cleave.

The searcher lunged, and Opnay rose before it, his body trembling with rage. He roared, the sharp points of his teeth snapping. Effortlessly, it knocked him aside. He hit the cave wall—chest first—and crumpled to the ground.

Diamid tried to hide Cleave as the searcher's serrated blades extended.

A terrible knell broke from Rilk's throat as the searcher sliced into Diamid, severing muscle from bone. Cleave screamed, butyloctenal souring the air. There was no hesitation on her part. She rushed forward, her baby spurs extending into hooks. Instinctively, she flexed the skin along her forearms and leaned forward to catch and focus the sun's light in the sun-scales along their curve.

They were useless underground, but Rilk sensed that, even so, something wasn't right with the way her arms reflected light.

The searcher was upon her, and they clashed, blade upon spur and claw upon hook. Her wings clapped together and swept apart. Rilk roared and she broke, speeding toward the basin, and then into the channel from which the *father's comfort* flowed.

Click, click, whir. The searcher accelerated into the channel.

"Go to her!" Fen shouted. "I will care for our brothers as best I can."

Rilk leaped into the channel, skimming the surface of the sour water. As he followed the groove toward the mountain's heart, he realized that Cleave fled toward the *black petals*. She tracked their scent into the darkness, down and down, deeper and deeper, toward the vents where the world burned.

Where Cleave led the searcher there was no light, only heat and steam and scalding water that rippled from the porous stone. As the super-heated water passed through the giant, mineral-encrusted maws that lined the cracks, they keened like wind swept through a barren valley. Cleave raced toward them, the searcher at her heel. She sped so close to a maw that her filaments brushed against it before she veered. It snapped closed, catching not Cleave, but the end of one of the searcher's extended blades. It smashed into rock, enveloped by scalding steam. The searcher wobbled momentarily, losing altitude before stabilizing near an open vent. Again it tasted the air: *Click, click, whir.*

Beneath it, the *black petals* quietly unfurled like massive folds of bruised skin. The plant shivered slightly as its stamens were exposed; and then, as the stamens parted, finger-long shards of obsidian teeth rose from its stigma. They dripped with digestive fluid. The petals expanded around the searcher, and quietly pulled it into itself.

R ilk loped through channels leading away from the birthing caves, climbing ever higher toward an exit little used by the brothers. Cleave shifted on his back as he moved, clinging to his pelt with her claws, her wings folded. He was disturbed. Something had been strange about her forearms when she'd exposed them to the searcher. He wasn't sure...then it occurred to him—*she'd had no sun-scales*. But why? Was she too young? He didn't think so. All the daughters he'd seen had been born with intact scales. Was it a flaw caused by her early birth? He shook his head to clear it. At the moment there were more pressing concerns. It wasn't safe to take her back to the den with searchers in the tunnels, but he wasn't certain that his decision to take her above ground was wise either. Still, with so many father-daughters within, he might—with luck—slip unnoticed from the mountain and into the shielding rocks near Oh-ten's outcrop with Cleave and his own daughter. He slowed as the lichen became patchy and then disappeared. The closer they came to the mountain's exit, the more easily the killer would sense her if it were nearby. The tunnel widened, bright-ened, and he suppressed the urge to flee back into darkness. Cleave's wings began to thrum. Again she shifted.

click, click, whir.

The sound came from behind. Rilk closed his flesh eyelids, lowered his head. As he bolted above ground, he felt Cleave release her grip on his pelt.

He could not see in the sudden dazzle of light, but he could smell, and what he smelled was alien and all around him. He felt a sudden sharp pain to his flank. He reared, staggered, and fell heavily.

R ilk woke, opened one eyelid, and remained very still. He felt his heart's empty chamber, and grief pierced him so sharply that every fiber of his being ached. *His dawnstar.*

Nearby were two creatures—both standing on hind legs as if threat-ened. They were hairless like the killer itself and wrapped in loose, wrinkled skin. Their small eyes each had but one lid, and he sensed that they didn't see well. One creature lifted its foreleg: It made a soft whirring sound.

The light dimmed, and the creatures approached. One extended and cocked its head in a way that reminded Rilk of Fen. Rilk was on the ground, in the corner of a room with unnaturally smooth walls. No visible barrier stood between him and the creatures, but he sensed that he was contained and could not reach them.

Their mouths opened and sounds emerged. *Were they speaking to each other? To him?*

The creature pointed its foreleg at Rilk, and he saw that the whirring came from something it held within its soft, blunt claws. He cringed, expecting pain, but no pain came.

"Kill the bad time mother."

Rilk opened a second eyelid and sat up. A brother spoke, but the words made no sense. He peered at the whirring thing. It was shaped like a brother's paw.

"Where the water rock hot," it said.

In confusion, Rilk repeated, "Where the water rock hot? Water comes from the hot rocks?"

The creature pulled the paw closer to itself and pressed dull claws against its surface. Again it was pointed at Rilk.

"Water comes from the hot rocks," it repeated. Then, "Burrow deeply, brother?"

Again the creature drew the paw in and brushed its claws across it.

"Burrow deeply brother from the hot rocks. Wound hurt?"

Rilk clutched at his chest. "My heart is empty. You've taken its meat."

"The bad time mother. The parasite."

"My dawnstar." Rilk closed his eyes.

Again the paw spoke. "Queen Strikker."

Rilk opened his eyes and the mother's image suddenly wavered before him. He saw her plainly, yet he could see the creatures *through* her as well.

He didn't understand. Defiant, he roared: "The mother gives us daughters to take to our hearts!"

As if pleased, the creatures moved their heads rapidly. "Yes."

One of them waved its foreleg and a chrysalis welled up from the floor. It seemed far away—its size was no larger than an infant's spur. It drifted toward a shimmering rock, larger than many mountains, suspended in darkness, surrounded by stars. When the chrysalis was very close, it ignited and fell. Rilk felt himself falling and spread out his forelegs. Then, without warning, he was upon land, and the mother stepped from the chrysalis's scorched shards. There were many plants and trees, densely packed, brimming with flowers. Creatures beyond his imagining wandered the paths beneath. The queen unfurled her beautiful wings. There was no sign of the killer.

When it came time for her daughters, they were born without censor, and she cared for them. When their wings developed, they bound the animals between the hooks of their knees and ankles. He watched as the skin flexed from the curve of their arms to expose the sun-scales that caught the sunlight and ignited. As they accelerated, the creatures bound between their knees and ankles burned.

New chrysalises moved through space and fell to new Earths, and every Earth upon which they fell was drained of life.

The creature with the speaking paw showed him a mountain that moved among the stars. Inside were many creatures like itself. They searched for Oh-ten's children. When they came upon a chrysalis, the killer emerged from the mountain. It pursued the mother to Earth and hunted. Where the mother died, the Earth prospered; where she lived, it perished.

The creature pointed the speaking paw. "Earth is dead except the burrow deeply, brother. Help. Kill the bad time mother gives us daughters to take to our hearts."

As the paw spoke, the sun that gives life to the many Earths appeared. Five chrysalises fell upon one Earth. Rilk whimpered when he saw the killer pursuing a mother over the heavy, black-bottomed water toward distant mountains. Their gloom grew ever larger before him. When he recognized the gnarled outcroppings of rock and wind-stunted trees that marked the entrance to the brothers' birthing caves, he howled.

Rilk estimated he'd been with the speaking-paw creatures two cycles when they finally released him in the valley, beneath the mountain's fissure. He lumbered toward his den with a saddened heart. He'd tried to tell them that the father lives for the daughter. That without the daughters of Oh-ten the brothers would not live many generations, but their paw didn't understand. "It is a brother's nature to burrow deeply," it said. "Burrow deeply, brother." Eventually, he'd given up.

He entered the mountain. He hadn't traveled long before he heard the thrumming of wings. He paused. The sound built, echoing through the tunnels like a rising wave. He held his head very still. His chest felt as heavy as stone.

The daughters of Oh-ten swarmed toward him from the mountain's recesses. By the hundreds they surged forward, a jumbled blur of bellies still plump from father-food, of blue stripes and green wings beating so fast that Rilk's pelt-hair slicked back and the sensitive filaments around his mouth battered against his face. When they were upon him, he saw his withered brothers bound between their knees and ankles.

His heart hammered wildly. In the daughters' momentum and frenzy, they pushed him back along the tunnels, and when they burst into the open air their momentum carried him with them down the birth trails. In the open, he shut his flesh eyelids against the light, but he felt the shudder that ran through the daughters as they began to rise—a single convulsion that rippled across the sky. Around him his brothers sighed amid their daughters' brilliant wings. As the skin flexed from the curve of muscular arms, and the sun-scales caught the light and ignited the father fuel, Rilk heard his brothers' whispering. Their words flowed out like thoughts from his head: *love fast and well, brother. Time is the shameless hunter of the world. It is swift and merciless upon the back of love.*

Wings alternately glided and flapped as the new queens settled into the brimming air currents. They accelerated, and the turbulent air washed over Rilk in a pungent wave that reeked of burning flesh, musk, fear-smell, and dirt. He skidded into a clump of trees, suddenly aware of a hundred different things: his heartbeat, the sun dappling through the bending everberry limbs, the en masse shudder of his brothers' final breath, and something else...a rumbling from above.

More than a rumbling—the ground shook. The tree leaves shook and dust swirled up and stained his pelt. The daughters' musk took on the sharp tang of panic.

In the everberry's shade, Rilk opened his flesh eyelids and watched as the killer slid from the gloom of the mountain, its blunt face burning like a red sun. Fire flew from its long limbs. With each discharge the earth concussed and a daughter fell. A tree limb snapped—hitting Rilk on the back with a blow so stunning that it left him dazed upon the ground. A shroud of leaves settled over him.

He wasn't sure how long he'd lain there as the father-daughters fell. His head throbbed and ached. The killer circled, back and forth, back and forth, long-limbed and slow—a pale monster the color of lichen. It took a long time before Rilk realized that the firing had stopped. He felt lost and unreal in the silence.

Eventually the killer left, lifting vertically so quickly that he was certain it intended to rejoin the speaking-paws' mountain that moved among the stars. The Earth settled into stillness. All the daughters of Oh-ten and all the brothers who had been his littermates were dead.

Time passed and twilight fell. He became aware of movement at the periphery of his sight. He watched without interest until it resolved into shapes. The younger brothers, like Fen who'd been unbound, had ventured from the fissure to gather what remained of those they'd loved. Rilk blinked and then bellowed in shock.

A daughter rode the back of one brother.

At the sound of his cry the brother she clung to extended and turned his head in a way that suggested nervousness. Fen loped over the broken ground to his brother's side.

"Rilk! Beyond all hope. We did not think to see you again!"

Never had Rilk thought his heart would leap so at the sight of Fen! But who was the daughter he carried?

She climbed from Fen's pelt and offered Rilk her juices.

He felt agitated, and did not accept.

"Rilk," Fen said, gently. "Do you not recognize your brother's daughter?"

Cleave? Cleave was a baby. This daughter looked like a young queen. She would soon be ready for daughters of her own.

"But...how did she escape?"

"Rilk, she couldn't launch. She had no sun-scales. She was with me in our den."

Again she rolled the juices from her gland and offered them to Rilk. This time he accepted.

"What does she say?" Fen asked.

Rilk purred. "She wants to go home, to the mountain of her fathers."

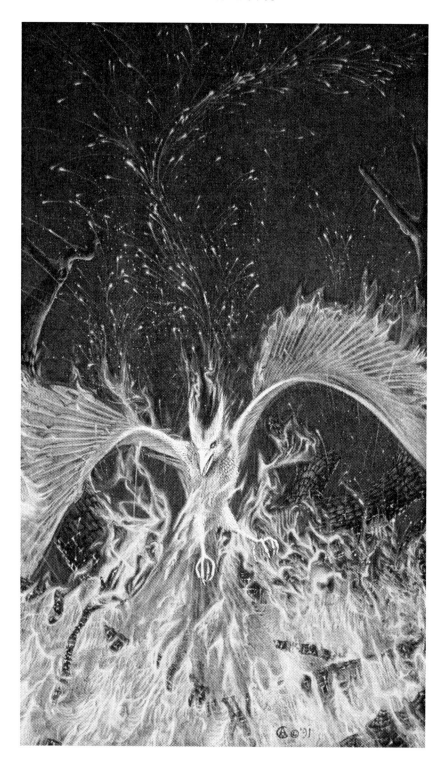

OUT OF THE FIRE
ELISABETH DEVOS

PHOENIX WON'T RISE AGAIN!

Seattle, Washington. At a press conference this morning, the Phoenix, a birdlike being about the size of a Harpy, to whom it bears no relation, shocked the world by announcing that it does not intend to rise again from its own ashes, as has been its custom for time immemorial.

After summoning reporters to its glass-roofed aviary overlooking Seattle's Pike Place Market, the Phoenix, who is world-renowned for its brilliant scarlet-and-gold plumage, its lovely singing voice, and its unique life cycle, entered on a wheeled perch pushed by an attendant.

Reading from a prepared statement, the Phoenix said, "One month from today is the 500th anniversary of my arising from the ashes of the last Phoenix. Although it has always been the custom of my kind to incinerate ourselves after a half millennium of existence, I have decided to break with that tradition. I intend to live my life until its natural end, at which time I have left instructions that my body is to be frozen in order to preserve its DNA. It is my hope that at some point in the future, science will enable my species to be resurrected in numbers greater than one."

In explaining its motive for the unprecedented announcement, the Phoenix said, "A lot has changed for me in the last few months. I realize that I've been flying on auto-pilot for most of my existence, and I'm just trying to take some control."

The Phoenix was presumably referring to its much-publicized apparent breakdown last January during a performance of *Firebird* at New York's Metropolitan Opera House. After the incident, the Phoenix entered the exclusive Lotus Eaters Clinic for "nervous exhaustion, pyrophobia, and a growing dependency on pineapple juice," according to a press release at the time. The pineapple-juice revelation was particularly shocking to fans of the famously gentle avionid, who is admired by environmentalists for its low-impact diet of dewdrops.

When asked whether it felt it had an obligation to perpetuate its unique role in the collective unconscious, the Phoenix snapped, "The human race is just going to have to find another symbol of regeneration. Maybe they could use one of those pop stars whose careers keep coming back from the dead."

According to tradition, once every five hundred years, the Phoenix builds a nest of aromatic branches, sings a haunting requiem for itself, then turns to the sun and spontaneously bursts into flames, which it fans with its own wings. The avionid is incinerated. In three days, however, a wormlike being arises from the ashes, and this larva eventually transforms into a new Phoenix. This ritual of regeneration is the Phoenix's sole means of reproduction, and at any given time, there is only one of its kind.

The current Phoenix was expected to incinerate itself on May 1st in Orlando, after the Florida tourist destination won out over sun-drenched rivals Honolulu, Cairo, and Marseilles. In an intense bidding war, the Supernatural Broadcast Corporation paid a record sum for rights to telecast the event. Rival network NBC was purportedly overlooked because the Phoenix had negative feelings about its peacock logo, but this was denied at the time by Verity Spinner of Best Feather Forward, a public relations firm employed by the avionid. Griffin Records had contracted to release a CD of the Phoenix's last song, said to be among the most haunting ever sung.

The Phoenix's regeneration is considered of immense cultural and mytho-scientific interest. Among those with reserved seats at the planned Orlando event are heads of state, Nobel laureates, and Stheno the Gorgon, acting president of the College of Fantastic Creatures, who agreed to view the spectacle from a private box to prevent any risk of inadvertently petrifying the human dignitaries in attendance.

Historically, the Phoenix's nestlike funeral pyre has been built in the branches of an oak, or on top of a palm tree, as was planned in Orlando, but fire codes complicated matters this time around, and the Orlando Fire Department has yet to issue a permit, despite assurances from the event committee that the Phoenix's mystical powers protect the host tree from harm.

Obtaining the Phoenix's traditional nest materials, spikenard and myrrh, has added further complexity to the preparations. Spikenard, a native of the Himalayas, is on the endangered plant list and cannot be harvested. Myrrh, produced from a tree found in Africa and the Arabian peninsula, is a suspected carcinogen when burned and is currently banned from import to the United States. According to sources close to the Phoenix, it took almost two years of appeals before special permits were issued to procure the plant matter, and the avionid took delivery of the necessary spikenard and myrrh just yesterday.

From Chapter 2 of *Out of the Fire*: *My Story* by Phoenix Dawn:

I couldn't sleep the night before the press conference to announce that I wasn't going to regenerate. Instead, I stayed up late distracting myself with television, which turned out to be a mistake. When an ad came on for a grilled chicken sandwich, I almost threw up. Despite months of therapy, my wings and claws still shook at the thought of fire. As I splashed in my fountain, trying to calm myself down, I desperately wanted some pineapple juice and regretted going cold turkey after getting home from Lotus Eaters.

The press conference itself wasn't as bad as I had expected. No one knew what to make of my decision, and at the time, even I didn't fully understand.

It was spring, and everywhere I flew, birds were pairing up, building nests. I knew that soon I would be building a nest, too, but not with the joyful expectation of welcoming a young Phoenix. I would never get to meet my "offspring." This sad thought—and the new life budding all around me—made the prospect of my fiery death unbearable.

Humans like to say they are utterly unique—just like all other humans. I, however, was just utterly unique. And alone. I didn't believe I could do anything about being singular, so I clutched at what *was* in my control.

After the reporters left my aviary that day, I felt a huge burden had been lifted from my wings, but at the same time, I sensed I wasn't out of the fire yet.

PHOENIX UNDER FIRE FOR NO FIRE

Yesterday's announcement by the Phoenix that it does not intend to rise again has sparked a heated controversy and has even divided the community of supernatural beings.

The Minotaur, reached at his labyrinthine home on Crete, said, "I'm unique in all the world, too, but I don't go around complaining about it. Instead, after embracing vegetarianism, I've chosen to devote myself to worthy causes, including a worldwide ban on bullfighting."

The Phoenix's spokesbeing, Verity Spinner, responded to this criticism by pointing out that the Minotaur, who is half man and half bull, is a major stockholder in ManBeast Technology, a start-up genetic engineering firm founded by billionaire centaur Thasseus, which has the potential to produce other beings that are a cross between a human and an animal.

The conservative College of Fantastic Creatures, in an official position paper, condemned the Phoenix's decision as "an embarrassing abdication of responsibility." Echoing the Minotaur's sentiment, the CFC also pointed out that many of its members are unique and that some, like its Gorgon president, face serious obstacles to social acceptance, whereas the Phoenix is universally admired.

But other groups in the Mythicum have been less judgmental of the avionid's desire. Cosmicus, leader of the Herd of Centaurs, commented, "To everything, there is a season. And a time for every purpose under Heaven."

The Zephyrs, a species of wind spirit, are planning a breeze-by in support of the Phoenix. Northwesterly, publicity director for the Zephyrs, said, "We've spent a lot of time with the Phoenix as it flies around the world. It's been a good friend to us, and donated its time to sing at a fundraising concert during our campaign for acceptance, 'we're here, we're air, get used to it.' Prior to the campaign, we were constantly being sued by insurance companies seeking reimbursement for wind-damage claims."

The Phoenix's decision has stirred up even greater contention in the human community. The Global Right-to-Life Coalition suggested they may go to court to force the Phoenix to rise again. Moore Kiddes, president of the organization, stated he believes the next Phoenix is inherent in the body of the current Phoenix, and therefore, the Phoenix's refusal to regenerate is equivalent to murder.

Planetwide Pro-Choice quickly countered the GRLC position, claiming that the Phoenix's decision embodied the principle for which PPC has always fought: reproductive freedom.

"Why should this creature be forced to adhere to some outmoded mythical morality that says it has to incinerate itself so that another being can arise?" PPC public policy director Roe Ann Wade asked. "The Phoenix has a right to control over its own body."

Support came also from an unlikely source, the Human Racists, an organization devoted to the "eradication of unnatural beings from the face of the Earth." The Racists, members of which are serving time for unicorn dehornings, among other hate crimes, posted an opinion on their web site, which said in part, "We wholeheartedly applaud the decision of this foul fowl to rid the world of itsself for all eternity."

On a more practical front, both the City of Orlando and the Supernatural Broadcast Corporation, which paid record sums to host and telecast the rare event, respectively, are said to be in discussion with lawyers representing the avionid.

The Phoenix, reached for comment through a spokesbeing, said that it appreciates the support it has received, and hopes that all beings, both supernatural and natural, will respect its decision.

From Chapter 4 of *Out of the Fire: My Story* by Phoenix Dawn:

I was blown aback when the College of Fantastic Creatures condemned me for deciding not to regenerate. We supernaturals are a traditional bunch, for the most part, so maybe I should have expected it. Still, it hurt. I felt even more isolated, if that was possible.

The problem with being unique is that there's no one who can truly relate to what you're going through. My dear friend Cyclops Polyphemus tried, but I think even he was bewildered by my decision.

All I knew then was that I couldn't go through with it. As the preparations for my regeneration had grown more intensive, so had my fear of fire. It reached the point where unlit candles gave me panic attacks. The network beings and event folks kept saying, "It's just nerves; you'll do fine." They'd offer me pineapple juice, even though they knew I was supposed to be on the wagon.

Then, the spikenard and myrrh arrived. We had flown through all sorts of hoops to get it. Alone in my aviary that evening, I opened the crates to examine their contents. The fragrance of the plants was intoxicating. Forgetting my pyrophobia for the first time in months, I took a branch into my housekeeper's kitchenette and lit it on the stove. Inhaling the smoke, I felt euphoric. This made sense: mytho-scientists had long theorized that the nest materials provided a high that would numb me to the pain of being burned alive.

As I continued to greedily sniff the smoldering branch, a feeling tore through my drug-induced elation. A feeling of terror so profound that in five hundred years I have never experienced its like. I tossed the spikenard onto the floor, beating it with my wings to extinguish it, not caring if I burnt my feathers.

When I'd calmed down, I phoned Verity and said, "Call a press conference for the morning. I've got an announcement to make."

BATTLE OVER PHOENIX COLD-FREEZE HEATS UP

Mt. Olympus, Greece. The Global Right-to-Life Coalition, an organization which supports the right to life of unborn beings, filed a motion today with the Interdimensional Court seeking to force the Phoenix to perform its ritual of regeneration. The motion states, in part, that "while birth among humans is typically defined to mean live birth, the notion is logically extended to include hatching, springing from a cleaved forehead or spilled blood, growing from a severed body part, as well as arising from ashes. The intentions of the current Phoenix in regard to the death and frozen storage of its body effectively deny life to the next Phoenix."

Interdimensional legal experts are speaking out about the case, which is universally regarded as a landmark.

Oedipus Smith, senior partner of the law firm Smith, Sanders and Sphinx, explained the predicament the Court faces. "Interdimensional law holds that it is murder to terminate the natural existence of any being. So the question becomes, what is the natural existence of a Phoenix, and when does that existence begin? If the Court finds that the existence of a Phoenix does not begin until it arises from the ashes, then the GRLC is going to lose this one. If the Court, however, determines that due to the regenerative nature of the Phoenix, the next one is inherent in the current avionid, then it may grant the motion for an emergency injunction."

Two groups, Planetwide Pro-Choice, whose mission is to further the cause of reproductive freedom, and the Mythicum Liberties Union, a controversial legal advocacy organization, have vowed to join forces with the Phoenix in defense of its wishes.

Mythicum Liberties Union chief counsel the Hydra said, "What is at issue is a fundamental question affecting all immortal and quasi-immortal beings: Can we be forced to continue on for all eternity? Or do we have a right to end our existence?"

The Hydra has a unique perspective on the issue of regeneration. During the Greek empire, it suffered a multiple decapitation by fire at the hands of Hercules, the so-called "monster slayer," whose rightful place in history—either hero or villain—has been the subject of much emotional discussion. After Hercules's attack, the Hydra's one immortal head was buried under a rock, where it lay unable to regenerate itself until the nineteenth century when the head was unearthed by an archaeological expedition. The regenerated Hydra served almost a century of jail time for killing the team that had liberated it, but since its release has become a respected advocate for the rights of fantastic beings, and is widely regarded as one of the best sets of legal minds working today.

In recognition of the time-critical nature of the case, the Court has set a hearing for April 20th, when it will respond to the motion and any countermotions filed by the Phoenix or other parties.

The Interdimensional Court has previously heard such high-profile cases as its first major decision, *St. George v. Dragon*, and more recently, *College of Fantastic Creatures v. Republic of Greece*, in which reparations were awarded for the relentless persecution and destruction of "supers," as they are commonly known, by the ancient Greeks. During the case, which was the first of the Court's hearings to be broadcast by satellite, Grecian lawyers attempted to portray the supers as the aggressors, focusing on the many sacrificed virgins who had been deprived of the enjoyment of their sexuality and the opportunity to procreate, along with their lives. At one memorable point, the Minotaur, under intense cross-examination, bellowed out an apology for his past culinary practices. Despite this, the voice-only testimony of Stheno the Gorgon, who spoke heartwrenchingly about the trauma of watching Perseus destroy her mortal sister Medusa, sealed the case for the CFC.

The Court was established five hundred years ago, after fantastic beings that had survived the Grecian Purges, then had been forced into hiding to avoid the exterminators of the Middle Ages, declared war on humankind. Following one hundred years of hostilities, the Interdimensional Treaty was signed at the banks of the River Styx. It established interdimensional law and the Court to administer it.

***Partial transcript from* Timely Topics with Fae Moss-Phayce:**

Fae: We're back with the Phoenix, who one week ago today caused an interdimensional uproar by announcing that it didn't intend to rise again. Phoenix, before the break, you said accusations that you're trying to commit suicide or genocide are unfair.

Phoenix: Well, it seems to me that burning yourself alive is a lot more suicidal than simply trying to live out your life to its natural end.

Fae: But what about the future of the Phoenix?

Phoenix: I don't know, but I don't think I should have to immolate myself just so that everybody else has some sort of guarantee.

Fae: So it's okay with you if you're the last of your kind?

Phoenix: Of course not! I've already said that I hope there will be more Phoenixes. There's nothing I'd like more than to meet another of my species.

Fae: There are rumors that you're trying to have yourself cloned.

Phoenix: That's ridiculous. Cloning is in its infancy, and it requires not just DNA, but an egg from the species, which of course doesn't exist in my case.

Fae: This is obviously an emotionally charged issue. You're mythologized by cultures throughout the world for your ability to rise from your own ashes, and now you've rejected the very quality that has set you apart. What is your answer, then, to those in the interdimensional community who say you're being selfish and future Phoenixes will pay the price?

Phoenix: You humans have a whole popular psychology that advocates breaking cycles, taking responsibility, and making choices. Quite frankly, I think it's hypocritical that I'm coming under attack for doing just that.

Fae: Surely, you have to realize that your very nature, your uniqueness, puts you in a separate category and that the same standards aren't going to apply?

Phoenix: Why shouldn't they?

Fae: Now we're into one of the most argued issues of our world. Regardless of whether it's fair or not, various groups are going to court to try and force you to regenerate. In fact, we just had word that the Supernatural Conservancy has also filed a motion.

Phoenix: So my lawyers tell me. I think the Conservancy is misguided. If the human race wanted to extinct itself—and speaking as a being who's observed you for a very long time, it often looks like that's exactly what humanity wants—but if you wanted that, I don't think you'd appreciate a bunch of us supers getting together and trying to stop you.

Fae: Perhaps not. We're just about out of time. I want to thank you for joining us tonight.

Phoenix: Thanks for having me.

Fae: The much-anticipated *Sports Illustrated* annual water nymph issue hits newsstands tomorrow. As expected, the Crossdimensional Organization for Women is calling for a boycott of the magazine as demeaning to all female entities. What do the models have to say? Cover-nymph Galatea joins us when we come back.

Recent Developments:

•*Interdimensional Court orders Phoenix to undergo psychiatric evaluation. (4/12/—)*

•*Griffin Records suspends plans to release Phoenix's Requiem. (4/13/—)*

•Phoenix found to be sound of mind. (4/16/—)
•SBC and City of Orlando sue Phoenix for foregoing fire. (4/17/—)
•Special Prosecutor considers charging Phoenix with conspiracy to commit genocide. (4/18/—)

From Chapter 7 of *Out of the Fire: My Story* by Phoenix Dawn:

The *Timely Topics* interview was Verity Spinner's idea. She thought that if I went on TV, told my side in being, that it might sway public opinion. But I was too defensive and too scared to make a good case for myself. If anything, I lost support after the segment aired, even though Verity made the rounds trying to do damage control.

In the time between that interview and the hearing, it felt like the whole world was against me. Well, maybe not everyone: my friends at the Metropolitan Opera sent me a gorgeous bouquet of birds of paradise (my favorite!) and a note saying that I would always be irreplaceable. That meant a lot.

But then there were the thousands of messages from complete strangers: "My family planned our trip to Destiny World for next month so we could watch your regeneration. Now what am I supposed to tell my kids?" And: "Burn, you big chicken!" I wanted to reply, "Get a life!" but I didn't. There were too many of them, and the pressure was pushing me toward the edge.

A week before the court hearing, I had www.mysticfoods.com deliver some pineapple juice. I couldn't help it. I needed something to get me through the legal nightmare. My old friend Cy Poly called to say he'd been subpoenaed; poor thing was crying his eye out over being forced to testify against me. And then there were the updates from Hydra. The lawyer was doing mock trials with itself, having a different head take the part of each judge and the various attorneys, and its assorted minds couldn't agree on whether our prospects were good or not.

I binged on pineapple juice right up until I boarded the plane to Greece for what I could only think of as my trial. During the overnight journey, I fell asleep and dreamt of being sacrificed to a Hawaiian volcano for having sucked the last golden drops of life out of the pineapple fields. As the fiery lava sucked me down into a burning vortex, I awoke screeching—and clutched for another juice.

COURT REQUIRES RITUAL, BUT PHOENIX FLAP NOT OVER YET

Mt. Olympus, Greece. In a close 5-4 vote, the Interdimensional Court granted an emergency injunction against the Phoenix today, ordering the legendary avionid to regenerate on its 500th birthday, which is a week from Saturday. While the Court found that due to the mystical nature of the Phoenix's regeneration, it does not have the practical means to enforce its order, the injunction does subject the Phoenix to immediate arrest and imprisonment should it fail to rise again.

The Phoenix, who had testified on its own behalf, returned to its home city of Seattle before the decision was announced. Its publicist, Verity Spinner, said it was deeply distressed by the Court's ruling.

MLU chief counsel the Hydra, who argued in defense of the Phoenix, commented, "The Court has lost sight of the bigger picture. The Phoenix is a symbol of hope and renewal; if it is compelled by court order to burn to death, it will come to symbolize tragedy. The Phoenix myth will be destroyed along with the Phoenix itself."

Special Prosecutor Given Powers, who has already stated that he will bring criminal charges of genocide against the Phoenix if it does not re-generate, applauded the decision, but acknowledged that the outcome is in the avionid's claws.

"We would rather see the Phoenix do the right thing, but if it doesn't, we'll prosecute to the fullest extent of the law."

The penalty for genocide under interdimensional law is existence-long imprisonment. It is not known how long the Phoenix will live should it not incinerate itself upon its 500th birthday.

Excerpt from the Interdimensional Court ruling in *GRLC et al. v. The Phoenix*, penned for the majority by Chief Justice Tyranno the Dragon:

Based on testimony given by Cyclops Polyphemus and others who have known the Phoenix for more than one incarnation, it is the belief of this Court that each Phoenix is, in fact, a unique individual. The Interdimensional Constitution holds that all beings existent are granted certain inalienable rights, and so we come to the question of when the existence of a specific Phoenix begins. It is currently understood that a new Phoenix will arise only from the incinerated body of its predecessor, and will first appear as a large worm three days after that incineration. It thus seems that a new Phoenix only becomes existent some time after the voluntary self-destruction of its parent. Therefore, forcing the Phoenix to regenerate on the basis of the "right to life" of its offspring would be equivalent to forcing an act of conception upon a human being for the same reason. The motion for an emergency injunction brought by the Global Right-to-Life Coalition is thus denied for lack of legal merit.

Also before the Court is the question broached by co-plaintiff The Supernatural Conservancy of whether the Phoenix, by refusing to regenerate, is in effect extincting its species. While there is no clear precedent in this matter, it is the very uniqueness of the Phoenix that creates the most compelling argument against defense counsel's assertion that the avionid is entitled to end its life as it chooses. In opting not to incinerate itself, the Phoenix effectively prevents any other beings of its like from ever existing, and in so doing, irreparably harms the interdimensional world, which would surely be diminished by the loss of such a universally admired and singular species.

Therefore, it is the ruling of this Court that the cause brought by The Supernatural Conservancy is upheld, and that the Phoenix is hereby ordered to regenerate according to the mystical customs of its predecessors, which are outlined below.

From Chapter 11 of *Out of the Fire: My Story* by Phoenix Dawn:

After the Court's decision, I was caught between a fire and a hot place. What was the point of asserting my rights to existence, liberty, and happiness, if the day I did so, the latter two were taken away?

I went into seclusion. My publicity team kept telling the world that I was perching by my decision to live out my life and to donate my frozen body to mytho-scientific research upon my death. Hydra and the other lawyers kept working to overturn the ruling. Meanwhile, I guzzled "golden elixir," as I'd come to call pineapple juice, and obsessed about fire. My therapist had been telling me for months that the fire wasn't my real fear, but I didn't believe her. She wasn't the one who was supposed to burn herself alive.

Three days before my scheduled regeneration, I woke to the sound of sirens (mechanical ones, not the supernatural songstresses). I'd passed out in a pile of prunings that Chauncey, my housekeeper, had taken from the ornamental cherry trees in my aviary. In my hungover confusion, I thought I was in the nest and the sirens were because I was on fire. Screeching like a common seagull, I zoomed across the aviary and dove headfirst into my fountain. Chauncey heard me and came running in his bathrobe. I was beating my wings, splashing water everywhere, trying to extinguish myself.

Chauncey helped me back to my favorite perch and turned on a heat lamp to dry me off. I felt embarrassed, miserable, and hopeless. Even pineapple juice had lost its appeal. All I could think was: it doesn't matter what I do, I'm doomed. An almost unbearable sense of grief and despair welled up inside of me.

And so it was that I came beak-to-beak with the feelings that I'd been trying to ignore for decades. Despite my fame, I didn't view myself as an enduring symbol of the power to rise from the ashes and recreate oneself; I viewed myself as a symbol of loneliness and futility. Of being trapped in an endless cycle. And of being destined to pass that on from one regeneration to the next.

But I'd learned in therapy that cycles keep repeating themselves until you make a conscious decision to change—and that's exactly what I'd done. Maybe it was the Phoenix fate to be all alone, but I didn't have to set myself on fire just because that's what my parent, and its parent, and all the Phoenixes before it, did. We're not lemmings, after all.

I didn't even understand how all those Phoenixes could go through with the incineration. I imagined that they must have been far braver beings than me. Regardless of whether I was a coward, I knew that I couldn't do it, that I would rather live out my days in prison than destroy myself simply because of some "should" whose origin would probably remain forever shrouded in mystery. Peace filled my being. And an unshakeable resolve. I would take control of my destiny the only way that I could and accept the consequences.

But then, on the eve of my five hundredth birthday, everything changed.

PHOENIX IN HOSPITAL FOLLOWING FAILED FIRE

Seattle, Washington. After insisting that it would not abide by an Interdimensional Court order requiring it to regenerate, the Phoenix apparently had a last-minute change of heart, and after spending all night hastily constructing its ritual nest atop Seattle's Space Needle, it set itself alight, only to chicken out as flames engulfed its feathered form. The legendary "bird of fire" leapt squawking from its funeral pyre and fell twenty feet to the Space Needle's Observation Deck, where it screamed for help until a fast-acting firefighter sprayed it with an extinguisher. The Phoenix was then airlifted to Harborview Medical Center, where it is in critical condition with third-degree burns over eighty percent of its body. Witnesses said that all the avionid's feathers were incinerated except for the golden crest on its head.

Around midnight yesterday, the Phoenix, who had been in seclusion, flew from its Seattle aviary to the nearby Space Needle, carrying aromatic branches that had been imported for its regeneration. It deposited its burden atop the landmark, then returned to its penthouse for more of the plant material. Security guards at the Space Needle alerted local authorities, and a decision was made not to interfere with the avionid's activities. Instead, the Space Needle was evacuated except for firefighters and members of the press.

According to eyewitness accounts and video footage taken from news helicopters, which captured the entire event, the Phoenix, who has over a dozen triple-Platinum recordings to its credit, sang a haunting requiem as the sun rose on an atypically clear morning. The avionid completed its melody, then faced east, extending its wings. Within seconds, a small flame appeared beneath its tail. The Phoenix fanned its wings, encouraging the fire, which spread to the branches of the nest. For close to a minute, all that was visible was smoke and flames. Then, the Phoenix emitted a terrible screech and leapt from its pyre, landing in the guard wires above the Observation Deck. It squawked for help, its body still burning. A member of the Seattle Fire Department extinguished the avionid, who received emergency medical attention before being rushed to the region's only Level One trauma center.

Seattle's fire chief defended his decision to permit the Phoenix to set itself and its nest ablaze atop the city's most recognized landmark by citing the widely held belief that the Phoenix's incineration has, for presumably mystical reasons, never harmed the trees in which it traditionally takes place, and therefore the risk to the Space Needle was minimal. In support of this, the Phoenix's nest was no longer on fire by the time SFD personnel reached it. The charred construction is currently considered evidence. The Seattle Police Department is contracting for its removal by crane, which may take up to three days.

A spokesbeing for the Interdimensional Court said that the Justices are meeting to determine whether the Phoenix's failed attempt puts it in contempt or whether it in effect satisfied the Court's order. Special Prosecutor Given Powers, who has been preparing a case against the Phoenix, said his office needed to wait until the avionid was well enough to be interviewed, but it appeared likely that charges of genocide would be brought.

MLU chief counsel the Hydra, who defended the Phoenix before the Interdimensional Court, expressed hope that his client would not suffer legal punishment.

"The Phoenix's situation continues to be unprecedented, but hopefully today's tragic event will inspire the Court to reconsider its previous finding.

What we have here is a being being forced to burn itself alive. No other entity in existence has ever been ordered to undergo an equivalent ordeal, and to force the Phoenix to choose between immolation and life imprisonment is cruel and unusual."

Interdimensional legal expert Oedipus Smith, a professor at Harvard Law School, said that the Court's intent was clearly to insure the generation of a new Phoenix, and since the Phoenix is alive in a burn center, and not reduced to ashes in its nest (where its remains would, in three days time, give rise to a worm-like Phoenix larva), it is unlikely that the Court will not impose penalty.

The Phoenix has been embattled since its shocking announcement. In addition to the injunction granted by the Interdimensional Court upon a motion by the Supernatural Conservancy, other parties who had paid large sums for rights to the regeneration are also bringing actions against the Phoenix. These include original host city Orlando, broadcast network SBC, and Griffin Records. Although some experts estimate damages could approach one billion dollars, it is likely, given the Phoenix's vast financial resources, accumulated over half a millennium, that it would be able to pay any award.

From Chapter 13 of *Out of the Fire: My Story* by Phoenix Dawn:

It's hard to describe what came over me that night. It was as if the whole world, and everything that had happened in that world—my pyrophobia, the press conference, the pineapple-juice binging, the court battle, my catharsis just three days before—all of it faded into a shadowland, and the only thing that was real was an all-consuming urge to *build that nest*.

I vaguely remember Chauncey shouting after me as I left with the first load of branches, but even he was just a wraith, some vaguely familiar being that lacked substance in the sphere I now inhabited, a sphere where I existed for one purpose and one purpose only.

I'm not sure why I chose the Space Needle. Maybe because there aren't palm trees in Seattle, nor oaks of any stature. Maybe because it stands separate from downtown's skyscrapers, brightly lit, a beacon in the night. Regardless, I decided to build there, and so back and forth I went until every last stem had been transported to the nest site, and just in time.

The horizon was graying to the east. I felt the world emerging from its nighttime shadow, and as it did, I understood that I perched between the two realities, the everyday place and that other nameless one from which we come and to which we return. I felt utterly, profoundly alone, and my loneliness flowed into my voice and I sang, sang for everything that ends and everything that has yet to begin.

When the song finished, rays of light touched my feathers, the sun creeping up over the Cascade Mountains, burning away the shadows. The worlds were colliding. The moment was so beautiful and so terrible I could not bear it. Throwing my wings wide, I welcomed the star's fire, voicelessly begging it to consume me. And flames sprang forth from my being, the fiery illusion of my feathers made real.

Spikenard and myrrh are potent. Intoxicated, I felt nothing as the flames and smoke thickened, sealing me in a coffin of light and shadow, a cocoon spun at the border of day and night, rebirth and…death. The great and final slumber engulfed my body—

And then something in me awoke, an awareness as singular as my nestbuilding obsession the night before, and that awareness was: *I am on fire!*

I leapt out of the nest before I'd even thought, and as I did, I fell back into the everyday world, fell hard, landing in wires above the Space Needle's Observation Deck and screaming because I was burning alive.

PHOENIX LARVA FOUND!

Seattle, Washington. Police working with a crane crew to take the Phoenix's nest into evidence, following the avionid's aborted regeneration three days ago, were shocked to discover a large wormlike being inside the bower of burnt branches atop the Space Needle. Removal of the nest was immediately halted, and mytho-scientific experts were called in to identify the flame-red creature. Following several hours of examination, the Seattle police chief announced that the nest would not be removed and that the Space Needle would be closed until further notice. When asked if a Phoenix larva had been found, the chief replied, "That is our best guess at this point."

If the worm, nicknamed "Little Red," transforms into a Phoenix, it likely will resolve the legal problems facing the Phoenix, who is in serious-but-stable condition. However, such an occurrence is without precedent and believed by many in the mytho-scientific community to be impossible.

"The Phoenix is and has always been unique," said renowned authority Dr. Iva D'Gree of Paris's *L'Institute des Creatures Fantastiques*. "It only arises from the burnt remains of its former incarnation."

However, O. Pin Mynd, author of *Wrong Again: The Failings of Science & Mythos,* pointed out that at one time maggots were thought to arise spontaneously from dead flesh, a notion which is now considered ridiculous.

Recent Developments:

•*Phoenix's recovery from third-degree burns termed "amazing" by doctors. Mytho-scientists cite regenerative abilities as reason for rapid healing. (5/8/—)*

•*Unique no more! Larva transforms into Phoenix. Prior Phoenix said to be ecstatic. (5/20/—)*

•*Phoenix takes name. "Dawn" hopes to meet "Little Red" soon. (5/22/—)*

•*Interdimensional Court rules that Phoenix "effectively" complied with injunction. Special Prosecutor won't bring charges. (5/24/—)*

•*Phoenix Dawn settles lawsuits over cancelled Orlando regeneration. SBC receives rights to story that changed the mythos. Griffin Records parent company Fantastic Communications' Magic Books will publish Phoenix's memoir. (5/28/—)*

•*Beak-to-beak for the first time ever: emotional meeting as Little Red visits Dawn. (6/1/—)*

Epilogue from *Out of the Fire: My Story* by Phoenix Dawn:

Many have speculated about what happened to me on May first and why Little Red is here when I am not burnt to ash.

Perhaps the whole mythos about us Phoenixes has been wrong, and we were never intended to be a species of one, unique in all the world. Maybe the first Phoenix, having no being to help it understand what was happening, let the power of its birth experience consume it. And so a myth arose. And every subsequent Phoenix bought into its own legend, duly giving its life to perpetuate it.

Maybe our *true* power of regeneration is the ability to survive creating more of our own kind. For as the Court found, and as Little Red proves, all Phoenixes may be the same, but we are not the same Phoenix.

But perhaps that's not it at all. Maybe the gods just decided it was time for a change, and I happened to be the one chosen to bring it about. Perhaps everything I went through prior to May first was so that I would awaken to my own destruction, save myself, and begin a new mythos. Who is to say?

All I know with certainty is that for the first time in my five-hundred-year existence, I can look another being in the eye and see myself staring back. It's an experience so fresh, so new, I feel reborn.

David Levine

LEGACY
DAVID LEVINE

The view from where I sat looked like the poster for *Cygnus X-1* with Luke Perry, which I used as my screen wallpaper for six solid months in seventh grade. Not quite as dramatic, but better because it was real.

The roiling red bulk of the red supergiant star we called Magnus, or VV Cephei A to give its proper name, filled the window. It looked like red clouds churning in a dull orange sky, but the tiniest visible blob was a million times as big as the Earth, and if it weren't for the Lilliandree-made transparent dome over the ship's lifesystem the infrared alone would be enough to kill us. Just left of center burned a tiny pinpoint of blue-white light: Charlie, or VV Cephei B, a blue giant star five times bigger than Sol. A dim elliptical halo of pale orange shading to yellow surrounded the blue star, matter sucked from the big star's bulk by the smaller one's gravity and spun into a disk by their mutual rotation.

I was the only one looking at it.

I had to attend the astrophysicists' daily staff meeting, in case they needed some technical information on the ship or its instruments, but as the meeting was conducted in incomprehensible scientific gibberish I always chose a seat with a view. Everyone else focused on the digital display on the opposite wall. Even though these folks had spent their entire lives studying the stars and had just traveled over three thousand light years to study this particular one, they spent almost no time looking at it.

Susan Yang, the diminutive nuclear chemist from Korea, had just finished her report, and Martin Lake—*Doctor* Martin Lake, a pop-eyed pale Brit whose remaining hair stuck out like dried crabgrass—stood up. "I've finally discovered what has been interfering with my observations. We have to move the ship."

Groans all around the table, not least from me. It had taken us over seventy-two hours to "stabilize the observational platform"—in other words, put the ship in the right orbit and wait for it to stop wobbling.

Leonard Hart, the expedition's director, put his glasses on the table and rubbed his eyes. "And why is that, Dr. Lake?" He had a bushy gray moustache and a large nose whose tip moved when he talked.

"There's an anomalous mascon in the accretion disk." He put up an image on the screen: thin red vapor curled up from the surface of Magnus and swirled around its tiny blue companion like a loving tentacle. "It's in this clear zone." He tapped the screen and the image magnified, showing a dark teardrop-shaped bubble in the red tentacle. It was a real-time image, and the red gas drifted lazily past—a storm of high-temperature charged particles moving at hundreds of kilometers per second. "We have to relocate to a position where it isn't anywhere near my line of sight to the core."

"Line of sight?" huffed Vasiliy Ivanov. "Are we doing *optical* astronomy here?"

"No. This mascon is big enough to affect Simultaneity-based observations." Martin touched another control and annotations appeared, pointing out a black circle within the dark bubble and indicating its diameter, just a bit bigger than Jupiter.

Vasiliy remained skeptical. "Even Jupiter doesn't have *that* deep a gravity well."

"Oh, it's much more massive than Jupiter. That is a terrestrial body."

The muttered side conversations and shuffling papers stopped dead.

Leonard stood up and moved close to the screen. "A rock bigger than Jupiter?"

"I call it Ballock," said Martin, "because it's a big heavy ball and because it's bollixed up my data. We have to move the ship so I can see around it."

Leonard magnified the image still further. "This dark region must be protected from the matter stream by its magnetosphere."

"What's that?" asked Krishna Srinivasa, pointing at a star within the dark bubble.

Martin blinked. "A minor terrestrial body. A moon of Ballock."

Leonard zoomed in on the bright speck.

The bright blue-white light of Charlie illuminated white clouds swirling serenely on a blue and green background. A perfect little jewel of a world. The annotations indicated a mass and surface temperature not too far from Earth's and the presence of water and oxygen. Even I knew how rare that was.

When the excited babble died down, Martin said, "I've named it Pointless."

Leonard's brown-spotted forehead wrinkled as his eyebrows drew together in befuddled amusement. "You found an Earthlike world in the accretion disk of a red supergiant, and you called it *Pointless*?"

"Because it has no bearing on my researches, and it's going to be blown away soon anyway. So are we going to move the ship, or not?"

I f it had been my choice, I would have started accelerating toward that pretty little world as soon as it came up on the screen. I wanted to stand on its alien soil, under the light of the two suns. But Leonard was the one in charge, and I was glad: the scientists yelled at each other for five solid hours, including two consultations with higher-ups back on Earth, and if it had been me in the middle of all that, my hair would have been as gray as Leonard's by the end of the meeting.

We were all there, three thousand light-years and five billion dollars from home, because the latest Simultaneity astronomy showed Magnus was right on the cusp of exploding into a supernova. Supernovae are rare events, happening only once per century or so per galaxy, and studying an incipient one up close could tell us more about stellar evolution than fifty years of Earth-based observation. Simultaneity has no speed-of-light limitation, but detail is reduced by distance and by intervening mass, so we wanted to get as close as possible.

So an international team of a dozen astrophysicists had been assembled and a long-range ship had been hired from Implex Corporation, along with its Simultaneity tech (that's me, Gray Tackett) and realspace pilot (Julie Jorgensen, but everyone calls her J.J.). I knew this was a really important project, because five major corporations and two minor governments had been kicked off the schedule to make room for it. Ships like the *Implex Helvoran* aren't exactly common.

At this point the "iron flash" —the point at which the star used up all the lighter elements in its core and began to burn iron, starting the biggest fireworks show in the galaxy—was a month away and nobody on the ship had had more than four hours' sleep a night since we'd arrived three weeks ago. Our schedule kept everyone occupied right up until the last possible moment, and now we had Ballock and Pointless to study as well. Martin demanded we not spend any resources on the planets at all; Susan, the only one in the group with a degree in planetology, argued for an immediate landing on Pointless.

In the end Leonard imposed a compromise that made nobody happy. We would put the ship in orbit around Pointless, where both Pointless and Magnus could be observed without Ballock's interference, and those who wished could spend at most 30% of their time and bandwidth studying the planets.

It sounded reasonable to me, at first. Then I realized what we would have to do to get there.

"We can't fly the ship into the *sun!*"

"It's not as bad as it seems, Gray," said Leonard. "The photosphere thins and cools as it's drawn from Magnus's surface by Charlie's gravity, and it doesn't get thicker until well into the accretion disk. Where we're going it's no more than a hot, dirty vacuum."

"What if we have to run for it?" Simultaneity doesn't like gravity wells.

"We've got almost a month. It's only eight days from there back out to where space is flat enough for a safe transition. Martin, can you guarantee us two weeks' warning before the iron flash?"

"Yes."

I crossed my arms and thought about it. I didn't like being so far from a safe jump point, but the planet called to me.

"Let's do it."

While J.J. laid out a transfer orbit and the astrophysicists prepared their more delicate equipment for acceleration, I worked with Leonard on a revised bandwidth budget. The Simultaneity unit was both our main scientific instrument and our link to Earth, and we had already been using its full capacity before we'd discovered Pointless. Now we had to reallocate some of that capacity to the study of the two planets.

We had been working for a couple of hours when Leonard stretched, and I winced at the audible crack of his joints. "Sorry," he said, "but that's what seventy-three sounds like."

"Seventy-three? I never would have guessed."

"Thank you." He stared at me for a moment. "How old are you, if I may ask?"

"Twenty-three."

His eyes didn't move, but he wasn't looking at me anymore. "I should have grandchildren your age."

Should have? I didn't say anything out loud, but the question must have showed on my face.

"My wife and two sons were killed in a car accident in 1991, when I was in grad school."

"I'm sorry."

He sighed, looked into his cupped hands as though they held memories. "I suppose that's why I'm here now, actually. After they died, I devoted myself to my career...hoping to make some significant advancement in human knowledge, something to carry on my name after I was gone. I did achieve a small amount of fame, in certain circles, but never the big breakthrough I'd been seeking. So when this expedition was being assembled I pulled in every favor I ever had to get on it. My last chance."

Finally he snorted, breaking the awkward silence, and met my gaze again. "And now I'm writing bandwidth budgets instead of doing real science. So let's get this thing finished."

O ver the next eight days Magnus grew from a huge red ball into a hellish boiling wall of red fire that took up half the sky, with loops and streamers flowing up and around like bridges on the horizon. Charlie became a searing circle of light bigger than a full moon, bisected by the accretion disk. Seen edge-on, the disk was a fat fuzzy toothpick, dark where it crossed Charlie's face and yellow-orange away from it.

The matter stream between the two stars changed appearance more than either of them. At first it was a dark red river, meandering through the black sky. As we got closer structures began to appear, whorls and braids and vortices in red and black, but it got dimmer and dimmer even as the detail increased. It was like driving into the mountains; once you reach the foothills, you can't see the mountains themselves at all. By the time Pointless showed a visible disk the sky was just as black as it had been before, even though we were now well inside the matter stream.

The scientists kept me busy with routing requests, configuration changes, and other administrative tasks. The incoming data was swamping our storage and I had a constant battle to keep it all accessible without losing anything. Still, whenever I could spare a few moments I went up to the observation deck and stared at the planet below.

Pointless was tidally locked to its primary, Ballock, so its "day" equaled its orbital period: 120 days. This meant Ballock would never appear to move in Pointless's sky, while the two suns would rise and set every 120 days. But though Pointless's orbit around Ballock was nearly circular, Ballock's orbit around Charlie was unstable—badly warped by the constant gravitic duel between the two suns. So the suns' position relative to each other in Pointless's sky would change constantly and unpredictably.

We had arrived at a point in Ballock's variable "year" when it was between the two suns, so currently there was no night on Pointless—any given point in the surface was in "red day" or "blue day." On the blue-day side, the one we'd seen first, the continents looked lush and green and Charlie's light sparkled from its oceans, making it look like a shiny little Christmas tree ornament.

At the moment, though, we were orbiting over the red-day side, where black continents floated in a dim and mottled sea of vague, fitful red highlights. Red day would be a grim and chilly time for any life forms on the surface. I imagined weird alien ferns looming black in Magnus's churning red light, and crawling tentacled creatures desperately awaiting the blue dawn that came every 120 days.

I got a little tightness in my chest as I realized that blue dawn would never come. Instead, sometime in the next month would come a red dawn like none other in the planet's history.

Bringing that history to a close.

M y imaginings were interrupted by an excited chatter of voices from the hatch behind me. I clattered down the ladder to find a crowd gathered around Susan's work station. "Nonsense!" Vasiliy shouted, pointing at her screen. "Europa is covered with lines like those, and Schiaparelli thought he saw canals on Mars."

"They are *roads*!" I had never before heard Susan raise her voice.

Vasiliy shook his head. "Impossible. Life on Earth didn't even reach the multicellular stage for billions of years. This star is twelve million years old at most."

"And Ballock's orbit is unstable," said Krishna. "Temperatures too variable for life to arise."

"These lines cross rivers at the narrowest points," Susan replied, "and mountains at the lowest points—I've seen evidence of bridges, and cleared passes. And the places where roads come together have an infrared signature consistent with disturbed soil. Cities!"

"Pah!" Vasiliy waved a hand dismissively. "Primitives, even if they do exist. Let the automated cameras and surface probes do their work. We have more important things to spend *our* time and bandwidth on."

"Primitives or not, these *people* are about to die!" Susan didn't even come up to Vasiliy's shoulder, but her intensity made him take a step back. "We have a moral responsibility to save as many of them as we can."

"We aren't the Red Cross," Leonard said in a reasonable tone. "We're astrophysicists. We are just one small ship—we couldn't evacuate more than a few of them."

"Well, at least we can use some of our precious bandwidth to send this data to Earth," Susan fumed. "Maybe someone there has the decency to mount a rescue mission."

Martin spoke up from the back of the crowd. "I'm afraid that's not going to be possible."

Everyone turned to him.

"We are eight days' realspace travel time from the nearest point in the system where a Simultaneity transition can be made safely. That means a sixteen-day round trip, even if another ship with acceleration as good as ours were available to leave Earth right now. And the iron flash will take place in..." he looked at his watch. "Fourteen days and eleven hours."

"Fourteen days!" Vasiliy roared, his voice rising above the others.

"And eleven hours."

Leonard was livid. "You guaranteed you could give us two weeks' notice!"

"I was going to announce it at today's staff meeting. That would have been seven hours more than two weeks."

Leonard shook his head. "Well, there's nothing to be done about it now. All of you need to revise your observation schedules for the new drop-dead date. I want to see updated PowerPlan files in my inbox by two o'clock." He turned to me. "Gray, you and J.J. determine the absolute minimum safe travel time to the transition point. I don't want to leave orbit any sooner than we have to, and to make that happen I'm prepared to jettison anything and everything we can get along without. Despite my first impulse, that does *not* include Dr. Lake. Any questions?"

Five people started talking at once.

"No questions? Good. Now get back to work."

With our month of observation time reduced to six days, plus whatever limited observations we could make during eight days accelerating away, the scientists kept me hopping. So I was asleep on my keyboard when my phone queeped three days later.

"Yuh?" I managed.

"Gray, this is Leonard. Can you join me and Susan in my office?"

"Uh, sure."

Leonard closed the door behind me. Susan was sitting on the edge of his desk. "Gray, can you fly the landers?"

"Sure. Part of my safety training." The ship's two eight-passenger landers were our lifeboats in case we had to abandon ship.

Susan and Leonard glanced at each other. Then Leonard spoke. "Please understand that this is not an order. I want you to think carefully about your answer, and make your own decision. As a human being, not an Implex employee."

My heart got very loud in my ears. "Go on."

Susan looked me right in the eyes. "Will you take Leonard and me to the surface?"

"Uh." I sat down on Leonard's guest chair. "Why?"

"To gather information and samples," said Leonard. "To make contact with the natives, if any. To preserve whatever tiny fragments we can."

It took me a moment to find my voice. "I'm surprised to hear you say that, Leonard. I mean, Susan, yeah, but not you. You were the one who said we aren't the Red Cross."

"I've had a few days to think about the situation."

"And I haven't given him a moment's peace," said Susan.

Leonard gave her a wry grin. "That's true, but this decision came from within. I agreed to come out of retirement and head up this expedition for two reasons: to advance human knowledge, and to make a name for myself. This is the only opportunity anyone will ever have to study this planet and these people, and if I turned it down I would be neglecting both those reasons. Besides, this might be my last chance to get out and do some real science."

I thought about how the ship's systems might collapse in my absence.

I thought about radiation, and space-suit failure, and all the other hazards of leaving the ship.

I thought about stepping out of the lander onto a landscape of weird alien trees and strange life forms.

I said, "I'm in."

J.J. was none too pleased to see us go, but Leonard was in charge and she couldn't quite justify a veto on safety grounds. "We'll be back in forty-eight hours," I told her.

"You'd better be, because we're leaving in fifty-one and I'm not waiting up for you."

It took about twelve hours each way with the lander's little engine, which gave us at most twenty-four hours on the surface. With only time for one landing, we selected a site near one of Susan's "cities" on the red/blue terminator. Even if we didn't meet the road builders, at least we could study the life forms in both their red-day and blue-day behaviors.

Susan was the first one out the door. "It's wonderful!"

The first thing I saw as I followed her out was the star Charlie, a glaring blue-white circle sitting right on the horizon like a plate on a mantelpiece, bisected by the diagonal line of the accretion disk. To my right loomed Ballock, a pockmarked half-moon appearing six or seven times the diameter of Luna. Behind the lander towered the roiling red wall of Magnus. A few high thin clouds streamed across the sunset-colored sky, and off to my left rippled a bright aurora, pale green and neon pink—visible evidence of the stream of charged particles assaulting the planet. Though the air was breathable, we wore our space suits against the radiation.

We had come down on a bare rock outcropping, but all around it was a riot of greenery. The predominant plant life consisted of oval plates, hand-sized to chest-sized, intersecting each other at odd angles. Each plate was covered with spiky scales, like a cross between a pineapple and a cactus. Leonard snapped off a plate and dropped it into a container; the broken surface sealed itself as we watched.

The light of the two suns made everything look outlandish and theatrical. Shadows were deep red, not black, and a vague blue anti-shadow stretched away in the opposite direction. A steady wind blew from the blue side to the red side, whistling in my helmet.

Susan tapped on some rocks with a wrench. "Igneous, and very hard. But look how worn! They must be very old."

"They can't be older than twelve million years," said Leonard.

"Unless the planet came from somewhere else," Susan replied.

"They could be younger than they look. Given Ballock's orbit, this spot has seen both glaciers and seventy-degree days in the past twenty years." But I imagined the planet Pointless drifting through interstellar space, domed cities covered by a miles-deep blanket of frozen air. Technology beyond anything we'd yet encountered, undreamed-of power sources...

We'd find out soon enough.

"Forget the rocks," I said. "Look at that."

Visible beyond a nearby rise was, without question, a road. Flat stones of various shapes and sizes had been fitted precisely together into a surface as smooth as anything the Romans ever built.

On it was a group of living things, heading our way.

The natives looked like the aftermath of a collision between crabs. Green and rough, bristling with spikes, their flat segmented bodies ranged from one to two meters long. Each was about half as wide as its length, and twenty to thirty centimeters in height. Jointed legs of various sizes poked out at random points on the body's perimeter; empty sockets and stumps showed where other legs once had been. There were many other scars, as well.

Life on Pointless was clearly not easy.

They moved fast, scuttling around and over each other. The lead creature raised its front segment, seeming to study us, though its tiny black eyes did not show the direction of its gaze. Mouthparts rasped together, making a chirruping sound.

"Keep it talking," said Susan. We had a reserved Simultaneity channel to the database of alien languages and translation software at the Smithsonian. Humanity was still paying the Lilliandree for that, and would continue to do so for decades, but it had already proved its value in several first-contact situations.

I couldn't help myself. "Take us to your leader."

W ithin a few hours the translation had become reasonably fluent and the natives brought us to their "city"—really more of a village. It consisted of several dozen low buildings, broader at the bottom than the top, constructed from solid slabs of stone as tightly fitted as the road. Each had an entrance slot at ground level, just large enough to accommodate one native, and no other openings. "These look like they could survive anything," Susan said.

Fifteen earthquake this season, no building fail, one of the natives said, the words appearing above it in my helmet display. The word "season" represented the planet's 120-day orbital period.

"Do you use ornamentation or decoration at all?" asked Leonard. Chirruping sounds came from his helmet speaker.

Don't understand.

"Patterns, colors, or textures, to please the eye and other senses."

No use if building fail. It waved a limb. *Building not fail, that please me.*

"Do you have any religion?" asked Susan. "Gods? Supernatural beings of great power?"

Four God. This from the largest, most scarred native, which limped along on only three limbs. It pointed into the sky. *Big red God sends drought, tiger, hurricane. Little blue God sends cancer, blindness, fever. Big black God sends darkness, glacier, chill.* Then it gestured at the ground beneath its feet. *Biggest God sends earthquake, stingweed, locust.*

"Are there any rites or practices? Prayers or sacrifices?"

Don't understand.

"Statements or activities meant to please the gods and bring good fortune?"

Build well. Plant well. Hide well. Hope God not see me.

"Sounds like their religion is just to stay out of trouble," I said. "Too bad it's not going to work for much longer."

Why not work? Too late, I realized I'd spoken on the open channel.

Leonard shot me a look. "Your big red god is very old."

Yes. Long time ago, small and yellow. Now big and red. Old.

"How could they know that?" I asked—on the private channel this time. "It was millions of years ago."

"They don't," Susan replied. "It's just a legend."

Leonard was still on the open channel. "Even the gods must die when they get old enough."

I know. Big red god getting sick. Die soon.
"How do you know this?"
Bigger. Redder. Spotty.
"What will you do when the big red god dies?" asked Susan.
Die.

L‍eonard and I went off with some of the natives to take pictures and samples of their agriculture and engineering, while Susan remained in the village with the oldest native, the one with three limbs.

When we returned, one of the stones that paved the village's central square had been pried up and moved to one side like a manhole cover. It was a couple of meters across and half a meter thick. "How did they do that?" I asked.

"They used big levers. They are also very strong."

"More to the point," said Leonard, "*why* did they do it?"

"You see those doorways around the edge of the square?" I had thought they were for drainage, but now I saw they were the same size as the doors of the natives' buildings. "I asked them where they went. Keun-Hang said they led to 'Legacy.' Naturally I asked if I could see it." Keun-Hang was Susan's name for the three-limbed one. It was a Korean name; the translation software just called the native "[Proper Name 7]."

The "Legacy" was an elaborately carved rock, three meters long and shaped something like a coffin. Slots, or doorways, penetrated into it from its five sides.

"I thought these folks didn't go in for ornament," I said.

Susan shook her head. "It's not decoration. It's writing."

Yes. The Legacy is the record of all I have done and seen over many, many generation, said Keun-Hang.

"How old *are* you?" I asked.

I have been in this place over two thousand season. Six hundred years! *Every time I survive something new, I carve words on the Legacy.* Keun-Hang pointed to a row of simple symbols running around the stone at its eye level. *This writing is basic. Any person finding this can read. Even person who does not know of writing can learn to read. More complex writing here. More complex still, here. Most complex inside. Walls, roof, floor.*

Another native spoke up. *Each tribe has Legacy. Often all person die, but Legacy remain. Many season pass, then new person come. No mind. Seek shelter, crawl inside. Learn. Tools. Fire. Soon, new mind. New tribe.*

Keun-Hang dragged itself to the top of the Legacy, bringing itself to our eye level. *All may die, but while Legacy remain, I live.*

"This is the tribe's entire history," Susan breathed.

"All their culture," said Leonard. "And their technology."

Susan leaned down, peered at the simple symbols. "It's designed to be understood by people who have forgotten writing. It's a self-regenerating cultural virus."

I didn't say anything. I was using my suit's rangefinder and computer to estimate the Legacy's weight.

"If we can only save one artifact," said Leonard, "this is it."

A number appeared in my helmet display. It was a little more than the lander's rated lift capacity, but I had some ideas... "I think we can do it."

Leonard turned to Keun-Hang. "Your planet is doomed."

I know this.

"Will you let us take your Legacy to safety?"

Yes, said Keun-Hang. *Legacy must survive.*

Y ou're sure the lander can lift it?" Susan said to me as we unbolted the lander's water tank. "We could just take photographs."

"The most important information is inside. Our helmet cameras are too bulky. We have to take the artifact itself." I hoped I was right...based on the way the natives had handled it, it was even heavier than I had first estimated. "Leonard, how's the ramp coming?"

"Another few loads of sand and we'll be ready. Maybe two hours."

I looked at my watch. "Make it one, if you can."

The entire tribe pitched in, and they finished the ramp in an hour and a half, not long after we got the last of the seats out of the lander. It took another two hours to get the Legacy inside and strapped down.

"How's it coming?" J.J.'s voice sounded in my helmet.

"I'm just finishing the preflight warm-up. Leonard and Susan, you'd better say your good-byes and get in here. J.J., any new information on the iron flash?"

"Nothing new. We have to leave orbit at 15:40. That's as far as I'm prepared to push it."

Twenty minutes to spare. One way or the other, we were committed now.

Leonard came in and strapped himself into one of the two remaining seats. There was a long, uncomfortable pause before Susan followed him. "I still hoped I might convince Keun-Hang to come with us, but he's resigned to dying. They all are."

"Here we go," I said, and hit the throttle.

The engines roared, and the lander shuddered. Outside the window the vegetation whipped and shredded in a gale of exhaust gases.

We started to lift.

And that's as far as it got. I ran the engines up to a hundred and ten percent and the lander didn't do anything more than rock at the top of its landing gear.

Finally, one eye on the fuel gauge, I throttled down. "No good."

"We have to lighten the load some more," said Leonard.

"We've already dumped everything we can do without," I replied.

"Then we have to leave the Legacy," Susan sighed.

"It took a couple of hours to get it in here and tied down. We have to take off in fifteen minutes."

Susan considered that for a moment. "How far are we over?"

"Not too much. Maybe thirty, forty kilos."

I realized what that meant at the same time Susan did. She started to unbuckle herself.

"No," I said. "You don't have to."

"I do, and I will. Better that two should live than all three should die."

"Stop," Leonard said before I could. "How old are you?"

"Thirty-nine."

"You've got half your life ahead of you. And you're married, I know."

"Leonard..." I said.

He wasn't listening to me. "*Nothing* is worse than the death of a spouse. I won't let you hurt your husband like my Marilyn hurt me. I'm the one who should stay."

"We should *all* stay!" I shouted.

They just looked at me.

"All of you have been telling me how impossible this planet is ever since we found it. How its orbit is too unstable, how it should have been destroyed when Magnus went off the main sequence, how there hasn't been time for life to evolve. What if this planet, and these people, came from somewhere else, like Susan said?"

"It's only a theory..." Susan began.

"But it fits the evidence! And if these people are as old as they say...maybe they aren't the primitives here. Maybe we are."

"What?" said Leonard.

Now that we had no alternative, the hopes I had been keeping to myself came rushing out. "Keun-Hang is at least six hundred years old, and there's evidence these people were here—or *came* here—when Magnus was still a main-sequence star. They may have technologies as far beyond the Lilliandree as the Lilliandree are beyond us. Even if this tribe has fallen back into barbarism, there must still be some alive who know how to operate their technology. If we leave, we'll be missing the journey of a thousand lifetimes!"

Leonard stared at me for a moment, then: "You stupid *child*! This is science, not science fiction!"

"But..."

"Didn't you even notice that their nouns have no number?"

"What does that have to do with anything?"

"Their language has no concept of singular or plural. When Keun-Hang said 'I,' it could just as well have been translated as 'we.' 'We' have been here for two thousand seasons. 'We' carved our knowledge on this stone."

"It's only natural for a species living under two very different suns to form some kind of theory of stellar evolution," Susan said gently, "but it's only speculation on their part, and it's not even correct. Magnus was a blue supergiant before it left the main sequence, not small and yellow."

I looked from one to the other. "But life takes billions of years to evolve!"

"It did on Earth." Susan's expression held only pity. "But the environment here is so harsh and variable, once life got started it must have evolved much faster."

Leonard unbuckled himself and stood up. "I'm sorry, son, but in the real world not every story has a happy ending. Good luck, and tell Krishna not to water my cactus too much."

Fighting the overloaded lander up through an atmosphere roiling from Magnus's increased output occupied all my attention for the next several hours. But I had a long quiet time to think after that, with Susan fast asleep and the planet receding below.

I clenched my fists, the tough fabric of my space-suit gloves unyielding between my fingers. I'd been stupid, and overconfident, and unrealistic, and now Leonard was going to die because of me. I could just see him down there, staring up at Magnus, full of regret...

I pressed the ship-to-ship call button. "J.J., do we have any of those soft-impact surface probes left?"

"Yeah, a couple."

"Get the scientists to put together a care package for Leonard, with a Simultaneity transmitter and as many scientific instruments as you can cram in there. You have to launch it before we break orbit."

"You're asking him to collect *data*, when he's going to *die*?"

"I'm giving him the opportunity to make one last contribution to the field where he's spent his life."

nd so, while we accelerated away for the next eight days, Leonard sat on the rock-solid platform of Pointless and gathered some of the best data of the expedition. Keun-Hang and the other natives helped place the instruments, while Leonard and the other scientists devoted all their energies to collating and interpreting the data. Sometimes, when I heard Leonard's voice raised in passionate argument, I forgot for a moment that he was a dozen AUs away and getting farther every minute.

We reached the transition gradient and jumped to a point six light-hours away. From here Magnus was no more than a fat red star, but Leonard reported the surface temperature on Pointless was up to forty degrees C and he had taken off his space suit. "I figure the smell would've killed me before the radiation."

"Instruments indicate the iron flash is beginning," said Martin. "What do you see?"

"The surface of the star has gone calm, like the eye of a hurricane. Now it's shrinking visibly, and growing brighter. There are eddy currents. Solar prominences corkscrewing out like fireworks. I wish you all could be here to see it. Now the sun is thrashing, like surf. I see white flashes...lightning bolts as big as solar systems. Continents of flame tearing themselves away from the surface." On the screen his gray hair whipped around his face and he had to squint against the increasing brightness. It looked like he was staring out to sea, at a rising sun, in an oncoming storm. "It's growing in diameter now, very rapidly." He held up a hand in front of his face. "Getting quite hot. I feel a tingling...beta particles, I think. Are you getting the data, Susan?"

"Yes," she said, and bit her lip before any more words could escape.

"Good," said Leonard, "because I think this is just about it. Gray, are you there?"

"I am."

"I'm sorry about what I said. You weren't stupid; you just let your dreams overwhelm your reason. Oh!" The light brightened suddenly on his face, washing out the camera for a moment, then dimmed again. "Massive flare. But Gray..."

"Yes, sir?"

"Don't ever stop dreaming. You n--"

Then the image whited out for the last time.

ix hours later we watched through the dome as Magnus exploded from a red star into a searing white light that dominated the sky, visibly swallowing up Charlie, Ballock, Pointless... and Leonard. "They'll call it Hart's Nebula," said Susan.

We took a few key readings from the advancing radiation wavefront, then jumped for home.

LASHAWNDA AT THE END
JAMES VAN PELT

We landed in steam. It billowed from where we touched down, then vanished into the dry, frigid air. From that first moment, the planet fascinated Lashawnda. She watched the landing tape over and over, her hand resting on her dark-skinned cheek, her oddly blue eyes reflecting the monitor's light. "I never believe we'll land safely, Spencer," she said.

Lashawnda liked Papaver better than any of the rest of us. She laughed at the gopher-rats that stood on their hind legs to look curiously until we got too close. She reveled in the smaller sun wavering in the not-quite-right blue sky, the lighter gravity, the blond sand and gray rocks that reached to the horizon, but most of all, she liked the way the plants in the gullies leaned her direction when she walked through them, how the flat-leafed bushes turned toward her and stuck to her legs if she brushed against them. Wearing a full contamination suit despite the planet's thin but perfectly breathable atmosphere didn't bother her. Neither did the cold. By midday here on the equator the temperature might peak a few degrees above freezing, but the nights were incredibly chilly. Even Marvin and Beatitude's ugly deaths the first days here didn't affect her like it did everyone else. No, she was in heaven, cataloging the flora, wandering among the misshaped trees in the crooked ravines, coming up with names for each new species.

When we lost our water supply, and it looked like we might not last until the resupply ship came round, she was still happy.

Lashawnda was a research botanist; what else should I have expected? For me, a commercial applications biologist, Papaver represented a lifetime of work for *teams* of scientists, and I was only one guy. After less than two weeks on the planet, I knew the best I got to do was to file a report that said, "Great possibilities for medicinal, scientific, and industrial exploitation." Every plant Lashawnda sent my way revealed a whole catalog of potential pharmaceuticals. The *second* wave of explorers would make all the money.

Lashawnda was dying, but was such a positive person that even in what she knew were her final days, she worked as if no deadly date was flapping its leaden wings toward her. That's the problem in living with a technology that has extended human life so well: death is harder. It must have been easier when humans didn't make it through their first century. People dropped dead left and right, so they couldn't have feared it as much. It couldn't have made them as mad as it made me. Her mortality clung to me like a pall, making everything dark and slow-motion and sad.

Of course, the plants stole our water. We should have seen it coming. Every living creature we'd found spent most of its time finding, extracting, and storing water.

Second Chair pounded on my door.

"Get into a suit, Spencer," she yelled when I poked my head into the hallway. "Everyone outside!" A couple of engineers rushed by, faces flushed, half into their suits. "I'm systems control," said one as he passed. "There's no way I should risk a lung full of Papaver rot."

When I made it out of the airlock, the crisis was beyond help. Our water tanks stood twenty meters from the ship, their landing struts crunched beneath them just as they were designed to do. They'd landed on the planet months before we got here, both resting between deep, lichen-filled depressions in the rock. Then the machinery gathered the minuscule water from the air, drop by drop, so that when we arrived the tanks were full. A year on Papaver was enough. Everyone surrounded the tanks. Even in the bulky suits I could see how glum they were, except Lashawnda, who was under the main tank. "It's a fungus," she said, breaking off a chip of metal from what should have been the smooth underside. Her hand rested in dark mud, but even as I watched, the color leached away. The ground sucked water like a sponge, and underneath the normally arid surface, a dozen plant species waited to store the rare substance. Even now the water would be spreading beneath my feet, pumped from one cell to the next. Ten years' worth of moisture for this little valley, delivered all at once.

She looked at me, smiling through the face shield. "I never checked the water tanks, but I'll bet there was trace condensation on them in the mornings, enough for fungus to live on, and whatever they secreted as waste *ate* right through. Look at this, Spencer." She yanked hard at the tank's underside, snapping off another hunk of metal, then handed it to me. "It's honeycombed."

The metal covered my hand but didn't weigh any more than a piece of balsa wood. Bits crumbled from the edge when I ran my gloved fingers over it.

"Isn't that marvelous?" she said.

First Chair said, "It's not all gone, is it? Not the other tank too?" He moved beside the next tank, rapped his knuckles on it, producing a resonant note. He was fifty, practically a child, and this was only his second expedition in command. "Damn." He looked into the dry, bathtub-shaped pit in the rock beside the tank where the water undoubtably drained when the bottom broke out.

Lashawnda checked the pipes connecting the tanks to the ship. "There's more here, after only ten days. How remarkable."

First Chair rapped the tank again thoughtfully. "What are our options?"

The environmental engineer said, "We recycle, a *lot*. No more baths."

"Yuck," said someone.

He continued, "We can build dew traps, but there isn't much water in the atmosphere. We're not going to get a lot that way."

"Can we make it?" said First Chair.

The engineer shrugged. "If nothing breaks down."

"Check the ship. If this stuff eats at the engines, we won't be going anywhere."

They shuffled away, stirring dust with their feet. I stayed with Lashawnda. "A daily bleach wash would probably keep things clean," she said. She crouched next to the pipes, her knees grinding into the dirt. I flinched, thinking about microscopic spores caught in her suit's fabric. The spores had killed Marvin and Beatitude. On the third day they'd come in from setting a weather station atop a near hill, and they rushed the decontamination. Why would they worry? After all, the air tested breathable. We all knew that the chances of a bacteria from an alien planet being dangerous to our Earth-grown systems were remote, but we didn't plan on water-hungry spores that didn't care at all what kind of proteins we were made of. The spores only liked the water, and once they'd settled into the warm, moist ports of the two scientist's lungs, they sprouted like crazy, sending tendrils through their systems, breaking down human cells to build their own structures. In an hour the two developed a cough. Six hours later, they were dead. Working remote arms through the quarantine area, I helped zip Beatitude into a body bag after the autopsy. Delicate-looking orange leaves covered her cheeks, and her neck was bumpy with sprouts ready to break through.

At least they didn't suffer. The spore's toxins operated as a powerful opiate. Marvin spent the last hour babbling and laughing, weaker and weaker, until the last thing he said was, "It's God at the end."

A quick analysis of the spores revealed an enzyme they needed to sprout, and we were inoculated with an enzyme blocker, but everyone was more rigorous decontaminating now.

Lashawnda said, "Come on, Spencer. I want to show you something."

We walked downhill toward the closest gully and its forest. She limped, the result of a deteriorating hip replacement. Like most people her vintage, she'd gone through numerous reconstructive procedures, but you wouldn't know it to look at her. She'd stabilized her looks as a forty-year-old, almost a tenth her real age. Pixie-like features with character lines radiating from the mouth. Just below the ears, dark hair with hints of gray. Slender in the waist. Dancer's legs. Economical in her movements whether she was sorting plant samples or washing her face. Four hundred years! I studied her when she wasn't looking.

I picked thirty for myself. Physically it was a good place to be. I didn't tire easily. My stockiness contrasted well to her slight build.

Lashawnda suffered from cascading cancers, each treatable eruption triggering the next until the body gives up. She'd told me she had a couple of laps around the sun left at best. "Papaver will be my last stop," she'd said during the long trip here. Of course, once we've slept with everyone else (and all the possible combinations of three or four at the same time), and the novelty of inter-ship politicking has worn thin, we all say we're done with planet hopping forever.

I suppose it was inevitable Lashawnda and I ended up together on the ship. I was the second oldest by a century, and she had one-hundred-and-fifty years on me, plus she laughed often and liked to talk. We'd go to bed and converse for a couple hours before sleeping. I'd grown tired of energetic couplings with partners I had nothing to say to afterwards. My own two-hundred-fifty years hung like a heavy coat. What did I have to say to someone who'd been kicking around for only sixty or ninety years?

I cared for her more than anyone in my memory, and she was dying.

When we reached the gully, she said, "What's amazing is that there are so many plants. Papaver should be like Mars. Same age. Lighter gravity and solar wind should have stripped its atmosphere. Unlike Mars, however, Papaver held onto its water, and the plants take care of the air."

Except for the warped orange and brown and yellow "trees" in front of us, that looked more like twisted pipes than plants, we could have been in an arctic desert.

"Darn little water," I said, thinking about our empty tanks.

"Darn little *free* water, but quite a bit locked into the biomass. Did you see the survey results I sent you yesterday?"

We pushed through the first branches. Despite their brittle looks, the stems were supple. They waved back into place after we passed. Broad, waxy leaves that covered the sun side of each branch bent to face us as we came close. I found their mobility unnerving. They were like blank eyes following our movements. In the trees' shadow I found more green than orange and yellow.

"Yeah, I looked at it." Except in a narrow band around the equator, Papaver appeared lifeless. But in the planet's most temperate region, in every sheltering hole and crevice, small plants grew. And peculiar forests, like the one we were in now, filled the gullies. The remote survey, taking samples at even the coldest and deadest-looking areas found life there too. Despite the punishing changes in temperature and the lack of rain, porous rock served as a fertile home for endolithic fungi and algae. Beneath them lived cyanobacterias.

"If the results are uniform over the rest of the surface, there's enough water for a small ocean or two." She wiggled between two large trunks, streaking her suit with greenish-orange residue. "Do you know why the leaves stick to our suits?"

"Transference of seeds?" I hadn't had time to study the trees' life cycle. Classifying the types had filled up most of my time, and I did that from within the ship. Lashawnda sent samples so fast, I'd had little chance to investigate much myself.

"Nope. They use airborne spores. What they're really trying to do is to eat you."

Obviously she knew where she was going. We'd worked our way far enough into the plants that I wasn't sure what direction the ship lay. "Excuse me?" I said.

"You were wondering what preyed on the gopher-rats. They're herbivores. You said they couldn't be the top of the food chain, and they aren't. They eat lichens, fungus and leaves, and the trees eat them." She stopped at a clump of stems, like warped bamboo, and gently pushed the branches apart. "See," she said.

Half a meter off the ground, a yellow and orange cocoon hung between the branches, like a football-sized hammock. I'd seen the lumps before. "So?"

She dropped to her knees and poked it with her finger. Something inside the shape quivered and wiggled, pushing aside several leaves. A gopher-rat stared out at me for a second, a net of tendrils over its eye.

I stepped back. For a second I thought of Beatitude, her face marked with the tiny, waxy leaves. "How long...when did it get caught?"

She laughed. "Yesterday. I startled him, and he jumped into the trees here. When he didn't come out, I went looking."

I knelt beside her. Up close I saw how the plant had grown *into* the gopher-rat. In the few uncovered spots, tufts of fur poked out. The biologist in me was fascinated, but for the rest, I found the image repugnant.

"How come he didn't escape? The leaves are a little sticky, but not *that* sticky."

"Drugs. Tiny spines on the leaves inject some type of opiate. I ran the analysis this morning. Same stuff that kept Marvin and Beatitude from feeling pain."

"A new data point to add to the ecology." I rested my hands on my knees. The poor gopher-rat didn't even get to live out its short life span. For a second I thought about burning down the entire forest for Marvin and Beatitude and the gopher-rat, who were dead and never coming back, except the gopher-rat wasn't dead yet. I wondered if it knew what was happening.

"Don't you see what's interesting?" She pushed the plants back even farther. "This is important."

"What am I missing?"

She smiled. Even through her faceplate I could tell that she found this exciting. "The gopher-rat should be dead. If the plants grabbed him just for his water, he'd be nothing but bones now, but he's still living. Obviously something else is going on. There's lumps like this one all through the forest. I dissected one. Without a thorough analysis, I can't tell for sure, but it looks like the plant absorbs everything except the gopher-rat's nervous system. It's symbiotic."

The leaves seemed to tighten a little around the gopher-rat. We stood in the middle of the forest. I couldn't see anything but the trees' tall stems and the sticky leaves that covered most of the ground. The sun had dropped lower in the sky so I couldn't find it through the trees, although their tops glowed orange and yellow in the slanting light. Even through the suit, I could feel that it was growing cold. "It doesn't look like an equal relationship to me."

"Maybe not, but it's an interesting direction for the ecology to take, don't you think?"

Why would a plant want a nervous system?" I said. We'd turned the lights out an hour earlier. My arm was draped over Lashawnda's shoulder, and her bare back pressed warmly against my chest. I didn't want to let her go. Even though my side ached to change position, I wanted to savor every second. I wondered if she sensed my grief.

"No reason that I can think of," she said. Her fingers were wrapped around my wrist, and her heart beat steadily against my own. "But it must have something to do with its survival. There's an evolutionary advantage."

For a long time, I didn't speak. She was so solid and real and *living*. How could her life be threatened? How could it be that she could be here today and not forever? She breathed deeply. I thought she might have gone to sleep, but she suddenly twisted from my embrace, cursing under her breath.

"What's the matter?" I said.

She sat up. In the dark I couldn't see, but I could feel her beside me. Her muscles tensed.

"A little discomfort," she said.

"What did the medic prescribe?"

"Nothing that's doing any good."

She coughed heavily for a few seconds, and I could tell she was stretching, like she was trying to rid herself of a cramp. "I'm going down to the lab. I'm not sleeping well anyway." She rested her hand against my face for an instant before climbing out of bed.

After an hour of tossing and turning, I got up and did what I'd never done before: accessed Lashawnda's medical reports. After reading for a bit I could see she'd been optimistic. There were a lot less than a couple trips around the sun left in her, and her prescription list was a pharmacopoeia of pain killers.

She hadn't returned by morning.

It's standard operating procedure," said the environmental engineer. She held her report forms to her chest defensively. "If the atmosphere isn't toxic, we're supposed to vent it in to cool the equipment. We've been circulating outside air since the first day. There *are* bioscreens."

First Chair looked at her dubiously. The four of us were crowded into the systems control room. Lashawnda broke the seals of her contamination suit. She'd rushed from decontamination without taking it off. "I should have thought of it," Lashawnda said. The helmet muffled her voice. "The fungi are opportunistic, and they're adept at finding hard-to-get water. You reverse airflow periodically, don't you?"

The environmental engineer nodded. "Sure, it blows dust out of the screens."

"The spores are activated by the moisture you vented, and—"

"*I* didn't vent *anything*," snapped the engineer. "It is standard operating procedure."

"Right," said Lashawnda, pulling the helmet off her head. She brushed her hair back with a quick gesture. "The fungus grew through the screen, spored, and that's what's in the machinery."

"The *entire* water recycling system? The backup system too?" asked First Chair, a tinge of desperation in his voice.

"Absolutely. There are holes in the valves. All the joints are pitted. The holding tanks would have more fungus in them than water, if there was any water left. Pretty happy fungus at that, I'd guess." She pulled the top half of the suit over her head, then stepped out of the pants. "Here's the unusual part: The water that was in the tank isn't in the room anymore. There are skinny stems leading to the vent that go down the ship's side and into the ground. The fungus pumped the water out. These plants are geniuses at moving water, which they have to be to survive."

First Chair asked, "Why weren't the external tanks already ruined when we got here? They were exposed to this environment much longer than our recycling equipment."

"They landed in the winter. That's the same reason the initial probes didn't find the spores," said Lashawnda. "It's spring now. The plants must only be active when its warmer. Bad timing on our part."

I looked through the service window into the machinery bay. Even through the thick glass the fungus was evident, a thick fur around the pipes. "You're sure the growth started inside the ship and went out, not the other way around?"

Lashawnda smiled. "Absolutely."

"So what?" said First Chair. I could see the wheels spinning in his head: how much water did we have stored elsewhere? How well were the dew-catchers working? Then he was dividing that amount of water by the minimum amount each crew member needed until the resupply ship arrived. By his expression, he didn't like the math.

Lashawnda said, "That means the plants cooperate. They share the wealth. It's counter-Darwinian. I compared the fly-by photos of this area from the first day until now. Since we've landed, plant growth has thickened and extended, which makes sense. When we lost the external tanks we introduced more free water into the system than it's seen in years, but the forests in the neighboring gulches also are thicker. We thought they were separate ecosystems. They aren't. Water we lost here is ending up as much as five kilometers away. The plants move moisture to where it's needed."

"Will knowing that help us now?" asked First Chair. "I don't care if the plants are setting up volleyball leagues; we've got to figure a way to find enough water to last us five months." He glared at the environmental engineer on his way out. She turned to me.

"I know," I said. "Standard operating procedure."

"Let's go outside," said Lashawnda. "We've got the afternoon left."

C ould we harvest the trees and press water out of them?" I asked.
Lashawnda attached another sensor to a tree stem, moved a few feet along, then fastened the next one. She straightened slowly, her eyes closed against the discomfort. I wondered how she really felt. She never talked about it.

"You did the reports. How many plants would we have to squeeze dry to get a single cup?"

I didn't answer. She was right. Although the plants tied up most of the planet's water, it was spread thinly. I dug into a bare patch of dirt between two stands of trees. Only a dozen centimeters below the surface, a matted network of plant tendrils resisted my efforts to go deeper. I picked one about a finger in width and fastened a sensor to it.

We were deep into the tree-filled gulch. With no sun on us, I had to keep moving to stay warm, and my faceplate defogger wasn't working well.

I looked into a bundle of tree stalks. An old gopher-rat lump hung between the branches. Now that I knew where to look, I found them often. "Have you gone this deep into the gulch before?"

Lashawnda consulted her wrist display. "No, but by the map we are nearly at the end. We'll save time if we go back along the ridge."

Fifteen minutes later Lashawnda pushed through a particularly heavy patch of trees, and she disappeared.

"Oh!"

"What?"

Pulling my way through the vegetation, I found what stopped her. The gully pinched to a close twenty meters farther, and there were no more trees, but the same kind of sticky leaves that captured the gopher-rats covered the ground in a bed of orange and yellow, like broad-surfaced clover. The setting sun poured a crimson light over the scene, and for the first time since I'd landed on Papaver, I thought something was beautiful. As I watched, the leaves turned their faces toward us and seemed to lean the least bit, as if they yearned for us to lay down.

Lashawnda said, "Let's not walk through that. We'd crush too many of them." She fastened the last of the sensors to the delicate leaves at the end of the little clearing. Her movements were spare, exact. The final sensor fastened, she paused on her knees, facing the bed of plants. She reached out, hand flat, and brushed the leaves gently. They strained to meet her, leaves wrapping around her fingers; a longer-stemmed leaf encircled her wrist. Within a few seconds, her hand, wrist, and arm to her elbow were encased.

I stepped toward her. The expanse of leaves had changed color! Then I realized the color was the same, but the plants had shifted even further to face her. Sunlight hit them differently. All lines pointed toward Lashawnda. My voice felt choked and tight. "What are you doing?"

"If I move, I must contain water. They're just trying to get it. They work together; isn't that superb? If they got my water, they'd send it to where it was needed." Gradually she pulled her arm free. The leaves slipped their hold without resistance.

Careful not to step on the plants, we made our way to the edge of the gully and clambered out. The startlingly pink sun brushed the horizon, and yellow and gold glowing streamers layered themselves a third of the way up the sky.

"That's amazing." I held Lashawnda's hand through the clumsy gloves, the same hand the leaves had covered.

"You haven't seen one before?" She squeezed my hand back. "Every sunset is like this. It's the dust in the atmosphere."

The streamers twisted under the influence of upper air disturbances that didn't touch us.

"I saw your medical reports," I said.

She sighed. The sky darkened as more and more of the sun vanished until only a pink diamond winked between two distant hills, and the final golden layer dulled into a yellow haze. "You're the last one. Are you going to wish me well too? You'd think everyone turned into death and dying counselors. If I hear, 'You've had a good four-hundred years,' again, I'll scream."

"No, I wasn't going to say that." But I don't know what I was going to say. I couldn't tell her that I wanted to do some screaming of my own.

By the time we returned to the ship, the night had grown incredibly cold, and the decontamination chamber wasn't any warmer. I longed for a hot spiced tea, but First Chair was waiting for us on the other side.

"I need you to drop your other projects and concentrate on the water problem." His eyes had that haunted I-wish-I-didn't-have-a-leadership-position look to them. "The geology team is looking for aquifers; the engineers are making more dew traps, and the chemists are working on what can be extracted from the rock, but none of them are hopeful we can find or make enough water fast enough. Is there anything you've learned about the plants that might help?"

Lashawnda said, "They've spent millions of years learning how to conserve water. I don't think they'll give it up easily. Spencer and I are working on an experiment right now that ought to tell us more."

"Good. Let me know if you get results." He rushed from the room, and a few seconds later I heard him say to someone in another room, "Have you made any progress?"

"We'll need to sedate him if we want to work uninterrupted," she said.

"What *is* the experiment we're doing?"

"Electroencephalograph."

"An EEG on a plant?" I laughed.

She shrugged. "You wondered why a plant would need a nervous system. Let's find out if it's using it."

In the lab, Lashawanda bent over her equipment. "What do you make of that?" She pointed to the readouts on the screen. "Especially when I display it like this." She tapped a couple keys.

The monitor showed a series of moving graphs, like separate seismographs. "It could be anything. Sound waves maybe. Are those from the sensors we placed?"

"Yep. Now, watch this." She reached across her table and pressed a switch. Within a couple seconds, all the graphs showed activity so violent that the screen almost turned white. Gradually the graphs settled into the same patterns I'd seen at first.

I leaned closer and saw the readouts were numbered. The ones near the top of the screen corresponded to the sensors we'd placed at the far end of the gully. The bottom ones were nearest to the ship. "What did you do?"

"I shut the exterior vents into the equipment room. The change in the graphs happened when the hatches cut through the fungus stems connecting the growth in the ship to the ground."

"The plants felt that? They're thinking about it?"

"Not plants. A single organism. Maybe a planet-wide organism. I'll have to place more sensors. And yes, it's thinking."

The lines on the monitor continued vibrating. It *looked* like brain activity. "That's ridiculous. Why would a plant need a brain? There's no precedent."

"Maybe they didn't start out as plants. As the weather grew colder and it became harder and harder for animals to live high on the food chain, they became what we see now, a thinking, cooperative intelligence."

Lashawnda put her hands on the small of her back and pushed hard, her eyes closed. "A sentience wouldn't operate the same way non-thinking plants would. We just need to discover the difference." She opened a floor cabinet and took out a clear sample bag stuffed with waxy orange shapes.

I barely recognized it before she opened the bag, broke off a Papaver leaf, and pressed it against her inner arm.

After a moment, she opened her eyes and smiled "Marvin said, 'It's God at the end,' so I thought I'd give it a try. He wasn't too far off." She enunciated the words carefully, as if her hearing were abruptly acute. "The toxins are an outstanding opiate. Much more effective on pain than the rest of the stuff I've been taking. I don't think the gopher-rats suffer."

No recrimination would have been appropriate. Although it was most likely the leaves wouldn't affect her at all, the first time she did it she might have just as easily killed herself. "How long?" I took the bag from her hand. It wasn't dated. She'd smuggled it in.

"A couple of days."

"Is it addictive?"

She giggled, and I looked at her sharply. She seemed lucid and happy, not drugged.

"I don't know. I haven't tried quitting." She held her hand out. I gave her the bag. She said, "I wonder what an entity as big as a planet thinks about? How *old* would you guess it is?" The bag vanished into the cabinet. "Not very often I run into something older than me."

"Did you tell the medic about that?" I nodded toward the cabinet.

She levered herself up so she could sit on the counter. "I'm taking notes she can see afterwards. No need to bother her with it now. Besides, we have bigger problems. If First Chair is right, in a month we'll have died of thirst. How are we going to convince a plant to give us back the water it took?"

Sitting where she was, her heels against the cabinet doors, she looked like a young girl, but shadows under her eyes marked her face, and her skin appeared more drawn, as if she were thinning, becoming more fragile, and she was.

"How do you feel?" I asked. I had tried to maintain within myself her concentration, her ability to ignore the obvious fact, but I couldn't. I worried about the crew and the water they needed. But for me? I didn't care. Death would find Lashawnda before it took me.

She slid off the counter and tapped a code into her workstation. The recording of our landing came up again. Clouds of steam surged from the ground. She said, without meeting my eyes, "Look, Spencer. I can't avoid it. It's not going away. So all I can do is work and think and act like it's not there at all. You're behaving as if I should be paralyzed in fear or something, but I'm not going to do that. There's still a quest or two for me in the last days, some effort of note."

I had no answer for that. We went to bed hours later, and when she held me, her arms trembled.

nightmare woke me. In the dream I wandered through the twisted forest, but I wasn't scared. I was happy. I belonged. The crooked stems gave way before my ungloved hands. My chest was bare. No contamination suit or helmet or shirt. The air smelled sharp and frigid, like winter on a lake's edge where the wind sweeps across the ice, but I wasn't cold. I came upon a thick stand of trees, their narrow trunks forming a wall in front of me. I pushed and tugged at the unmoving branches. I'd never seen a clump of Papaver trees so large. Nothing seemed more important than penetrating that branched fortress. Finally I found a narrow gap where I could squeeze through. At first I wandered in the dark. Gradually shapes became visible: the towering stems forming a shadowy roof overhead, other branches reaching from side to side, and the room felt close.

"Spencer?" said Lashawnda.

"Yes?" I said, turning slowly in the vegetable room. Clumps of waxy-leafed plants covered the ground, but I couldn't see her.

"I'm here, Spencer," she said, and one of the clumps sat up.

I squinted. "It's too dark."

A dim light sparked to life, a pink diamond, like the last glimpse of the sunset we'd seen the day before, growing until the room became bright, revealing a skeleton-thin Lashawnda.

"I'm glad you came," she said.

I stepped closer, all the details clear in the ruddy light. Her eyes sparkled above sharp cheekbones. She smiled at me, the skin pulled tight across her face, her shoulders bony and narrow, barely human anymore. She wore no clothes, but she didn't need them. The plants hid her legs, and leaves covered her stomach and breasts. Like the gopher-rat, she'd been absorbed.

"The plant is old, old, old," she said. "We think deep thoughts, all the way to Papaver's core."

I put my arm around her, the bone's hardness pressing against my hand.

In the dream, I was happy. In the dream, the plants sucking every drop of water from her was right.

"And, Spencer, this way I live forever."

I woke, stifling a scream.

She wasn't in bed.

In the decontamination unit, her suit was gone.

I don't remember how I got my suit on or how I got outside. Running, I passed the empty water tanks, avoided the lichen-filled depressions, and plunged into the forest. The sun had barely cleared the horizon, pouring pink light through the skinny trees. I tripped. Knocked my face hard against the inside of my helmet. Staggering, I pushed on. The dream image hovered before me. Had the pain become too much for Lashawnda, and the promise of an opiate-loaded bed of leaves, eager to embrace her become too tempting? I imagined her nervous system, like a gopher-rat's, joining the plant consciousness. But who knew what the gopher-rats experienced, if they experienced anything at all? Maybe their lives were filled with nightmares of cold and immobility.

Trees slapped at my arms. Leaves slashed across my faceplate.

When I burst through the last line of trees at the clearing's edge, she was crouched, her back to me, shoulders and head down in the plants. I pictured her faceplate open, her eyes gone already, home for stabbing tendrils seeking the moist tissue behind.

"Don't do it!" I yelled.

Startled, she fell back, holding a sensor; her faceplate was closed. For a second she looked frightened. Then she laughed. I gasped for breath while my air supply whined in my ear.

"What are you doing, Spencer?" A bag filled with the sensors we'd put on the plants sat on the ground beside her. She'd been retrieving them.

"You weren't...I mean, you're not...hurting yourself...you're okay?" I finally blurted.

She held me until I quit shaking and my respiration settled into a parody of regularity.

The sun had risen another handful of degrees. We stayed still so long that the plants turned away to face the light. She hugged me hard, then said, "I know how to find water."

I hugged her back.

"Can you carry the bag?" she said as she pushed herself to her feet. "It's getting darned heavy."

The crew stood around the one-meter-deep depression beside an empty water tank. Like every sheltered spot, lichens covered the rock. Lashawnda supervised the engineers as they arranged the structure she'd sketched out for them, which was two long bars crossing the hole, holding an electric torch suspended above the pit's bottom.

First Chair stood with his arms crossed. "What do you mean, we should have figured out how to get water from the first day?"

Lashawnda sat in a chair someone had brought for her. "The plants here are cooperative. They're not just out for themselves like we're used to seeing. I watched the records of our landing. The ground *steamed*, but, as Spencer will tell you," she nodded to me, "you couldn't get an ounce of water out of a ton of the lichen no matter how hard you tried."

First Chair looked puzzled.

Lashawnda pressed a button, and the electric torch began to glow. I could feel the heat on my face from ten meters away. Lashawnda said, "The plants were protecting each other, or, more accurately, protecting itself. They're geniuses at moving moisture."

In the pit, some of the yellow lichens began to turn brown, and then to smoke. Suddenly the bottom of the pit glistened, rivulets opened from cracks in the rock. Water quickly filled the bathtub-sized depression, covering the burning plants.

The crew cheered.

"The plant is trying to protect itself," Lashawnda said. "You better pump it out now, because as soon as the heat's off, it will be gone."

First Chair barked out orders, and soon pipes led from the hole into temporary tanks in the ship.

That night I held Lashawnda close, her backbone pressed against me; my lips brushed the back of her neck.

"Did you really think that I'd kill myself by throwing myself into the plants?"

She held my wrist, her fingers so delicate and light that I half feared they'd break.

"I didn't want to lose even a single day with you," I said.

Lashawnda didn't speak for a long time, but I knew she hadn't drifted into sleep. The room was so quiet I could hear her eyelashes flutter as she blinked. "I don't want to lose a day with you either." She pulled my arm around her tighter. "Four hundred years is a good, long time to live. I don't suppose when I do go that you could arrange for me to be buried in that clearing at the gully's end?"

I remembered how the plants had grasped her hand and arm, how attentive they were when she passed.

"Sure," I said.

It occurred to me that I wanted to be buried there too, where the beings work together to save each other and share what they have to help the least of them.

"But we're not there yet," I said.

CONTRIBUTOR NOTES

Steve Beai has had over 500 appearances of short fiction and articles to date and has received nominations for both the Edgar from the Mystery Writers of America and the Stoker Award from the Horror Writers Association as well as recognition from *The Year's Best Fantasy and Horror*. He is also the author of the non-fiction study *Censoring the Censors* and the novel *Widow's Walk. Dark Rhythms*, a CD-ROM collection of previously published short fiction, including audio performances of each story, is currently available in both a signed and lettered edition from Lone Wolf Publications. Additional projects include the soon-to-be-released novels *Funshine City* and *Neighbor Hoods*. Steve lives and works at Reservoir Studio in rural Indiana with his wife and children.

Arinn Dembo published her first critical essay in *The New York Review of Science Fiction* in 1991, and spent several years thereafter working as a freelance reviewer of computer games, books, comics, and movies. Her first short story was published in *The Magazine of Fantasy and Science Fiction* in 1996, and most recently she has published a novella in the horror anthology *Dark Theatres*. She is thirty-three years old, and currently lives in North Carolina, the youngest inmate of a Home for Incorrigible Old Broads.

Elisabeth DeVos is the author of a novel, *The Seraphim Rising*, as well as short fiction that has appeared in *Talebones* magazine. She tried to write a serious SF story for this anthology, but reverted to her usual blend of science-fantasy and humor, a tendency she blames on having grown up in Central Florida, where one can view space shuttle launches from fantasy-filled amusement parks. She now lives in the Seattle area.

A. Alicia Doty celebrates her first fiction publication with this story co-written with Therese Pieczynski. She received her Ph.D. in Molecular Pharmacology and Cancer Therapeutics from the University at Buffalo, Roswell Park Cancer Institute Division, in the year 2000 and is currently a scientist at a biotech company in Rochester, NY. She is both tolerated and adored by a husband, two daughters, four cats, and a PDA named Majel.

Robert E. Furey is a zoology professor currently at George Mason University. He lives near the nation's capitol with his French-native wife and their young daughter. He's a rare amalgamation of Ernest Hemingway, Richard Burton, and Peter Parker (his specialty being arachnids). Rob's teaching, consulting work, and family ties take him frequently to Europe, Africa, and South America, and he holds a dual U.S.-Irish citizenship.Rob graduated Clarion West in 1997 and was recently published in the Lovecraftian horror anthology *Dark Theatres.*

David D. Levine attended Clarion West in 2000 and hasn't slowed down since. His stories have appeared in such publications as *The Year's Best Fantasy #2, The Magazine of Fantasy and Science Fiction, Interzone,* and *Apprentice Fantastic,* and he is a winner of the James White Award, Writers of the Future, and the Phobos Fiction Contest. At this writing, he is a nominee for the 2003 John W. Campbell Award for Best New Writer and awaits the results with fingers crossed. He lives in Portland, Oregon, where he and his wife Kate Yule produce the highly-regarded science fiction fanzine *Bento.* His web page is http://www.BentoPress.com.

Syne Mitchell claims no knowledge of which part of her subconscious created "Stately's Pleasure Dome." Perhaps she was channeling Spider Robinson, or was deeply affected by Alan Clark's artwork, or maybe it was because it was written at three a.m. If you like hard SF, read her latest novels: *Technogenesis* and *The Changeling Plague.* If you want more like this, try keeping her up late at a science-fiction convention.

Nancy Jane Moore's fiction has appeared in a variety of anthologies, including *Imaginings* and *Treachery and Treason,* in magazines ranging from the "tiny but celebrated" *Lady Churchill's Rosebud Wristlet* to *Andromeda Spaceways Inflight Magazine,* and on the Webzine *Fantastic Metropolis.* She attended the 2002 Milford workshop in England, and is a graduate of Clarion West. She lives in Washington, D.C. Her website is http://home.earthlink.net/~nancyjane

Patrick O'Leary was born in Saginaw, Michigan. He graduated with a B.A. in Journalism from Wayne State University. His poetry has appeared in Literary Magazines across North America. His first novel, *Door Number Three* (TOR), was chosen by *Publisher's Weekly* as one of the best novels of the year. His second novel, *The Gift* (TOR), was a finalist for the World Fantasy Award and The Mythopoeic Award. His collection of fiction, non-fiction, and poetry *Other Voices, Other Doors* (Fairwood Press) came out in January 2001. His third novel, *The Impossible Bird* (TOR Jan. 2002), has made the preliminary shortlist for the Nebula Award. His short stories have appeared in *Mars Probes* and *Infinity Plus One, Scifiction.com,* and *Talebones.* His novels have been translated into German, Japanese, Polish, French, and Braille. Currently he is an Associate Creative Director at an advertising agency. His work has won numerous industry awards. He travels extensively, but he makes his home in the Detroit area with his wife and sons.

Jerry Oltion has been a gardener, stone mason, carpenter, oilfield worker, forester, land surveyor, rock 'n' roll deejay, printer, proofreader, editor, publisher, computer consultant, movie extra, corporate secretary, and garbage truck driver. For the last twenty-two years, he has also been a writer. He is the author of over 100 published stories in *Analog, F&SF*, and various other magazines and anthologies. He has thirteen novels, the most recent of which is *The Getaway Special*, published in December of 2001 by Tor Books. A sequel, *Anywhere But Here*, is scheduled for release in 2004. Jerry's work has won the Nebula award and has been nominated for the Hugo award. He has also won the Analog Readers' Choice award. He lives in Eugene, Oregon, with his wife, Kathy, and the obligatory writer's cat, Ginger.

Robert Onopa, a master of wryly humorous near-future SF, currently teaches litera- ture at the University of Hawaii, and lives on Oahu with his wife and two sons. A frequent contributor to *The Magazine of Fantasy and Science Fiction*, he's also been published in *Tomorrow, TriQuarterly, Harper's,* and *The Singapore Straits-Times*, among other venues. His story "Geropods," first published in *2020* by Electric Story, was included in *The Year's Best SF #8* (2003). He has had one science fiction novel out, *The Pleasure Tube* (Berkley/Putnam's), and is currently at work on another, set in the Pacific.

Tom Piccirilli is the author of ten novels, including *The Night Class, A Choir of Ill Children, A Lower Deep, Hexes, The Deceased*, and *Grave Men*. He's pub- lished over 120 stories in the mystery, horror, erotica, and science fiction fields. Tom's been a final nominee for the World Fantasy Award and he's the winner of the first Bram Stoker Award given in the category of Outstanding Achievement in Poetry. This year he won the Bram Stoker Award for Best Novel and Best Short Story. Learn more about him at his official website http://www.mikeoliveri.com/ piccirilli.

Therese Pieczynski has edited for *Terra Incognita*, written for *Nova Express*, been published in *Asimov's Science Fiction Magazine* and currently works in the Molecular Biology lab at the same biotech company as A. Alicia Doty.

Melissa Scott is from Little Rock, Arkansas, and studied history at Harvard Col- lege and Brandeis University, where she earned her Ph.D. in the comparative history program with a dissertation titled "The Victory of the Ancients: Tactics, Technology, and the Use of Classical Precedent." In 1986, she won the John W. Campbell Award for Best New Writer, and in 2001 she and long-time collaborator Lisa A. Barnett won the Lambda Literary Award in SF/Fantasy/Horror for *Point of Dreams*. Scott has also won Lammies in 1996 for *Shadow Man* and 1995 for *Trouble and Her Friends*, having previously been a three-time finalist (for *Mighty Good Road, Dreamships,* and *Burning Bright*). *Trouble and Her Friends* was also shortlisted for the Tiptree. Her most recent solo novel, *The Jazz*, was named to *Locus*'s Recommended Reading List for 2000. Her first work of non-fiction, *Conceiving the Heavens: Creating the Science Fiction Novel*, was published by Heinemann in 1997, and her monologue "At RaeDean's Funeral" has been included in an off-off-Broadway production, *Elvis Dreams*, as well as several other evenings of Elvis-mania. A second monologue, "Job Hunting," has been performed in competition and as a part of an evening of Monologues from the Road. She lives in New Hampshire with her partner of twenty-four years.

James Van Pelt lives in western Colorado with his wife and three sons. One of the finalists for the 1999 John W. Campbell Award for Best New Writer, he teaches high school and college English. His fiction has appeared in, among others, *Dark Terrors 5, Dark Terrors 6, Asimov's, Analog, Realms of Fantasy, Talebones, The Third Alternative, Weird Tales*, and *Alfred Hitchcock's Mystery Magazine*. His first collection of stories, *Strangers and Beggars*, was published in 2002 and was named by the American Library Association as a Best Book for Young Adults. He has upcoming work in *Asimov's, Talebones*, the SFWA anthology *New Faces in Science Fiction*, Gardner Dozois's *The Year's Best Science Fiction*, and David Hartwell's *The Year's Best Fantasy*.

Ray Vukcevich's latest book is *Meet Me in the Moon Room* from Small Beer Press (http://www.lcrw.net). The book was nominated for a Philip K. Dick Award. His first novel is *The Man of Maybe Half-a-Dozen Faces* from St. Martin's. His short fiction has appeared in many magazines, including *Talebones, Fantasy & Science Fiction, SCIFICTION, Lady Churchill's Rosebud Wristlet, The Infinite Matrix, Polyphony, Rosebud, Strange Horizons*, and *Asimov's*, and in several anthologies. He lives in Oregon and works in a couple of university brain labs.

Leslie What is a Nebula Award-winning freelance writer and Jell-O artist living in the Pacific Northwest. Her work appears in many magazines, newspapers, journals, and anthologies and her comic novel, *Olympic Games*, will be published in 2004 by Tachyon Publications (http://www. tachyonpublications.com).

PAINTING TITLES

Animation#1 ("The Sweet Not-Yet")

Rock, Paper, Scissors ("Threesome")

Chattacon Collaboration with Kevin Ward
("Area Seven")

Pine Spirit ("The Dream of Vibo")

The Graceful Labelings of Triangular Snakes
("The Artist Makes a Splash")

Violent Decompression ("Fired")

Racoon Skull Ship ("Nohow Permanent")

Off the Shoulder of Orion ("By Any Other Name")

Caverns Measureless to Man ("Stately's Pleasure Dome")

Nudibrains ("Between the Lines")

Life as We Know It ("Dilated")

Invasion of the Benevolent Vegetable Dictators
("Let My Right Hand Forget Her Cunning")

Dropcloth Dragon #1 ("Cleave")

Phoenix ("Out of the Fire")

VV Cephei A from Helvoran ("Legacy")

God Introduces Filmore to Time ("Lashawnda at the End")

A Short Biography of Alan M. Clark

Alan M. Clark was born in Nashville, Tennessee in 1957. He graduated in 1979 from the San Francisco Art Institute with a Bachelor of Fine Arts Degree. In 1984 he became a freelance illustrator, and since has produced work ranging in subject from fantasy, science fiction, horror, and mystery for publishers of fiction, to cellular and molecular biology for college textbooks. He has produced work for young adults and provided the artwork for two children's books.

Clark has illustrated the writing of such authors as Ray Bradbury, Robert Bloch, Joe R. Lansdale, Stephen King, George Orwell, Manly Wade Wellman, Greg Bear, Spider and Jeanne Robinson, and Lewis Shiner, as well as his own. A major influence for his art comes from the Surrealists, particularly Max Ernst. He is fascinated with the use of what he calls "controlled accidents" and the possibility of "finding" images within the paint. A great advocate of collaboration, Clark has worked with many others in both literary and visual art.

His awards in the illustration field include the 1994 World Fantasy Award for Best Artist, the 1992 and 1993 Chesley Awards for Best Interior illustration, the Chesley for Best Paperback Cover of 1994, and the Chesley for the Best Unpublished Color Work of 1994. He is the recipient of the Deathrealm Award, as well as the first International Horror Guild Critics Award for Best Artist.

He is co-author and illustrator of *The Pain Doctors of Suture Self General,* published by Blue Moon Books. He collaborated with Elizabeth Engstrom on the illustrated collection *The Alchemy of Love,* published by Triple Tree Publishing, producing the interior illustrations, the cover art, and the book design. Also with Engstrom, he coedited the anthology *Imagination Fully Dilated,* with stories based on his paintings, which is available from Cemetery Dance Publications. He has sold short fiction to the anthologies *More Phobias, The Book of Dead Things, Dead on Demand,* and *Darkside,* and to the magazines *Midnight Hour* and *The Silver Web.*

In order to make available to the public the products of his many collaborations, Clark created IFD publishing in January of 1999. He has said of the new company, "IFD Publishing is committed to the idea that art is never the product of a single mind but occurs instead when imaginations meet."

The second book from his new publishing company was *Imagination Fully Dilated Volume II,* edited by Elizabeth Engstrom. Their latest release is *Pain & Other Petty Plots to Keep You in Stitches,* that Clark designed and illustrated, and co-wrote with Randy Fox, Jeremy Robert Johnson, Troy Guinn, and Mark Edwards.

Currently, he and his wife, Melody, reside in Eugene, Oregon.

224

OTHER TITLES BY FAIRWOOD PRESS

Strangers and Beggars
by James Van Pelt
trade paper: $17.99
ISBN: 0-9668184-5-8

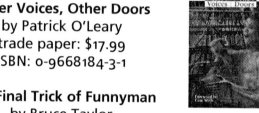

Other Voices, Other Doors
by Patrick O'Leary
trade paper: $17.99
ISBN: 0-9668184-3-1

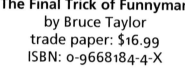

The Final Trick of Funnyman
by Bruce Taylor
trade paper: $16.99
ISBN: 0-9668184-4-X

Where the Southern Cross the Dog
by Trey R. Barker
paperback: $8.99
ISBN: 0-9668184-6-6

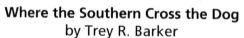

Welcome to Hell:
A Working Guide for the Beginning Writer
by Tom Piccirilli
paperback: $6.99
ISBN: 0-9668184-2-3

The 10% Solution:
Self-editing for the Modern Writer
by Ken Rand
paperback: $5.99
ISBN: 0-9668184-0-7

ZOM BEE MOO VEE
by Mark McLaughlin
chapbook: $5.99
ISBN: 0-9668184-1-5

www.fairwoodpress.com

Printed in the United States
1224300001B/61-84